Man in the Shadows

Man in the
SHADOWS

GORDON HENDERSON

HarperCollins*PublishersLtd*

Man in the Shadows
Copyright © 2014 by Gordon Henderson.
All rights reserved.

Published by HarperCollins Publishers Ltd

First edition

HarperCollins books may be purchased for educational, business,
or sales promotional use through our Special Markets Department.

HarperCollins Publishers Ltd
2 Bloor Street East, 20th Floor
Toronto, Ontario, Canada
M4W 1A8

www.harpercollins.ca

Library and Archives Canada Cataloguing in Publication
information is available upon request

ISBN 978-1-44343-180-4

Printed and bound in Canada
WEB 9 8 7 6 5 4 3 2 1

For Pam

The fate of our land
God hath placed in your hand;
He hath made you to know
The heart of your foe,
And the schemes he hath plann'd;
Think well who you are,
Know your soul and your star;
Persevere—dare—
Be wise and beware—
THOMAS D'ARCY McGEE

The fate of our land

≡

May 1867
Fenian Brotherhood Headquarters
10 West Fourth Street
New York City

"I don't care how many of them you have to kill," Colonel Patrick O'Hagan said. "I don't care what you have to do. I want that damned country destroyed."

The man receiving the orders stood ramrod straight. The high collar on his long grey coat obscured much of his face. The only distinguishing feature the colonel could see was his eyes, piercing out of the shadows. He stayed a step behind the ray of late-afternoon sunlight shining from the only open window and let the colonel talk.

"Take your time. Plan your moves carefully. But when you do strike, strike swiftly. Strike ruthlessly."

The colonel's long, flowing moustache was perfectly coiffed, his skin smooth and delicate. He spoke with authority, but the man in the shadows was not impressed. He knew about Patrick O'Hagan. O'Hagan worked closely with General John O'Neill, the "commander-in-chief" of an Irish military force that vowed to free Ireland from Britain's control. He even had a new sign on his desk: the Irish Republican Army—the IRA. But they were better known as the Fenian Brotherhood, or simply the Fenians. Romantically named after the Fianna, ancient Celtic warriors, the Fenians had recently targeted North America as a battleground, a way to attack Britain from its frontier—from its back door.

"I am talking about nothing less than a reign of terror," he said. "Soften up the enemy. Prepare the ground for our attack."

Silence.

"How long have you been in America?" Colonel O'Hagan asked, filling the empty air.

"Long enough."

Patrick O'Hagan was an American citizen. He had no plans to return to his homeland, but he would always be an Irish rebel. He wiped a bead of sweat from his brow and stamped his fist on the table. "We are at war with England; we must do our part."

The man in the shadows just nodded.

"You will be the first soldier behind enemy lines, the advance guard. You can become a great hero."

He had stopped paying attention. He was considering O'Hagan's accent. He was from the northern counties. Maybe Armagh. Probably Monaghan.

The colonel was starting to feel unnerved under the spell of this man's cold stare.

"How ruthless?" he asked O'Hagan, barely moving his lips.

"You will be working as a spy and soldier in enemy territory. You'll have to do whatever it takes to survive." O'Hagan rubbed his sleeve against his forehead, paused and said solemnly, "And your job includes eliminating key targets."

"Money?"

"It's in this pouch."

For the first time since the meeting began, he took his eyes off Colonel O'Hagan as he reached for the pouch and slowly counted the stack of bills. When he had finished, he allowed a slow, sinister smile. "You have the right man." His voice was a murky undertone.

The right man. O'Hagan felt sure of it. This person in front of him emanated icy, heartless efficiency.

A year ago, General John O'Neill had led a raid across the border into British territory at Ridgeway, near Buffalo. O'Hagan was at his side. They had proven how easy it was to cross the barely defended frontier.

But O'Neill lost his nerve and retreated when the American reinforcements he expected didn't arrive. It became clear to O'Hagan that O'Neill should have done the groundwork first. If he had created confusion in the British territory ahead of time, a better-organized invasion would have succeeded. The Fenians needed something—or someone—to throw British North America off balance. A few perfect murders would do the trick. That would create chaos. Chaos would bring panic. The world would see that this fledging country couldn't cope. And they could move in. But the normally squabbling politicians in the north were actually starting to work together. In a month, some British colonies planned to unite to become Canada. "Confederation," they called it. A new British country. The very thought of it made him fume.

He—and this mysterious man—must see to its early end.

Colonel O'Hagan knew little of the person in front of him. He had been instructed in a coded dispatch from the Fenian commander in Dublin to be in his office alone at 4 P.M. on May 29. The man arrived at precisely four o'clock, wearing an old grey coat. He kept it on despite the heat. In fact, he did not even remove his black hat when he entered. He just walked in, dropped the appropriate letters of introduction on O'Hagan's desk, muttered the password and moved back, out of the light.

The colonel held up a piece of paper. "Here are some names and addresses of people who might help you."

The man put it in his pocket without glancing at it.

"You know your targets?"

He didn't react. The question was idiotic and insulting.

"While you are in Canada," O'Hagan continued, "I will work with O'Neill to amass an army. He doesn't know about your mission. No one does except for me and our contact in Ireland. If you want to get in touch with me or need help—"

"I won't," he cut him off, "need help. I know how to find you. You won't need to find me." He adjusted his coat. It was as if a statue moved. "Is that all?"

"Umm . . . yes," O'Hagan answered, stumbling to his feet. "Except to say, I meant what I said about this being a holy war. Good luck to you, my man, and God bless you."

"Neither luck nor God has anything to do with this," he muttered disdainfully, and turned to leave.

O'Hagan felt a refreshing breath of evening air as the man stepped out of the shadows, opened the door and silently left.

PART ONE

July 1, 1867

1

The first of July. Maybe it was his birthday. Conor O'Dea wasn't sure how old he was. He assumed he was twenty-one, but his date of birth was unclear. He knew he had been in Ireland during the late 1840s or early 1850s, but his father rarely talked about those years. Conor only knew life in British North America. He may not have known how old he was, but he knew he was a child of the New World.

July 1, 1867. In Ottawa, the day began with fanfare, and now the bells rang. Conor lay in bed, savouring the sounds. History would be made today. The prospect filled him with excitement. He knew some people thought that today's union of three British colonies was doomed to failure. *A rung on a ladder leading nowhere.* He had thought up that phrase a few nights ago and written it down; it might be a line he could use someday.

It was just past dawn and already the summer air was stifling. The night had barely cooled the musty basement flat. If it was this hot at dawn, imagine the rest of the day. He relished the thought. He imagined it would be a day of . . . he tried to muster the right word . . . *distinction*. Not bad, but he could do better. He needed a D'Arcy McGee–type word. He was a speechwriter, after all, or at least a junior parliamentary assistant. The bells signalled something . . .

portentous. Sounds important, but he wondered, did that mean something good, or something bad?

"In any event," he said to himself, "happy birthday," and he jumped out of bed. He grabbed a mildewed towel and headed to the bathhouse behind the flat. The residue of past users in the public privy disgusted him, but this was all a meagre rent provided. The landlord had promised he would have the filth cleaned up. Fat chance. And there wasn't much anyone could do about the smell. At least, he thought, it wasn't as horrid as a logger's shanty, and it was inside.

There was still some warm water in a pannikin. He heated it slightly on the wood stove, soaped his face and started shaving. The razor was old and tired. "But I'm young and agile," he told the mirror. "Handsome—well, sort of. Dashing and suave, in a homespun way. A young man on the rise."

Conor O'Dea was an Irish Catholic in a land dominated by Scottish Presbyterians and Church of England elitists. He had spent a short lifetime trying to be accepted by those in power. He had learned the catchphrases: "For Queen and Country." "The Empire. The Glorious Empire." His charm, hard work and perseverance had manoeuvred him to the sidelines of politics. Close, but he wanted to get even closer. He knew that most people in the neighbourhood thought he was overreaching. An upstart from the rowdy lumber camps with delusions of glory.

He scratched away at his red stubble and rubbed the condensation off the mirror so he could examine his handiwork. Some soap was trapped in his bushy right side-whisker. In the American Union Army, General Ambrose Burnside had started the fad and a new name for sprouting whiskers. Conor was eager to look modern, and growing sideburns was cheap.

Back in the tenement flat, he considered his wardrobe. His one old suit would have to survive the day's proceedings, and with a little adornment, maybe get him into a proper party that night. Apparently there would be evening fireworks at Major's Hill Park. His pants were threadbare; the seams were too thick, the stitching unrefined. Good enough for the poor Irish section, but he wanted better. He had tried to iron his shirt by pressing it between books. It worked as long as he ignored a persistent wrinkle across his chest. He expertly put the finishing touches on his tie's knot, twirling the silk with dexterity. D'Arcy McGee had bought him the tie, but he had taught himself the procedure. He put on the slightly too snug waistcoat and wiped off a few dried food stains. He squeezed his feet into freshly polished shoes that had once fit him. He proudly put on his jacket. One last look at his hair and his stylish red whiskers, and he was ready.

He knew there wasn't much that was dashing about a political apprentice still living with his father. He was only as suave as he could pretend. But he was smart, or at least smarter than most people he knew, and he was definitely on the rise—heading upwind from this shabby flat in Lowertown.

Before leaving, he had a final duty. His father had slept through the morning symphonies of roosters and bells, but he had to get ready for work. Conor gingerly shook the snoring mass in the other bed, dreading the reaction. Thomas O'Dea had worked the late shift at Lapierre's Tavern and was working today. Conor wanted to let him sleep, but he knew Thomas had some deliveries to make before the first shift. Somehow, his father's problems became his fault. He had better make sure Thomas wouldn't be late.

"It's time to get up, Da," Conor whispered. His father moved with the prodding.

"Yeah, off with you, then," he growled.

And Conor O'Dea scurried into the streets of Ottawa's Lowertown.

LOWERTOWN. Market stalls, taverns and brothels. Yelling hustlers and haggling customers, fishmongers and farmers, butchers and bullies all peddling their wares amid hungry street urchins and deft pickpockets. The Byward Market in Lowertown was a frenetic opera stage featuring the best and worst of humanity just under Parliament's tower. Conor absorbed it all. The sun had been shining throughout the week, and for a change the streets were not covered in mud. Instead, Conor coughed dust and gagged on the sulphuric stew of outhouse and sawmill smells.

Conor smiled at those he recognized as he passed by. Mrs. O'Connell was putting some fruit on a wheelbarrow. He wandered over. "And how's my favourite woman?" She threw him an apple. Breakfast.

"You're skin and bones, my boy. Those books you read don't give you strength."

"I'll pay you on a Thursday," he promised, emphasizing the Irish lilt. He would sound very different a mile from here.

"You'll not be payin' me, and you know it. You and your fancy clothes."

He bit into the fruit. "Thanks, Mrs. O." It sounded more like "tanks." This was a daily ritual, and Conor appreciated it. He knew that many of the older women in Lowertown worried about him—a determined young man and his sometimes-derelict father. They kept an eye on him and helped the O'Deas with the occasional meal, especially during the holidays. A few of the mothers thought Conor might be a good match for their daughters, but he had never shown much interest in the neighbourhood servant girls and dressmakers.

Conor looked completely out of place in his suit and tie, amid labourers and layabouts in open shirts and ripped jackets. He dodged the farm animals roaming about the squalor in the streets—pigs, cows, hens and those noisy roosters—trying to protect his worn but well-polished shoes. He nodded to a few women sweeping out doorways or throwing out night soil and avoided more than one rumpled man lying on the street, fast asleep. One drunk was still desperately hugging an empty bottle. He looked familiar. Conor had probably seen him at Lapierre's over the years. And, of course, there were the street people huddled in doorways. A mother holding her child looked up at Conor as he walked by. If there had been any spare money in his pocket, he might have given her some.

"Hey, Cookie," someone called from an open window, "why the getup?" Conor knew the voice. It was a skidder from up the Opeongo Line; a logger in town throwing his money around. The madame of the house would soon be sending him packing. Conor waved a friendly but simple hello. He hated being called Cookie. He'd grown from a cook's assistant in a logging camp to a parliamentary assistant in a logging town. His other nickname in the logging camp was Bookie, because his nose was so often stuck in a book. He didn't like hearing any reminders of his rough past.

"Will you make me breakfast, Cookie?" the skidder joked.

Conor ignored him. He crossed the Rideau Canal at Sappers Bridge and headed along the wooden plank sidewalk on Wellington Street into another world. From Lowertown to Uppertown.

THE height of land that dominated Ottawa's Uppertown had been called Barracks Hill, and it housed soldiers before 1857, when Queen Victoria surprised everyone and chose the backwoods town as the capital of Canada. "An arctic lumber village," some wag said, and he wasn't far off. But any place could be refurbished. So out went the soldiers and in came the architects, stonemasons and tradesmen. A grand stone building burst out of the ordinary streets on the bank of the Ottawa River. Barracks Hill became Parliament Hill, and a palace of power peered down on the citizenry below.

Uppertown was a grid of new houses and shops. The streets were wider and the buildings more substantial than in Lowertown. Water was routinely delivered by horse and wagon, and night soil was picked up daily. Often Conor would linger along Rideau or Wellington Street, admiring the merchandise on display. But not today. He had his sights on Parliament Hill.

He arrived far too early—the ceremony would not begin until eleven o'clock—but he knew he would have some conniving to perform to earn a front-row seat, and that would take time. Beads of sweat were already forming under stray hairs on the back of his neck. It was going to be a swelteringly hot day. He slapped at a mosquito and looked at his hand. There was blood. How the mosquitoes love me, he thought, and flashed that engaging, vulnerable smile his father had told him was so like his mother's.

"I'm here," he said to no one in particular. "So let's get started."

A mile away in the new suburb of Sandy Hill, John A. Macdonald was nursing a hangover. He had toasted the new Dominion perhaps a dozen times too many the night before. He had shaken the hands of his opponents, slapped the backs of his colleagues and shocked many of their wives with a ribald story or two. He had had a wonderful time. And now he sought help.

"Agnes, where's my blasted sash?"

"Hanging up, dear."

"Where's my damned sword?"

"Where you left it, I suppose."

By the time John Macdonald was ready to leave Quadrilateral, his rented house on Daly Street, he had asked his young wife the whereabouts of just about every piece of formal clothing he owned. He had found the headache potion himself, not wanting to disturb her with his problems, or open the door to a scolding.

"A cocktail suits me more than a cocked hat," he muttered to himself.

His headache wasn't helped by the stench on the main floor. "Those damned useless drains," he whined. "This house smells like a . . ." He almost used a coarse word, then smiled to himself. "It smells like a necessary room." His wife could hardly disagree. Since coming to Ottawa, she had consulted carpenters and handymen, but there was little anyone could do to relieve the unpleasant smell until the city built a new drainage system. In London, modern water closets were being installed—at least for the few who could afford them—but that was not on anyone's plan for this aspiring lumber town.

"It's no worse today, dear. It may just be that you're feeling a bit under the weather."

"No, I'm fit as a fiddle." And, he thought, three fingers of whisky would be just the ticket right now.

Agnes Macdonald knew the day's schedule by heart. Her brother, Hewitt Bernard, was her husband's private secretary, and they often conspired to free some of his time for her. Lunch with his cabinet would mean drinks with his cabinet, so she had convinced Hewitt to book him a few hours of rest in the afternoon. But one afternoon meeting with an insistent policeman could not be moved. "Irish business," her brother said. And she resented it.

She looked her husband over judiciously. A peculiar face, she thought, but one that emanated distinctive charm. Or devilish charm. He loved dressing well and had somewhat flamboyant tastes, at least in Agnes's view. Today he could indulge his love of colour. He was dressed in full formal regalia: bright red jacket with gold embroidery. A sword was sheathed treacherously by his side. She thought he looked a bit wobbly this morning.

"Watch your step or you'll trip," she warned. "You don't know what you may cut off."

He took a few practice steps, trying not to let the sword swing. Deftly, Agnes moved the sword out of harm's way. "What did you ever do without me?" she asked gently.

"I don't know," he answered, clutching his sword. "I really don't know."

There were many things John A. Macdonald didn't know on that sunny July morning. He was uncertain about the political union he was forging. Was there really the will to build a nation? He was unsure of the West. Would he be able to talk British Columbia into entering Confederation if he could build a railway? And could they build a road through those infernal mountains? He was nervous about the East. Nova Scotia was talking of leaving before they had even started. He knew he had practically bought the New Brunswick election. Could he talk the East into helping fund the railway? He was always doubtful about his own political power. Would he stay one step ahead of his enemies? Could he control the factions in this land of religious and language divisions? He had won more battles than he had lost, but there were many ahead. What compromises, what chicanery would be needed to stay the course?

He grimaced and closed his eyes to relieve the pain.

He knew it would be a day of both celebration and mourning—festivities and funerals staged side by side, buildings covered in flags confronting buildings draped in black. Amid the cheers and toasts of the new Canadians, there were many who preferred being Nova Scotians, New Brunswickers, Ontarians or Quebecers. They had not asked for this political union, and they didn't care if it lived or died. Distinct, squabbling, practically ungovernable British colonies would be pasted together today. It would be his job as the first prime minister of Canada to make the glue stick.

And there was something else he didn't know. When he and his wife left Quadrilateral, they had no idea that they were being watched. The newly laid-out streets of Sandy Hill, just east and a little south of Parliament Hill, were filled with people from all walks of life—gentry, servants, shopkeepers—so John Macdonald paid no attention to a man lingering across the street.

As he helped her into the carriage, Agnes Macdonald whispered demurely, "I can lean on no other arm like yours." Macdonald sat back contentedly and called out to the driver, "Buckley, take us to the office."

It would have been simple, the man across the street thought, lifting the collar of his old grey coat. A flick of the blade and a slit throat. So easy. But the time wasn't right. Not yet.

He pulled from his pocket the piece of paper that the insufferable colonel had given him. He checked the address on Sussex Street and the name. "O'Dea." He decided he had best hurry.

2

onor O'Dea looked at his timepiece. It didn't work properly, but it gave an approximation of the hour. And it looked sophisticated. Parliament Hill was starting to fill with people, but to his dismay they were mainly common folks who were happy to stay outside and enjoy the weather. He needed a contact, someone to get him in the building. From afar he spotted Will Trotter, in his formal pageboy outfit, and a plan came into shape.

"Will, how are you?" In their fraying black suits with tails, starched collars propping their heads up, Conor thought the pageboys looked like penguins, and he often told them so.

"I'm fine, Conor. What are you doing here? Do you have an invitation to go inside?"

"Not exactly, but you might help." He flashed a smile.

As a pageboy, young Will had a pass into the Centre Block. He was only sixteen years old, but he had influence beyond his position and his age because he had long been a favourite of John Macdonald's. Rumour had it that Will served Macdonald gin in his water goblet during long debates.

"Where's Mr. McGee?" Will asked. "I didn't see him this morning."

"He's in Toronto. That's why I'm here." Conor built on his story, knowing Will would go along with whatever he said. "Mr. McGee couldn't be here, so he wanted me to take his place. Be his represent-ative. He just never got around to getting me a pass."

Will Trotter knew D'Arcy McGee well. McGee rented a room at his mother's boarding house when he was in Ottawa. He looked at Conor with mocked sternness. "Are you lying?" he asked.

"Of course." Conor smiled impishly.

Will grinned back at him. "In that case, follow me. I'll get you in."

"You wouldn't have a flask of water handy, would you?" Conor asked mischievously as they entered the Centre Block.

JOHN and Agnes Macdonald arrived on Parliament Hill just before eleven o'clock. They paused outside, greeting people and smiling at the crowd until the other politicians and dignitaries had arrived. She was escorted off to sit with the ladies and he waited outside, chatting with Buckley. Macdonald wanted to be the last person to enter the building, to create a grand entrance, and he wanted a little more time for the headache potion to take effect before he had to meet his col-leagues. Even today, someone was sure to say something that would only make his head ache even more.

Inside the foyer, there was a stir of excitement. A police constable pushed Conor O'Dea aside. It was approaching eleven; the proces-sion was beginning. Conor held his ground and watched as each pol-itician entered. The July sun glowed like a spotlight on them, but as they entered the building, they faded into darkness.

George-Étienne Cartier, the lawyer and great nation builder from Canada East (or Quebec, as it would now officially be called), arrived first. He looked very much in charge: his back straight, his eyes fixed forward, and his manner at once cavalier and dignified. Conor was always surprised at how short he was. The talk of his mistress in Montreal who wore trousers and smoked cigars intrigued

Conor. The portly Alexander Galt strutted a bit. Macdonald often joked that Galt's constituents were the rich and the powerful, but Conor knew it was Galt who had come up with the original design for Confederation nine long years ago. He had the right to strut a bit. Leonard Tilley, the teetotaller from New Brunswick, followed as if sprinkling the holy water of religious calm and resolve. The parade continued. One bewhiskered gentleman after another.

Finally, John A. Macdonald entered, walking jauntily but still seeming to take his time. While his eyes adjusted to the darker hall, he winked at friendly faces and waved to admirers. With each step, he did his best not to damage himself with his ceremonial sword. Meanwhile, his head continued to pound, steadily and unrelentingly.

Conor savoured the performance. Macdonald did more than acknowledge the crowd; he befriended it, played to it and rose above it. Most of the so-called Fathers of Confederation ambled into the building as if going to a meeting. They were businesslike and dutiful. Macdonald swept in, clearly the leading man. Politics was his stage play. Parliament was his theatre. He loved being the star.

Conor knew you shouldn't always believe John Macdonald, you couldn't always trust him, but you had to admire him.

CONOR passed by young Will Trotter standing at the entrance. He really did look like a penguin in an ill-fitting uniform. "Cheers," he declared, as he entered the stone building. "I owe you one, Willy."

The politicians had assembled. Fourteen members of Canada's first cabinet, with a beaming John A. Macdonald, "The First of Equals," standing in the forefront. Conor studied them with a critical eye. D'Arcy McGee had told him to assess a scene as if he were a newspaper reporter. Think how a Tory paper would write it up. Then imagine how the Grits would see it. Conservatives vs. Liberals. Look at it from all perspectives. But report it as you see it.

So what did he think? Not a bad group overall, but not the best. Within Her Majesty's first Canadian Privy Council, there were a few glaring omissions. Charles Tupper, who had fought so hard to convince Nova Scotia to enter the union, was in Halifax, waiting for different political awards. George Brown, Macdonald's arch-rival but Confederation's indispensable supporter, was back in Toronto, ensuring that his newspaper, *The Globe*, gave him and not Macdonald full credit. Their exclusion from cabinet didn't bother Conor. After all, Tupper was better off chasing skirts in Nova Scotia, and Brown, the steadfast Liberal, or Grit, would never stand being in Macdonald's shadow. Brown and Macdonald had worked together for this one great cause and were more comfortable as enemies again.

For Conor, there was a more painful omission: the Honourable Thomas D'Arcy McGee. And Conor wasn't alone. Throughout Parliament Hill, questions were being asked. "Where's D'Arcy?" "Where's McGee?" "Where's the Irishman?"

Conor eased his way to the front and settled beside a rather pompous man in an oversized beaver felt hat. A little warm for a summer's day, Conor thought, but it was a celebration, and what's more Canadian than a fur hat?

Conor knew where D'Arcy McGee was, and he knew why he wasn't here. McGee had accepted a speaking engagement in Toronto, out of the limelight, away from the humiliation of watching others sworn into the cabinet. John A. Macdonald often said he was never much of carpenter but was a master cabinetmaker. A certain number of Protestants balanced by a certain number of Roman Catholics. A quota from Quebec, from Ontario, from the Maritimes. McGee and Tupper had agreed to decline posts in Canada's first cabinet to make room for someone named Edward Kenney. Kenney was Irish, a Catholic and from Nova Scotia. Macdonald could, as he boasted, kill three birds with one stone. It was unfair, and Macdonald knew it. No harm or insult was intended. It was . . . well, it was politics. But it made Conor furious. McGee spoke for Conor and other Irish-Catholic Canadians. He represented Conor's ideals and his aspirations.

Conor O'Dea had tied much of his ambition to D'Arcy McGee's coattails. He liked to say he was a speechwriter and parliamentary assistant, but he was really McGee's researcher and errand boy. He transcribed McGee's essays and letters, acted as a sounding board for some of his speeches and helped prepare his frenzied days.

"You're not qualified for the job," McGee had told him. "But you've a good Irish name, a studious nature, a youngster's eagerness, and best of all, you won't cost me much money."

Like an Irish labourer, Conor thought.

"And another thing, Conor," McGee had bellowed. "You're almost as ambitious as I was at your age. Not as smart, certainly not as handsome. Oh hell, you're nothing like me. Now get back to work."

Conor was determined to make something of his life. But what exactly? He might become a businessman, and his political contacts would serve him well. He might go into politics himself. What he really wanted was to become a newspaperman, and there were few people better able to teach him than D'Arcy McGee. McGee had edited and published his own newspapers. He had written, and was now revising, his *Popular History of Ireland*. But most important, he was easily the most eloquent orator Conor had ever heard. When he spoke, he lifted an audience out of the monotony of life, he thrilled and inspired, but patience was not a word in McGee's vast vocabulary. He was temperamental, volatile and sometimes intolerant, but he liked to lecture, and Conor was eager to learn.

McGee was teaching him the language of power; Macdonald was showing him the ways of leadership. Soon he would need someone to help him fill his bank account. But not today. Today was a day of grandeur. It was . . . *portentous*. And, he thought, I wonder if I'm pronouncing it right?

Conor had invited himself to the ceremony on Parliament Hill because he wanted to see history being made, because he didn't want to miss anything that might help fill his appetite for knowledge, but also because he wanted to honour his boss. He was there in the name of the greatest Irish-Catholic Canadian of the day: Thomas D'Arcy McGee. And no one was going to stop him.

Let people call him an upstart; he didn't care. Let them think he was reaching beyond his grasp; his day would come. He smiled at the stuffy man in the fur hat. He didn't smile back, but Conor didn't expect him to.

3

By late morning, Thomas O'Dea was already wincing with pain. Tension, anxiety or that old ache from lifting one pine log too many, it didn't matter. He stood behind the bar and braced his back.

Lapierre's was a typical Lowertown tavern. Nothing quaint about it. No pictures on the wall, just price lists, bottles and barrels. It was built for serious drinking. The dingy tavern was as dark as a jail cell, and Thomas O'Dea's downcast expression didn't make it much more inviting.

O'Dea took a yellowing sketch from his pocket and placed it on the bar. The crumbling drawing of his wife, Margaret, looked up at him. It was just a rough likeness drawn by Margaret's cousin; they could never afford a daguerreotype or one of those new photographic pictures the rich were posing for. Still, like a miracle, the fading image smiled at him. The rugged lines on his face couldn't resist the impulse; he smiled back at the innocent picture of youth. "I promised you he would get an education," he told the picture. "I did it for you, but what has it done for me?" He was gently returning the picture to his pocket when a stranger walked into the bar, ordered a Jamesons and sat in the back.

The bar started filling up. In the daytime, most men—they were all men; no self-respecting woman would walk through those doors—drank beer with the occasional watered-down whisky chaser. Some customers would order "grunts," or as much whisky as they could swallow in one swig. A grunt cost only pennies. The grunt drinkers were usually part of the nighttime crowd; the daytime patrons were either committed drinkers or people just too beaten down to face the day. Thomas passed a foaming beer across the counter to a rosy-cheeked regular who cheerfully raised his glass. "Will you toast the new Dominion?" he asked.

"I'd rather not, if you don't mind," Thomas answered firmly.

"Ah, not a believer," the customer chuckled. "Well, I'll drink to anything." And he did, with a hearty gulp.

Across the smoky public house, the man in the back listened attentively. Thomas O'Dea was the first name on the list the colonel had given him. A "potential supporter," it read. "Not confirmed, but worth pursuing." He rubbed his fingers along his new black moustache and scrutinized this Irish bartender. He looked intelligent enough and he was obviously strong willed. Already, through various sources, he had learned that O'Dea had worked as a lumberjack up the Ottawa Valley for more than a decade, until a runaway log almost killed him. Since then, he'd tended bar here at Lapierre's. It was backbreaking work in the lumber camps. Irish work. It could make any man bitter. He had also learned that O'Dea's wife was dead and he still mourned her. He must find out more about her. That might be a way to get at him. The real mystery was the son. He apparently worked for D'Arcy McGee. *That bastard McGee!* His son might have the will of his father, but he must have the heart of a traitor.

"Stand easy," the customer at the bar persisted. "All that's happening is the Canadas are joining up with some other British colonies. It could be the start of something grand. More land. More people. The more the merrier, I say."

Thomas O'Dea looked the man straight in the eye. "Well, I don't say so, sir, and I'm sure you won't mind if I don't share your enthusiasm."

The man in the back raised an eyebrow. Thomas O'Dea was a man of conviction. Barmen usually just agreed with their customers. Keep them talking and they will keep buying beer. After all, conversation was cheap; the liquid costs the money. This man valued his beliefs. Interesting. Useful to know.

The customer banged his empty beer mug on the bar. "I think I'll be off to Parliament Hill to catch the end of the party." He paid his money and tipped his hat to Thomas, who was busy drying mugs. As the door closed, Thomas O'Dea muttered to himself, "My son is up there."

The man in the shadows heard him and was curious. *His son was up there.* There was a complication here, so he should be leery. But maybe, just maybe, that complication could help him. Yes, there could be potential with this Thomas O'Dea.

"Would you like a drink over there?" Thomas shouted across the room. The customer waved his right hand, indicating no, while his left hand covered his face as if he were checking something in his eye. And he left. He knew Thomas O'Dea had barely seen his face. He would never remember the first time they had met. He also knew they would meet again.

THE dignitaries had moved into the Parliament Buildings' Privy Council Chamber, their wives staying back with the select observers. Each cabinet appointee in turn swore his oath of office. Conor noticed Governor General Viscount Monck whispering something to John Macdonald. Monck's long beard covered his mouth, and Conor couldn't tell what he was saying, but it certainly got Macdonald's attention. The prime minister smiled broadly, then almost gasped in horror.

McGee's instructions came back to him: "If you want to know what's going on, don't just observe what's happening; think about it and mull it over in your mind." Conor knew something was certainly going on here.

He was sure that Macdonald would be enraged by Lord Monck's attire. He was dressed in an everyday business suit, while the members of Parliament were resplendent in full ceremonial garb. The governor general seemed to be treating Confederation as just another working day. But Macdonald was reacting to something else. It was something Monck had said. Conor watched carefully as the prime minister left Monck's side. Macdonald turned to the crowd—the actor to his audience—and smiled at each familiar face. When his eyes met Conor's, he looked astonished and slyly winked. Yes, something was happening, and Conor was determined to find out what.

"Don't just watch events," McGee would say. "Wonder. Brood. Get out of the margins and into the page. Be curious. Never lose your curiosity."

"Someday that curiosity will get you into trouble," his father had told him.

It's funny, Conor thought, how D'Arcy McGee and his father gave him such contrary advice.

CONOR had met John Macdonald many times. There were few better places to find Macdonald and D'Arcy McGee on a cold winter evening—or any evening of the year, for that matter—than in the public houses and taverns around Ottawa. The Russell House, Macdonald's favourite haunt, was stately and sophisticated. Lapierre's, on Sussex Street, was shabby, simple and loud, more to McGee's taste. Occasionally, when Macdonald wanted to prove that he too was a man of the people, he would join McGee under the flickering gas lights of Lapierre's. The two men mingled with voters and held court surrounded by the sights and sounds—and smells—of Ottawa's people.

That's where Conor first met the politicians.

While his father tended bar at Lapierre's, Conor earned extra money in the back, washing dishes and cleaning up. The former cook's assistant was handy in a kitchen. To his father's horror, Conor would sometimes sneak into the front to hear McGee and Macdonald spin their countless yarns. He was in a boyish trance as they exchanged quips and each tried to outdo the other's last joke. As the hour got late, the conversation became spicier. Macdonald would beg McGee to sing the song McGee wrote, though it hardly took prodding for McGee to quote himself:

I drank till quite mellow
Then like a brave fellow
Began for to bellow
And shouted for more.

His voice would build until he screamed "shouted for more." Then Macdonald would join in:

But my host held his stick up
Which soon cured my hiccup
As no cash could I pick up
To pay off the score.

To the applause of the room, Macdonald would roar, "You've got to quit drinking, McGee. This government can't afford two drunkards." Then he would wink. The same mischievous wink as today.

Macdonald fascinated Conor. Cartoonists made fun of his bulbous nose, but Conor felt his eyes defined him. He used them to express his many moods. His eyes could be playful, pleading, melancholy or full of cheer. Macdonald was a careful man, his actions were almost always well planned and rehearsed, but the glint in his eye was spontaneous.

"His eyes are shifty, it's as simple as that," Thomas growled one night after Conor had actually been invited to sit down at the same table as Macdonald and McGee. "Shifty and untrustworthy. Stay away from him."

To Thomas O'Dea, everything was simple: Macdonald was a Protestant, and that made him an oppressor. Protestants controlled the best jobs in Ontario and kept the Catholics down—especially Irish Catholics. "'Romanists,' they call us. 'Papists.' And don't think they say it with any affection." Thomas had spent too many hours working for low wages and Protestant bosses to ever forget. Or forgive. D'Arcy McGee's sins were different, but no less enraging. To Thomas, McGee was the most damnable of creatures: a turncoat. McGee may have stayed true to his Catholic faith, but he had criticized Irish freedom fighters, so he had turned against his own people.

Catholic traitor and Protestant oppressor—that was how Thomas O'Dea summed up two lives. At times, Conor wondered what his father thought of *him*, but he dared not ask.

A voice came out of nowhere. "What are you doing here?" Conor had been daydreaming. A firm tap on his shoulder brought him back to reality. He was not in McGee's messy office, or in Lapierre's dingy bar; he was in the Privy Council Chamber on Canada's first day of business.

"I said, what are you doing here, young man?" It was that man under the beaver hat. His voice was stern and authoritative. Before Conor could respond, John Macdonald himself stepped forward. "Don't worry, Ambassador; this young gentleman is here representing a great Canadian."

And again, that wink.

Conor looked at Macdonald, as he so often did, in sheer amazement. How did he know his purpose here? How was he able to come to his defence at the precise moment of need? Still, he had better watch his step. Ambassadors can be a touchy breed, and he was, after all, nothing more than a lowly assistant without an invitation to the event.

The prime minister whispered in his ear, "You seem to have a knack for getting a front-row seat on history." And he added wryly, "Tell D'Arcy we miss him."

"I will, Mr. Macdonald," Conor answered respectfully.

"Actually, you can soon call me John," the prime minister said with a teasing smile. "Sir John."

So that was it. Macdonald would be knighted. That was what Governor General Monck had told him. "Don't just observe, damn it, interpret." There must have been some bad news, too, or Macdonald would not have also looked aghast. "Look at the story from all angles." Maybe Galt had not been given an equal honour? Or Cartier?

Sir John. He mouthed the words. It sounded right. Sir John A. Macdonald. He deserved it. Conor couldn't imagine Confederation without him. He was the negotiator, the compromiser, the architect, and now he would be the administrator.

George-Étienne Cartier might be a brilliant lawyer, but he was too much of a stuffed shirt to lead a new country. George Brown had played a crucial role in forging an alliance between the Liberals and Conservatives, but he was too abrasive to ever win a national election. Charles Tupper was too much of a bully, Leonard Tilley too

28

sanctimonious and Alexander Galt far too impatient. As for McGee, his fame stretched as far as Macdonald's, but he was simply too bombastic, too belligerent. His fiery eloquence could stir a crowd or sting an opponent, but too often his words left a wound. McGee's rhetoric gave Confederation its soul, but Macdonald's skill gave it skin and bones. Of all the politicians, John Macdonald was the most adaptable, the most pragmatic and the most politically astute.

But that was Conor's opinion. He knew Macdonald's enemies would heartily disagree. Many thought that Macdonald degraded the political process; that he was a rogue in power and a rascal in private. Macdonald never disagreed with his detractors; he just deflected the blows. He once told George Brown, "The people would rather have me drunk than you sober." And the polls proved him right.

There was a story Macdonald loved to tell. A year or so ago—Macdonald was always unclear about dates in his anecdotes—he led a delegation to Washington. One evening at a reception in Georgetown, he struck up conversation with a senator's wife. "I understand you have a very smart man up there in Canada," she said. "John A. Macdonald."

"Yes, ma'am, we do."

"But they say he's a dreadful man."

"Yes indeed, a perfect rascal." Conor could picture Macdonald smiling wickedly as he toyed with her.

"But why do you keep such a man in power?"

"Well, you see, ma'am, Canadians just can't seem to get along without him."

Apparently, at that moment, the senator arrived and said to his wife, "My dear, I see you have met John Macdonald."

The woman was aghast, but Macdonald put her at ease. "Now, don't apologize. All you've been saying is perfectly true, and it's well known at home."

The Fathers of Confederation. It was a group of able men, but only Macdonald was essential. Conor looked into those watery eyes and proclaimed, "Congratulations, Sir John."

LIKE a cat, he prowled the backstreets of Ottawa's Lowertown, his hand clutching a knife concealed in one of his coat's deep pockets. Ready and alert. In case. Always just in case. He couldn't stomach the thought of the pointless morning festivities on Parliament Hill. It was a national holiday, but he was at work. He had to get to know this dowdy, dusty town, learn the back alleys, understand the patterns and rhythms of the place.

Children were playing lacrosse down a side street. A missed ball hurtled toward him. He stepped out of the way. Rather than pick up the ball and throw it back, he watched cautiously as one of the young boys ran past him to retrieve it.

He had a decision to make. Whom should he choose first? He felt like God. He held the power of life and death.

A tall, gangly man approached him on the street, disturbing his thoughts. The hair on the back of his neck stiffened. Quickly, he readied his knife hand. "G'day to you, sir," the tall man said with an Irish-infused Ottawa Valley twang. The man in the grey coat looked away and said nothing. The tall man thought how rude this stranger was, especially on this happy day. How was he to know that he had killed people for lesser crimes than a simple hello?

The colonel—was he really a colonel, or did he just call himself that?—had talked of targets, and he considered the options. What would happen to Canada if Macdonald were found with a bullet in his skull? And what would happen to this fragile child they called Confederation if an Irish Catholic murdered him? What a pleasant thought. But what if McGee fell and his traitorous blood coloured the streets? That would send a clear message. Macdonald or McGee? Both scum. Both deserving to die. The self-important colonel had hired him to create confusion and anarchy. "A reign of terror," he had said. His wish would be granted. But there was more to this than a job. He had a personal score to settle. He thought back on his childhood in Ireland and how a man's eloquence had inspired him. He pictured his father dying in desperate, dreadful pain. A so-called martyr. He remembered his vow to his mother. And to his father's memory. Yes, there would be revenge; sweet revenge. He knew his first target. The colonel would approve. He smiled at the prospect, wondering, was there ever any doubt?

4

For a week, Ottawa's townspeople had been collecting material to burn: stray wood, packing cases, tar barrels, old newspapers, anything. They had assembled it all in a gigantic pyramid in Major's Hill Park, overlooking the river to the east of the Parliament Buildings. At exactly noon it was set ablaze. At the same time, from their drill shed in Lowertown, the Ottawa Field Battery fired a 101-gun salute. It looked like an inferno and sounded like war.

Conor watched the fire and wondered what to do next. He probably should simply go home, hang up his suit, read a bit and try his luck at a Confederation party that night. Or maybe he should help his father out at the bar, give the old man a rest and make some money in tips.

Then everything stopped.

In the fire's glow, he saw a girl with shimmering black hair weave through the crowd. She was tall, stately and alluring. He was spellbound. She was dressed in a hoop skirt pulled tightly around her waist. Stylish and modern, definitely not a dress made by an Ottawa seamstress. She stopped to talk to . . . Conor craned his neck to see who it was . . . It was Will Trotter. Why was she talking to *him*? Her right hand brushed her hair, and he glimpsed her profile. But only for a tantalizing second. My God, she is beautiful, he thought. He summoned his courage.

"Will, what's next?" he called and moved toward them.

"Conor, how are you? Say, have you met my sister, Meg?"

So that's who this vision was—Meg Trotter. She had changed so much that he hadn't recognized her. He tried not to stare. He hadn't seen her in years; he wondered if she would remember him, or if she had ever noticed him.

Thomas O'Dea had worked upriver from October to April and, like many loggers, moved to Ottawa in the off-season, so Conor had spent most of his summers in town. But he had never really been part of any "crowd." He was quiet and shy and had accumulated few friends. He spent the summers reading, doing odd jobs and trying to keep Thomas away from the bottle. And, of course, he studied the people who lived in Uppertown, people like Meg Trotter. She had always been one of the prettiest girls in Ottawa, but now she was stunning. Her long black hair struggling to pull free of the combs framed a face both strong and delicate. *Porcelain*, Conor thought, was the word they used for her kind of complexion. Her eyes were sky blue, an uncommon colour with such black hair, but there was nothing common about this woman. She had a wise, inquisitive pout, which he desperately wanted to transform into a smile. He affected a tone of confidence. "Hello, Meg. We may have met last year . . ." She returned his gaze with those blue eyes that commanded attention, and his confidence withered.

"Last year, I was in London," she corrected him. "No, I don't believe we've ever met."

While he was tripping over his words, she was looking him over. Red hair, green eyes—very Irish. Tall but not lanky; fashionable whiskers, she supposed, in an American sort of way. His clothes spoke more of Portobello Market than Savile Row, but he was clearly trying. There was something interesting about him. She surprised herself when she added, "I'm sure I would have remembered you."

"So, umm . . . how was London?" he said, trying to ignite conversation and recognizing that this was a feeble start. He wondered how she could afford such travel, but remembered Will saying something about a wealthy aunt.

"London is like nowhere else," she enthused. "It's the centre of the world."

Conor wondered about the people she would have met there, the parties and balls, and considered the backwater she was in now. He started to feel like the low-rent son of a lumberman. He hated that. But he persevered. "Are they still building the statue of Lord Nelson in London?" He had read about the extraordinary construction.

She looked at him, confused.

"I think they were going to call it Trafalgar Square."

"Dear me," she said. "That was finished years ago." Unlike Will, she had a slight English accent. "It is quite magnificent."

Damn it, he thought. Why are my hand-me-down books and magazines so old? Sometimes he mispronounced words because he knew them only from seeing them in print. It made him sound ignorant. And now he wasn't up to date. He stared at her, considering what to say next. Something current. Something upper-crust. She seemed to take some delight in watching him squirm.

"The Queen," he said, trying to restrain his Irish accent. "Queen Victoria. How is she? I mean, is she still in mourning for Prince Albert?"

"Well, I didn't actually look her up," she said with an upturned eye. "But Her Majesty seems to be back in society a little more."

Nelson. Victoria and Albert. What else? He was babbling to fill time, to sound learned, but he was going blank. "And why were you in London?"

"To study."

He could have asked, "To study what?" or "How long were you there?" or even "How did you like your studies?" But he was afraid to engage her in a conversation in which he couldn't keep up. Instead, he turned to Will. "What are you doing this afternoon?"

"I don't have to work. Some of us are going swimming."

Pause.

"Maybe have a picnic by the river."

Another pause.

"Do you want to come, Conor?"

Finally!

Conor regained his composure. "Will you be coming, Meg? I'd love to hear more about London."

Her eyes sparkled like sapphires and there was a glimmer of a smile. "You know, I might. I just might."

WALKING back to Lowertown, Conor was in a daze. Everything about the day's political spectacle now seemed dulled compared to the moment he saw Meg Trotter. He had never felt sure of himself around girls. There weren't any women up in the lumber camps. The women the loggers chased in the off-season were nothing like Meg. He would have to improve his performance if she was going to buy his act.

But there were practical matters to deal with—endless practical matters. A picnic meant food. He could get some from his father at Lapierre's. No, he'd pick something up at the Byward Market. Better yet, he would come late—fashionably late—and say he had already eaten. That would save him some money. A bathing costume? He'd never owned anything that unnecessary. Growing up in the North Country, you went into the cold river waters to wash, not play. And if you swam at all, you swam naked. A bit risqué for an Ottawa afternoon. He would just have to say he didn't want to swim. He would bring a book, some bread and a beer. He would come armed with clever stories and bright repartee. He would not betray his simple background and clumsiness. And, most important, he would try not to babble on this time.

THE market was still bustling with activity, but the smell had hardly improved. No regular night soil pickups here. The middle class would travel below the salt to Lowertown to shop for food and then retreat upwind as soon as they could. The upper class would send their servants. Conor was heading home.

There was a lineup at a butcher's stand. He looked at it with dismay. He hated waiting in line. One summer when he was about ten years old, his father took his hand and announced, "We're going to get some new clothes for you." Conor hoped that they would go to one of the new dry-goods stores on Rideau Street, or maybe a proper tailor shop, but they headed in the other direction, down Sussex to the Élisabeth Bruyère Church. The Grey Nuns were handing out used clothes to Ottawa's poor. When Conor saw the line of people outside the church, he stopped. He yanked his hand from his father's grip.

"You said new clothes."

"They'll be new for you, and they'll fit you better."

Conor looked at the people in the queue: orphans, beggars, the waifs and strays of Lowertown waiting patiently to get something for nothing. He saw children he knew standing uncomfortably with their mothers or fathers, shuffling their feet, trying to preserve their dignity. Humiliated, but in need.

"I won't wear someone else's discards."

"You'll wear what I tell you. You're growing like a weed, and this is all we can afford."

Conor figured that his father had squandered his winter's wages gambling or drinking or something worse. He saw the look of shame in his father's eyes. He could have taken pity, been understanding, but there was no way he was going to line up with the others. He was not desperate. He would never allow such a disgrace. He ran away, furious and determined.

It was the first time he defied his father.

"**CONOR**, do you want an apple?"

He knew the voice. Her name was Polly. He wasn't sure of her last name. Ryan, maybe. Or Reagan. She was friendly with Thomas. Polly was a washerwoman of dubious reputation. She was a widow, but there was talk of a mysterious past. A bit of the scruff, in Conor's mind. She repeated, "Would you like an apple?"

"No, I'm fine," he answered and kept walking.

Was he a snob? Sure. He didn't like Polly and he didn't care if she knew it. But he did smile at Mrs. O'Connell as he ambled toward her stall. "I'll be t'anking you again for the breakfast, Mrs. O."

THERE weren't many people on the banks of the Ottawa River. The Rideau Canal was a safer place to swim, but Meg had always liked the drama of the river. It was a place of stories and adventure. By mid-afternoon, she had grown bored with sitting by the river with her brother's dim-witted friends. She had found that Conor character interesting, with his clumsy talk of Nelson and Victoria. She rather liked watching the boys get flustered around her, but she had a sense that this one wouldn't stay flustered long. There was a resolved look behind that scrubbed face. But those whiskers! Who did he think he was, General Burnside?

She had acted as if she didn't know him, but she did remember him from Ottawa summers, his face always hidden behind a book. Her mother had recently told her about D'Arcy McGee's bright young assistant. An Irish boy without a chip on his shoulder. A very promising young man pulling himself up from the dirty streets. Meg thought the Irish were a homesick people who prayed and swore and drank too much. In London, they were always causing trouble with their appeals for Home Rule and their violent ways. They were colourful, she'd give them that, but curious, too, with their extravagant churches and pompous priests. She stopped herself. This is terrible. "Live and let live," was how her mother had brought her up. "Be respectful of others."

She had been raised as a Protestant—a Methodist, actually—by her father, but she hadn't been to church since his funeral five years ago. At his death, her mother turned away from organized religion and declared herself "a free thinker." She didn't reject the existence of God, but took a dim view of the practice of religion.

Will was never really interested in philosophical discussions, but Meg embraced the freedom of her mother's eccentric and, to some, heretical beliefs. She read Ralph Waldo Emerson and Henry David Thoreau, the transcendentalists from New England, who believed that the individual was the spiritual centre of the universe. That made sense to her. People, not priests or pastors. Like her mother, she found power in poetry and the divine in the miracle of nature— and there certainly was a lot of nature in this wild country. Her father would not have approved of these ideas. In fact, most people didn't, so the Widow Trotter and her free-thinking daughter usually kept their radical views to themselves.

Meg looked at the river and up to the beautiful Gatineau Hills.

Rather far from windswept Galilee or the busy River Thames. These Canadians wanted to create "Westminster in the Wilderness." They saw themselves as empire builders, more British than Yorkshire peers. What rubbish. Why didn't they accept the wonders they had? The vastness of the land. The wild green forests. The freedom of open spaces. London was grandiose, with its statuesque buildings and magnificent promenades, but this land was glorious, with its untamed beauty and changing seasons. Better to worship nature's might than perpetuate old prejudices—or fight yesterday's wars.

And where was that Irish boy? She wanted to taunt him some more.

THE walkway behind Parliament Hill was sometimes called Lover's Walk. Conor walked it alone. It was mid-afternoon when he carefully descended the steps to the river. He quickly spotted Will Trotter's group sitting by the water's edge. He knew most of them vaguely, and cared little for them. He preferred the company of older people. In fact, he found most people his age vacuous and a little silly. He had befriended Will more as a younger brother than a contemporary. He liked Will's sense of humour and they shared a love for the game of politics, but he glanced past Will, ignoring his friends, looking for . . .

Meg.

She sat calmly reading. The very picture of serenity. It was clear to Conor that she was not concerned about when, or even if, he might arrive. He decided to be forthright and approached her with the lines he had been practising for an hour.

"May I join you?"

She nodded, slightly.

"What are you reading?" he asked.

"Tennyson."

Damn it. He'd expected her to say Charles Dickens, so he could go on about the Artful Dodger and sound learned. Or even Edward Bulwer-Lytton, in which case he could show wit and well-placed sarcasm—"It was a dark and stormy night . . ." She put the book down and filled the pause. "Have you read him?"

"No, I'm not much of a poet," he stuttered. "But I love to read."

"And what are you reading these days?" She had already noted with disdain that neither her brother nor his friends had brought along anything to read.

"I just finished Macauley's *History of England*, and now I'm reading an account of Wellington at Waterloo," he said, proudly.

"Nelson. Wellington. Trafalgar. Waterloo. Are you aiming for the service?"

"No, I like studying strategy. And I'm fascinated by the glory of empire."

Here was his plan: He had rehearsed a conversation about England and empire and queens and dukes—the stuff a pretty, sophisticated girl from London would want to talk about, the stuff she would never expect an Irishman to care about. He would demonstrate the depth of his knowledge, show how much they had in common, and then start asking her about life in London, the greatest city in the world. He would initiate, manage and control the conversation. He would impress.

Instead, she took command. "I don't know how anyone could think of the glory of war these days after the war between the American states," she said. "It disgusts me."

He answered truthfully. "It fascinates me. The willingness of men to run into the fire, of brothers who kill each other, of the power of hate."

"Is hate more interesting than love?"

"More interesting, but not as appealing." He was satisfied with his answer. Clever. Sensitive. Even a bit daring. He'd rarely thought much about love, and he was uncomfortable talking about it. He'd never seen love in his father's life, and he was not sure he would recognize it in his own. The institution of marriage appealed to him. It was proper. He took for granted that he would eventually find a suitable wife who would help guide him up the social ladder. Was that love, or just the appropriate thing to do?

"You are different," she said and returned to her book.

Will and his friends were talking about some sport called "base ball" that was becoming popular in the United States. Conor considered joining their conversation, then thought better of it and opened his book, pretending to concentrate. Did I go too far with the empire bit? he thought. Probably. He decided to retreat and attack later.

Meg called over to her younger brother, "Come on, Will. Let's go swimming." She dropped her towel and stood up. Conor discreetly watched her walk into the water in her long, flowing bathing costume. Not for the first time, he wished someone would devise more revealing bathing garments. After all, they would dry faster.

DOWN the cliff, under the Parliament Buildings, the river was misleadingly treacherous. The current quickened and swirled, and the water turned angry and shrill. The voyageurs had said the water boiled, and named the rapids Chaudière. By the 1860s, there were modern dangers. Stray logs from the rafts upriver floated freely in the river's current, many bearing lethal, rusting spikes. Those implanted in the river bottom were called deadheads. The worst ones were hidden just under the surface.

Meg confidently swam a few breaststrokes, then turned and floated on her back. Conor watched her intently. What gave her such self-assuredness? Her education? Her beauty? Good Lord, she even swam with poise. Then, out of the corner of his eye, he saw a log right behind her. *A deadhead.* He looked closer. There was a spike jutting out of it.

"Meg!" he screamed, but she couldn't hear him. He called to a boy who was splashing around uselessly near her. He screamed at her again. But she kept floating toward the rusting nail, gently kicking and propelling herself toward disaster.

He had to react. And fast. He dove into the water, kicked away and swam frantically toward her. Head up, staring at her, arms pulling water, feet kicking wildly, he was a man possessed. His clothes weighed him down, but he found strength he didn't know he had. Gasping for air, he reached out and grabbed her. He pulled her tightly toward him, away from the deadhead, away from danger. He felt he was in heaven. Meg Trotter was actually in his arms. Then he saw the look of horror on her face. My God, he thought, she thinks I have attacked her. He coughed water and breathlessly sputtered, "You were going to hit a deadhead."

She looked behind her and saw the log with the sharp nail sticking out. It was just off to her side, out of harm's way. She smiled. "Thank you, Conor. Thank you very much. I've been in London so long I forgot how dangerous the river can be."

She held on to him so tightly that Conor thought maybe it really was his birthday.

5
===

It was mid-afternoon in Sandy Hill, and John Macdonald was supposed to be relaxing. Immediately after the Privy Council ceremony, at a private working lunch with his cabinet, he had to face the fury of his slighted colleagues. He knew only time—and a few more knighthoods, if he could help arrange it—would heal the wounds.

Agnes sat peacefully knitting as her husband paced the drawing room, dodging the cluttered side tables. Now that his headache had subsided, he poured himself a glass of sherry. "Medicine, my dear," he insisted.

While they were on Parliament Hill, the staff must have tried to soften the smell from the rotting wooden drains by disinfecting them with chloride and lime. He didn't know which scent he detested more: yesterday's excrement or today's disinfectant. He held the sherry glass to his nose. And looked at the clock. Fifteen minutes late. The nerve! Of course, Macdonald had been deliberately late for many meetings in his career. Arriving last showed who had the busiest schedule, who was most important. But when someone kept him waiting, it was inexcusable and damnably rude. He continued pacing anxiously.

It was Confederation Day, and already there were problems to iron out. He looked at Agnes, knitting by the window. The aristocrat's daughter, so much younger than him, and so damned content. Well, he wasn't content. In fact, he was starting to find the peace and quiet in the room infuriating. Fifteen minutes late. Imagine!

"So what do you think, milady?" he asked, with an affected accent. A Scot from Glasgow trying to sound like an Englishman from Belgravia. "I guess we're all just petty provincial politicians to the likes of you."

"Not all of you." She smiled coyly. Agnes Macdonald was a child of the British bureaucracy. Her father had been attorney general in Jamaica. While cash had been scarce, status had not. She grew up in a world of butlers, cooks, maids and servants. She would often say that her people were poor as church mice, but what a splendid church they had. That was as close as she came to joking. The minor aristocrat's daughter was more commanding than charming; more severe than sweet. Although Agnes was twenty years younger than her husband, it seemed more natural to call her Lady Macdonald than to call him Sir John.

Macdonald's first wife, the sickly and long-suffering Isabella, had died ten years earlier. For thirteen of their fourteen years together, John Macdonald tended her sickbed, watching her health decline. She took laudanum, liquid opium, to relieve her pain, just as her husband often turned to alcohol for a spark of joy. He rarely spoke of Isabella and never talked of her death. Agnes wondered whether, in the end, he had felt relief. Isabella had been sick for so long, what kind of life could they have had together? Agnes occasionally looked at Isabella's picture. She was rather beautiful in a grave way, with her aquiline nose, long dark hair and sad, thoughtful eyes.

John and Isabella had two sons together: John Junior, who died as a toddler, and Hugh John, who had been brought up by his aunt in Kingston and rarely came to Ottawa. Agnes once asked her husband about John Junior and learned quickly that this was treacherous territory for her to enter. There were doors of sadness and hardship in his past he preferred to keep shut.

Theirs was a brief courtship and a quick marriage. John had actually proposed to Agnes in Ottawa a few years before, but she had turned him down. He seemed too reckless and overbearing, and she too young to control him. Then, last year, between readings of the British North America Act in London, the most eligible bachelor in British North America took a stroll along Bond Street and saw Agnes Bernard across the road. A chance encounter, and a few weeks later, an engagement.

"It's a time of union," he said. And it was.

Macdonald did not like being surprised, but he loved surprising others. He took special delight in announcing the unexpected wedding. D'Arcy McGee was as astonished as everyone else when Macdonald informed him, "There will be fewer nights down in the bars, D'Arcy. I'll be staying home a bit more."

Since moving to Ottawa and taking residence as the wife of a leading politician, Agnes Macdonald had found most of these Canadians rather gauche. The nation, like her husband, had to learn how to behave. Already, many in Ottawa found her haughty and stuffy. She didn't mind; she was a great man's wife.

"Some of us may yet rise to become national statesmen," Macdonald pronounced without breaking stride. He was determined to carry on a conversation.

"Preparing a speech, are you, dear?" she said softly, her eyes focused on the wool.

"Just think about what happened. That damned fool Monck gave me a higher honour than the others. Cartier and Galt were so insulted they'll probably refuse theirs, and they're supposed to be my partners. Cartier keeps saying that I'm forever taking all the credit, and that my behaviour is not gentlemanly."

She looked up in wonderment. What an intriguing and insecure bundle of nerves she had married. Never satisfied. So rarely able to relax. She cringed as he poured himself another glass of sherry.

"Didn't you have enough at lunch?" she inquired delicately, trying not to sound too scolding.

"And what of McGee?" he continued, ignoring her question. "There was no room in the cabinet for either McGee or Tupper, and they're supposed to be my friends."

"Friends?" she asked. "Do you really have friends in this business?"

"Well, Tupper brought Nova Scotia to the union and McGee helped talk me into the damned idea in the first place—me and half the country."

She liked D'Arcy McGee, even though he was a Romanist with a controversial past. She was impressed that Dr. Tupper carried his medical case with him, even into the parliamentary chamber. But this day wasn't about them; it was about her husband. She laid her knitting on her lap and sighed. "John, how do you think they'll remember today?" She paused for an answer. Oddly, he had none, so she continued. "Mr. Cartier's right; you're not always 'gentlemanly,' but that's not the point. Confederation will always be *your* achievement. The others helped you design it. McGee, Tupper, Galt, even Cartier, they'll soon be forgotten, but you won't be."

There was a knock at the door. She carried on regardless. If her husband wanted to talk, he would have to hear her out. "It's been a hot, gusty day but these are gusty times," she said, amused by his astonished reaction. "You're the leader. Make sure this new country of yours—of ours—doesn't break apart before it has a chance to grow."

John A. Macdonald just stood there, feeling like an impetuous child who had just been soothed by his mother and, not for the first time, marvelling at the insight of this strong-willed young woman he had married.

"You do speak your mind," he said.

"As I said to you before, 'I do.'" With that, she turned her attention to the closed door and pleasantly commanded, "Come in."

The butler entered awkwardly, rather like an understudy, she thought, playing a British servant but not quite understanding the subtleties of the role. The leaders of the country were such an odd assortment that one could hardly condemn the staff for missing the grade. She smiled at the butler as he cleared his throat and announced, "Gilbert McMicken to see you, sir."

"I'll leave you to your serious business," she whispered in her husband's ear. "Keep your temper down, and don't forget the fireworks are tonight, not this afternoon." She nodded politely to a particularly severe man who marched into the room, and she departed, along with her knitting.

GILBERT McMicken was one of Macdonald's more successful political appointments. When he was attorney general, Macdonald had named him a stipendiary magistrate and justice of the peace. McMicken oversaw police activities and appointments. He had proven to be such a capable administrator that Macdonald charged him with heading a clandestine mission spying on Fenian activities in the United States and Canada. Macdonald was impressed at how McMicken exercised power shrewdly and secretively, although the man's persistence sometimes annoyed him.

McMicken could be a stuffed shirt, in Macdonald's view—not the sort of man he would want to socialize with—but he was extremely loyal to Macdonald, and there was nothing the prime minister admired more than people who admired him.

John Macdonald had come to British North America when he was five years old with his kindly, but not very successful, father. The family settled in Kingston amidst a welcoming contingent of relatives. Gilbert McMicken had emigrated on his own when he was nineteen. He settled in the Niagara region, just across the American border. Macdonald had only the trace of the Scottish brogue in his voice. McMicken spoke with a pronounced accent. Macdonald was clean-shaven with a cheerful smile. McMicken's beard was thick and heavy, his nose looked as if it had been broken a few times and his yellowing teeth were barely visible in a mouth that rarely smiled.

"McMicken, I wonder if God ever made a man as earnest as you look?" Macdonald said, glancing dramatically, and uselessly, at the clock. "May I offer you a wee glass of sherry?"

"Not while I'm on duty," McMicken answered and watched with interest as Macdonald topped his glass to the brim.

"It's been a great day," declared the prime minister.

"That it has." Small talk was not a part of McMicken's social armour. And this was no social call.

Macdonald chuckled to himself. He got the message. "All right, man, you've taken me away from a rare afternoon rest, so get on with it. What do you have to report?"

Irish extremists had recently staged a series of invasions, the so-called Fenian raids. The first, on New Brunswick's Campobello Island, had been quickly checked, but in early June 1866 almost a thousand Fenians had crossed the Niagara River and actually captured Fort Erie. At the ensuing Battle of Ridgeway, ten British—or Canadians—were killed and thirty wounded before the Fenians fled back to Buffalo. The same day, there were two other attacks in Quebec.

To add real insult, it took five full days for the American government to denounce the raid. It was well known that William Seward, the influential American secretary of state, wanted to see the Stars and Stripes fly up to the North Pole. Seward had often said that British North America's absorption by the United States was as inevitable as the Mississippi flowing south. President Andrew Johnson was not as vocal in his ambitions—he had enough trouble just staying in office—but Macdonald had never forgiven Johnson for taking so long to condemn the Fenian raid.

Macdonald responded to the Fenian threat in two ways, one public and one private. Publicly, he used the threat of an Irish-American invasion as a key argument for Confederation. "We are in a state of semi-war," he would tell his audiences. "We must gather together, if only for protection." This was for show and political purpose. Privately, he ordered the real work. He commissioned McMicken to find out how serious the Fenian threat really was. McMicken had all the resources he needed, and he used them well, building a spy ring that impressed even Macdonald, who in his darkest moments felt the Fenians were a society too cold and sinister ever to penetrate. About six months ago, one of McMicken's men had actually infiltrated a cell in New York. He faced possible torture and certain death if discovered. On the first day of Confederation, McMicken insisted on delivering the first substantive report from his undercover agent. "The news is not good, Mr. Macdonald," he began. "I mean, Sir John."

Macdonald waved his hand impatiently. This was no social call, indeed.

"The reports we've been getting from the United States indicate that the movement is spreading and the Yankee government is turning a blind eye to the treason."

The prime minister knew this, so why the meeting?

"The Fenians have renewed vigour," McMicken continued. "The New Jersey officer who led the Ridgeway invasion—"

"Raid," Macdonald objected.

"Sir, John O'Neill, who led the soldiers across the border into Canada last year—and I remind you, took Fort Erie—has been named president of the Irish Republican Brotherhood. He also has some fanatical people advising him and urging him on. They have actually started calling themselves the Irish Republican Army."

"A republic, is it?"

"Yes, and an *army*, and one well connected to a Republican president."

Macdonald dismissed this. "President Johnson has other problems on his plate." But the prime minister's eyes were alert and probing. "You said the movement is spreading. Well, by how much?"

"Twenty-one Fenian regiments have been allowed to parade this spring without being bothered by any authorities."

Again the prime minister was unimpressed. "Children can parade."

"These are not children, Prime Minister." McMicken was not the kind of man to overstate a case, or have his reports dismissed, even by his patron. "They brag in Massachusetts that there are enough men in Boston alone to ensure a successful invasion. In Chicago two thousand men are armed. In all—"

"Enough. I get the point."

"With respect, sir, you must hear the rest. They claim to have six hundred circles—or cells, as they call them." He paused to give full effect to his next sentence. "Twenty of them are here in Canada."

Macdonald's eyes dropped, and with them, much of his spirit. He asked with some trepidation, "How many men do you think they could assemble for an invasion?"

McMicken noted that the prime minister was now saying *invasion* and not *raid*.

"Forty, maybe fifty thousand are ready."

Macdonald did not need to check the arithmetic to know that if that number was accurate, and the attack was well planned, it could—no, it *would*—succeed. He guessed the Fenian strength was much exaggerated, and he was certain there was more bravado than substance to their claims. Still, he thought, what if they *did* attack?

Even with twenty thousand men? Would there be Fenians in Canada to welcome them with open arms? Would the American government, and that damn meddler Seward, rush to the Fenians' side? Did this weak, defenceless thing called Canada really stand a chance?

He had recently received a dispatch from Great Britain. His fellow Conservative Benjamin Disraeli had declared, "It can never be our policy to defend the Canadian frontier against the United States. What is the use of colonial dead weights which we do not govern?" So British help was out of the question. That was what McGee had been telling him for years. British North America must learn to stand alone.

"Have you heard of any invasion plans?" Macdonald asked calmly. There was no reason to let McMicken know the full extent of his fears.

"Yes, Sir. The plan is to attack at three places simultaneously. Where, we're not sure."

"And I suppose you don't know when."

"This is the shocking news," he responded, almost sounding sympathetic. "After a rash of assassinations."

"You mean murders?" the prime minister asked, in astonishment.

"Yes, sir. We have reason to believe there is a man in Canada right now whose purpose is to start what they call 'a reign of terror.'"

Macdonald looked dazed.

"If our informant is correct, your life and the lives of your colleagues are most seriously threatened. He is as dangerous as a poisonous snake."

The prime minister did not say a word. He glanced around the room as if seeking another opinion, searching for someone with more comforting words to offer. He took a long, hard drink from his sherry glass.

McMicken noticed the decanter was empty.

6

≡

Will Trotter had asked Conor to watch the Confederation night fireworks on Major's Hill Park with him and his mother. Meg smiled demurely and offered, "I might join you."

Conor had hung up his wet clothes and eaten a questionable piece of chicken for dinner. He agonized over what to wear. Even if his suit dried out, was it too formal? What do you wear to a fireworks display? What would he sit on? He couldn't ask Thomas. His father was still at the bar, and he would simply bark, "Don't go."

Luckily, he had taken his suit jacket off before diving into the water, so it wasn't wet. The jacket might cover his ragged pants. Looking right, sounding right, acting right—it was such a lot of work.

At the corner of Rideau and Sussex, Mrs. Trotter greeted Conor warmly. "You are my hero," she said.

"Mother," said Meg, "Conor saves damsels in distress every day, I'm sure." Meg had tied her hair back, but ribbons couldn't control the curls. He wanted to run his hands through the wild tangle, and he found himself staring, again.

Will broke the moment's spell. "Let's sit over there," he said. Conor was relieved to see that Will was carrying a blanket.

They sat to the side of the park, not with Ottawa's elite and a bit too close to the "scruff section" for Conor's taste. Mary Ann Trotter didn't seem to care about issues of class and status, and this spot would give them a nice view of the fireworks. He saw people he knew: loggers enjoying the freedom of summer, some tradespeople, some patrons of Lapierre's and that Ryan woman. That was her name. He remembered it now: Polly Ryan. He could tell she was watching him, but he avoided her stare.

Conor saw John Macdonald sitting with Lord Monck in a box in the centre of the park. They were both with their wives. If the prime minister and the governor general were in attendance, the suit coat was the right choice, the company was appropriate, and this was the proper place to be. Good.

Conor took the blanket from Will and placed it on the ground for the ladies. In the midst of his gallantry, he noted that there wasn't enough room for them all. He wondered how hard it would be to remove grass stains from his old pants.

It was a clear, star-filled night. A warm breeze softened the air. With the Parliament Buildings as a backdrop, the sky exploded in thunder and light, and the glow from the fireworks lit up Meg's face. She gasped with each bolt of colour. Conor was mesmerized. He had given up trying not to look love-struck.

Mary Ann Trotter watched him and smiled. People didn't often see her smile. When her husband died, she was devastated. She moved her family from Toronto to Ottawa and opened a boarding house on Sparks Street. The capital seemed like a place that would grow and attract "the right sort." She checked out many sites in Ottawa before settling on Sparks Street, in the Desbarats Block. Mr. Desbarats, the Queen's printer, was a fair landlord and the building's stone entranceway and thick wooden door spoke of substance. She named it the Toronto House. It was Meg's idea. She said it would bring in clientele from the West. It was also a nod to Mary Ann's sister in Toronto, who had married a banker and had been so generous to her family.

The boarding house became a favourite of those who liked a lively debate. Mary Ann insisted that conversation around her dinner table be clever, informed and challenging. She was the instigator, moderator and sometimes judge and jury. D'Arcy McGee loved it and fit right in. Once he quit drinking, McGee stayed at her boarding house when Parliament was in session. He often said that she was an argument to give women the vote. Conor found her intimidating and was actually rather afraid of her. Tonight, though, the Widow Trotter treated him as one of the family.

Mary Ann watched Conor gawk at her daughter. Men will always be boys, she thought. She suspected what Meg thought of him, but that was for this impressionable young man to find out, not for her to say.

ACROSS the park, someone had brought a fiddle. Someone else had a flute. A few people were dancing a country jig. Meg's blue eyes brightened and she turned to Conor. "Do you want to ask me to dance?"

Conor had grown up watching Irish workers stomp to jigs on Saturday nights in the lumber camps. He could do a two-step, even a rough Morris dance, but that was country music, peasant music, West Coast Irish and Highland Scots. Meg was too sophisticated for that. But she took his hand and pulled him off the ground, toward the music.

She manoeuvred her left hand around his waist, and before he knew it they were twirling to the scampering chords. When time came to change partners, Conor hesitated and lost the rhythm. Meg teasingly left him, and he found himself with a freckled Irish girl he knew from Lowertown. He moved with her to the music, remembering the pattern, faking some steps, improvising, having fun . . . and missing Meg. Soon she was back in his arms, just as the sky brightened with a blast of fireworks. They roared in laughter. And she was off, with a musical promise left in the air that she would soon be back. The musicians kept a steady, lively pace and the couples squared off, energetically dancing their rounds. The next time Meg was his partner, he held her a little tighter. She didn't seem to mind. In fact, she wilted in his arms and said, "I'm getting tired. Let's join the others."

Conor sat back on the grass, still feeling the joy of the dance. His hands on her waist, turning her, holding her, touching her. A girl in his arms. A worldly, cultured girl. He realized he was practically swooning.

SIR John A. Macdonald—that sounded nice to his ear: *Sir* John A. Macdonald—watched the fireworks from the makeshift splendour of the governor general's box. Normally, he liked such spectacles. They were celebrations, friendly gatherings and a peaceful use of gunpowder. He imagined festivities like this across the county and smiled proudly to himself. Then he glanced over at one of the plain-clothed guards Gilbert McMicken had stationed nearby and thought of the country's modest financial reserves. He took a discreet sip from a silver flask he had brought along, and growled, "It looks like a waste of ammunition to me."

Lady Macdonald sighed. The governor general ignored him. The electorate sat below him, unaware of his concerns. It was a fairly typical moment.

It was Canada's day—or *his* day, as Agnes had said. He had wrangled, cajoled and negotiated the governmental system he wanted:

essential powers in finance and defence staying with the central government. The provinces got powers that didn't really interest him, like social policy, education and health. He was no reformer. He had resisted any talk of secret ballots at elections. "Stand up and be counted," he would say. "Don't be afraid to state your views in the open." Only those who owned property could vote, and Macdonald wholeheartedly supported that. He abhorred the idea of "mob rule" practised in the United States. People with a vested interest in the country, he felt, deserved power. "The shareholders have earned the right to choose their leaders." After all, he had invested in this country, although not always wisely. He cringed at the thought of some of his business decisions.

And there was the Senate. He certainly got what he wanted there: a British-style House of Lords with the prime minister—him, to be exact—controlling the gate. "The purpose of government is to protect minorities," he quipped. "And there are fewer rich people." The appointed Senate gave him control as long as he had the power, and he couldn't imagine ever losing it. He still had elected members of Parliament to contend with, though. They could be unruly and undependable. He turned to Governor General Monck, who was avidly watching the fireworks. "Don't you think I should be able to put members of Parliament in the penitentiary when I want?" The governor general pretended not to hear him, and Macdonald went on watching the spectacle, grumbling to himself about the cost and chuckling at his little joke.

CONOR never wanted this day to end. He walked back to the boarding house with the Trotters, falling a little bit behind the others with Meg. He was gaining confidence by the stride, telling her about the morning, about Macdonald's knighthood, about the ambassador he stood beside, everything. Along Wellington Street, down Metcalfe, across to the south side of Sparks to the Toronto House.

Mrs. Trotter shooed Will inside with her, and Conor was left alone on the doorstep with Meg. He froze. This was not a moment to talk politics. This was a moment to—

She softly touched his cheek. "Good night, Conor. And thanks." Then she quickly went inside.

A man in a long grey coat was standing on the corner of Sparks and Wellington, chewing tobacco and spitting on the boardwalk. He fit right in. They had walked by him, unaware. He had discreetly followed them to the boarding house. He already knew the address. McGee's address. He had checked out where the turncoat had started living when he was in Ottawa. A nice, dark street because the cheapskate politicians often failed to light the gas lamps. A nearby alley for escape. That must be the landlady and her children. He would have to find out who else boarded there. And he must discover who this young man was, standing in front of the boarding house like a proud peacock. He couldn't quite see his face, but the girl called him Conor. An Irish name. A Catholic name. Wasn't that also the name of Thomas O'Dea's son? The girl certainly was pretty, but he had no time for that. Maybe later.

AS Conor walked back along Sparks Street, pictures from the day flashed in his head. It was like the light cast by the fireworks or the magnesium the photographers used to capture an instant of life. An explosion, a blinding light and a clear picture. A flash—and he saw Macdonald savouring the excitement of the morning. Another flash—there was the cheering crowd, and again Conor felt the achievement of being a part of something bigger than himself. Yet another flash and an explosion—and Meg Trotter. Meg swimming. Meg talking to him. Meg holding his hand. Dancing. Holding her. Meg's breath in his ear when she talked.

It was possible that tonight would be the end of it, that she was just thanking him for the incident on the river. Possible. Maybe probable. But after just a few hours with Meg, he felt happier than he had in his life. He was more than an upstart posing in second-hand clothes; he was a man about town wooing a sophisticated lady.

7

onor crossed Sappers Bridge toward Lowertown. A few Irishmen, like Nicholas Sparks and Daniel O'Connor, had made names for themselves in Ottawa, but the capital was dominated by Englishmen, Ulstermen and Scots. Most Irish-Catholic immigrants worked on the canals, along the train tracks and in the forests, and like Thomas O'Dea, lived in the slums. He looked in the windows of Howell's Grocery Store and considered how little he had eaten today. As he neared his father's basement flat, he felt a shiver of dread. He took a deep breath and opened the door.

Thomas O'Dea was a mess. After working the day shift at Lapierre's, he had stayed on throughout the night shift, drinking away the money he had made. "Where have you been, boy?" he drawled, his breath reeking of dusty, cheap whisky.

Conor hung up his suit coat, hoping to avoid a confrontation. He knew his father would be impossible to deal with tonight.

"Did you hear me? I said, where have you been?"

"I was at the Confederation celebrations, watching the fireworks."

"With who?"

"Will Trotter." Conor didn't dare say Meg's name.

"With some Protestant thug?"

"With a pageboy who happens to be a friend of mine, if that's

59

what you mean. Please, Da, let's not argue." Tonight, of all nights, Conor wished he could talk to his father. He wanted to share the evening with him, tell him about Meg, ask about girls, about his restless, anxious longing. He had spent many nights making love to his pillows, but tonight he had actually found a girl who seemed to like him. He had saved her life, her mother had called him a hero and he dared not tell his own father a word of it.

Thomas had often said that Conor had his mother's happy disposition. He had apparently inherited her red hair and green eyes— "the look of the Irish." Margaret O'Dea, that mystery who bore him . . . how he wished he knew her and could confide in her.

Long ago, he had stopped talking politics around his father. Thomas's hatred for England was too deeply rooted for a decent discussion. Conor knew his "Britishness" pushed every nerve in his father's body. He knew he could be insensitive to Thomas's pain, but then, he thought, what's wrong with wanting to fit in? What's wrong with trying to get ahead? They were in a British country, after all; why not accept it?

He found Thomas's lack of imagination frustrating. His father always wanted to dismiss issues, avoid conversation and damn those in power. Maybe he was afraid he couldn't keep up, or maybe he had just stopped trying. When he wanted to, Thomas could hold his own at the pub; why not at home? Why did he stay so sullen?

"The fireworks were spectacular," he said, searching for neutral ground.

"I suppose your fancy politicians were there."

"Macdonald has been made a knight."

Thomas didn't care. "You think this Confederation nonsense is wonderful, don't you?" There was contempt in his voice. "Well, I think—"

"I know what you think," Conor interrupted, surprising himself

60

with his rudeness. "You don't need to tell me. I know everything—and everybody—you hate." He had wanted to be conciliatory and reach out to his father, but he had lost the moment and the inclination.

Thomas O'Dea's face grew red with rage. "You fool. You know nothing, boyo. Nothing!" He spit out two words he knew Conor would hate: "Did you hear me, Bookie? Or is that Cookie?" Thomas persisted, delighting in Conor's outrage. "You're a pompous idiot." In his thick accent, it sounded like *eejit*, an Irish inflection that sometimes had a funny, light tone. Not tonight. Tonight, it sounded like the hiss of the devil.

"I'll tell you what I know," Conor said, glaring at him; once his anger had been awakened, it continued to rise. "I know that if you hate Canada so damned much, you should never have come here. I know—" Thomas tried to cut off his son's speech, but Conor's voice rose even louder. "I know you don't believe in Canada, or Canadians. You barely believe in yourself. And I don't care. I really don't."

Thomas O'Dea was in his forties, but his mind had withered with ancient hatreds. Conor looked at him with pity and disgust. It was a poisonous mix. "Tell me, Father," he jeered. "What *do* you believe in?"

"I believe in Ireland," Thomas answered contemptuously. "I believe in my homeland."

Conor buried his head in his hands. Ireland. Ireland. Ireland. Why can't people forget yesterday's pain? We have a new homeland now. He studied his father. Thomas sat on an old wooden chair beside a battered table, leaning on a cold stovepipe. His shoulders were stooped, his eyes blurry from the whisky. He was the very picture of failure. And Conor felt ashamed.

"Don't look at me like that," Thomas roared. "I'm not one of your hoity-toity Brits."

"No, you're a bitter wreck." Conor regretted his words as he heard them come from his mouth. "And you're drunk."

61

At that, Thomas threw himself at his son, preparing to strike him, but he stumbled getting out of the chair. Conor held his ground and blocked the blow. He grabbed his father's arm and twisted it behind his back. "I'm sorry," Conor said sternly, releasing his father's arm. "I shouldn't have said that. I'm not Cookie, Bookie, boyo or any petty putdown you may come up with. Not after today."

His father dropped to the muddy floor, a defeated man, sobbing in self-pity. "It's that McGee. He's turned you against me. To you, I'm nothing but a worthless barman and he's," he said mockingly, "a great politician."

"It has nothing to do with Mr. McGee." Now that he had control, maybe he could manoeuvre this dreadful confrontation from spite to reconciliation. "No, Da, it's not that at all." Conor's tone now was soothing as he bent down. "You know what I was thinking today?" he said. "I was thinking about Mother. How she would have felt about today. A new country. A new start."

Thomas looked up at him from the ground, barely believing that Conor would talk like this.

"Da, think of Mother. Is this how she would have wanted you to act?"

Colour slowly returned to Thomas O'Dea's pallid face. "Think of Mother," this boy said. As if he hadn't thought of Margaret every hour of every day since she died. What impudence. What stupidity. What on earth had he reared? Life was surging into his limbs. How could he make this boy understand? Yes, he was jealous of McGee, with his fancy talk and fancier friends. Yes, he despised the Protestant leaders like Macdonald and their railway cronies. He would admit that. But his anger was deeper than envy. Far deeper.

An old, almost forgotten vitality started to flow into his bloodstream, clearing the haziness of the whisky. This son of his spouted the empty slogans of politics, but he knew the full sting of

British politics, and British politicians. He lifted himself up. This self-righteous boy—yes, "boyo"—hadn't experienced enough of life to be called a man, yet he dared lecture him about life. About Margaret.

He took a deep breath and steadied himself. His eyes locked onto his son's, and in a hushed but powerful tone, he said simply, "Sit down. Let me tell you about your mother."

8

The flat was drab and dreary. Conor couldn't remember the last time his father could afford enough fuel oil to keep the lamps properly lit. The ceiling was black with smoke and the window frames green with mould. An old wood stove kept the room sweltering hot in the winter, but it was dangerously close to the walls and Thomas hung a frightening number of inflammable objects near it. A wooden plank balanced over two barrels created a table; two old mattresses on the floor served as their beds. It was a place to leave, not call home.

Thomas was now standing, looking down on his son. "I'll tell you what Canada did for your mother," he began slowly. "It was 1847, the start of the famine in Ireland. Millions of us were starving." He paused and looked Conor directly in the eye. "Not hungry, boyo, but starving."

Conor ignored being called "boyo." He didn't want to quell the new life in his father's voice. Thomas pulled up a rickety chair and sat down. Conor could tell that his father's back was aching even more than usual.

"The British landlords didn't care about us. Year after year, the potato crop was in ruin, but all they worried about were their prices, their precious investment. We weren't people; we were just Irishmen."

Conor knew the story of the famine. Thomas rarely spoke about it—and certainly never to his son—but other Irishmen spoke of little else. He was about to say something, but stopped himself and let his father continue. "The English had the means to help us, but they just sat back and watched us suffer. Finally, when the landlords' profits really started to decline, they took some action. They evicted us." Thomas kept his eyes focused on the mud floor. "Then we started to die. By the thousands, good farmers, good people . . ." His words drifted off, but only for a few seconds. "They wouldn't give us freedom. They wouldn't allow us our own government, but their bloody government didn't give a damn." Thomas swallowed hard; he was breathing deeply, almost gasping. "Oh yes, they sent commissions over—not to help us or feed us, but to count the dead. And they sent journalists over to watch us slowly waste away. I guess we were quite a story: Irish peasants in tattered rags, dying in ditches; children eating gravel while their parents lay dead beside them; typhus killing those who didn't starve; undertakers building coffins with trap doors so that dozens of bodies could be buried from the same wooden box. We were a great story."

Then, strangely, Thomas's expression changed, as if a dim memory had come to light. He rubbed his weary eyes. "It's hard to fathom, but amidst the horror, your mother and I were so much in love that we could almost ignore our hunger and the despair all around us."

Conor was about to tell his father about Meg, the stirring within him, but again he stopped himself.

"You were just a baby," his father continued. "And dear Lord, how we loved you. You were good, very good. We barely had enough food to feed you, but you seemed to understand. You cooed and giggled from the day you were born, and made everything so . . . so . . ." Again his words drifted off, but his distant smile faded as he stared deeply into the past. "But we couldn't bring you up in that poverty. And anyway, they evicted us, too. Your mother and I had to leave a land that could have been—should have been—heaven on earth to come to a strange new place we knew almost nothing about."

Thomas gingerly stood up and carefully paced across the tiny room. "Your grandparents scraped together every bit of money they could find. And so did we. We wanted a future for our family—for you—in the New World." He walked the length of the small room twice, pressing on the small of his back. "They held a wake for us before we left. Not a going-away party, but a wake. Our leaving meant we would never see any of our family or friends again. Margaret and I danced the steps of the living dead—the expelled."

Just hours before, Conor had been dancing with Meg with carefree joy. How long had it been since his father was carefree?

Thomas stretched his back and sat down. "We left Galway Bay in the spring, boarding the ship almost in sight of the farm my family had once worked. Margaret cried terribly when she said her final goodbyes to her mother and sisters. I practically had to pull her onto the ship— the ship that would take us on a voyage into hell." He anticipated Conor trying to defend his precious Canada and raised his voice to cut him off. "Yes, hell! We were packed into that ship like slaves in a hold."

It had never occurred to Conor how little he knew of the details of his father's life. He had heard snippets of this story over the years, but he hadn't pushed for more. Perhaps he was afraid to. One winter night in a lumber camp, when Thomas thought Conor was asleep, he told a fellow teamster about the terrible years of famine and death, and the cruel reception he had received when he arrived on Canadian soil. Conor listened from the next cot, but somehow he let it waft by him. It became a dream, a story from another land, another time. Thomas had never mentioned his wife to the teamster. Conor would have remembered that.

Now his father was not just retelling the story but reliving it.

"It took only a few weeks before the fevers began. We were terrified that you would get it. You were little more than a year old, but you were strong. Your mother, she was strong, too." He stopped talking and rested, alone with his memories. "I'll never forget one woman who died. Jenny was her name. She was travelling alone. Her husband had been in Toronto for two years earning the money for her trip—her final trip. When the fever first struck, your mother tried to care for her. Then, one night, when the seas were high, poor Jenny started screaming, calling out for her husband. She wailed and shrieked all night as your mother struggled to bring down her rising fever."

Thomas was now choking back tears, but he was determined not to give in. This boy who loved the Union Jack so much had some lessons to learn, lessons about British justice.

"By the morning, her feet had swollen to twice their normal size and they were covered in putrid black spots." Conor looked down in disgust, but Thomas howled, "Look at me, boy, and listen. When she died a few days later, her head had swollen so much it was sickening just to look at her. This beautiful young woman had turned grotesque and ugly." He chose his next words carefully. "And do you know why? Because she was poor. Because she was Irish!" The memories seemed to drain Thomas. He sat down again. "We were at sea for two months, rotting like the blackened potatoes we had left behind. When we spotted land, we thought we were saved, but we were fools. Nothing would save the likes of us. As we sailed up the Gulf of St. Lawrence, the nightmare only worsened. Land was all around us, but we were still adrift."

Conor felt he should say something, but what? His father's story was unrelenting.

"And then we ran out of drinking water. While the sick screamed for mercy, and the dying lay helpless in their own shit, people desperately tried to drink salt water from the Gulf."

He looked deeply into his son's eyes, reliving the worst memory of all. "That's when your mother got the fever. She died just two days before we reached shore."

Conor leaned over to touch his father, hold him, hug him, anything, but Thomas rejected his affection and carried on as if in a trance. "I wouldn't let them throw her overboard. I held her body until we reached Grosse Isle. We sailed into the quarantine station flying the flag of sickness. There were four hundred people crammed onto that ship. Thirty-six died at sea and a hundred others were gravely ill. I thought I had witnessed horror in Ireland, but Grosse Isle was the most repulsive place I had ever seen. It was little more than a graveyard on the St. Lawrence River. By day, people lay on the beach, crawling in the mud and dying like fish out of water. By night, you could hear the wailing in the sheds and tents of those lucky enough to die in a makeshift hospital. At least your mother never had to see it."

Thomas stopped. He reached for a handkerchief to wipe tears from his eyes and sweat from his brow. "When we got off board, I helped dig her grave. I placed two stakes together in a cross. I didn't have the schooling to write her name, but I vowed by that simple cross that I would never forgive those English bastards who did this to her."

He spoke his next words directly to Conor. "Before she died, she made me promise not to tell you how wretched her death was. She wanted to save you from it. Well, I have broken my vow. You asked me, and I have told you."

Conor could only imagine the pain in his father's heart, how it had grown and festered like a cancer. He wanted his father to continue; he wanted to hear it all. He searched for a tone of understanding in his voice. "Then what happened to you? To us?"

"We survivors carried on to Montreal, where they divided us

like cattle. Those with any strength left after the voyage were sent up the Ottawa River—up the Opeongo Line—to fell the white pines. A job. It sounded good, but it was gruelling, treacherous work in the lumber camps. You know that, boy. You saw it. Working from dawn till dusk for less than a dollar a day. Some went to dig the canals in the United States. Many of us died. Those too weak for 'Irish' labouring jobs were left to rot in Montreal, where there was little or no prospect of work. Some people I knew headed for Toronto, and what did they find? Signs staring at them everywhere: 'NINA—No Irish Need Apply.' They didn't mean Irish, they meant Irish *Catholics*. Romanists. Papists. 'The Queen City' was as Orange as Belfast's Shankill Road. You've seen the signs yourself. 'No Irish wanted.' 'No Irish employed here.' There's your Canada for you."

Conor had listened in silence. Finally, he took his father's large, weathered hand and asked softly, "How do you remember Mama?"

Thomas held his son's hand tightly, but looked at the ground. Conor wondered whether he was trying to conjure up her image on the mud floor. "I remember two things about her," Thomas said softly. "I remember our childhood in Galway. I remember us dancing with such delight on Saturday night; then at Sunday morning Mass I'd watch her praying with such conviction. I remember her smile." Thomas brightened as he spoke, and his voice grew stronger. "Yes, I remember her conviction that life was good, that no matter how dreadful it seemed, things were going to get better." Instantly, his face darkened as if he dared not remember too vividly the happiness of youth. "And I remember her dying on the ship's floor like an old woman. I can never forget her just . . . wasting away."

Conor squeezed his hand. "Father, I know it's been hard, terribly hard. I know you've been lonely—"

Thomas would have none of it. "Don't give me your pity," he snarled, and cast his son's hand away.

"It's so much better for the immigrants today," Conor said, sounding far too much like the politicians he worked for. "The voyage is safer, people are better cared for and there are much better conditions when they arrive in Canada now. When Mr. McGee was in the cabinet he made sure—"

"McGee!" Thomas bellowed. "How dare you bring his name into this?"

Conor knew instantly that he had made a stupid mistake, but he compounded it. "And Mr. Macdonald—"

"Macdonald!" Thomas spun from anger to fury. He spit out the name as if he were speaking of the devil. "Mc-Gee . . . Mac-don-ald!" Rage that had been building within him for days, for months, for years exploded. He shrieked, "Get out!" The explosion echoed through the small room. Shocked, Conor hesitated. "I said, get out of my sight!"

Guilt choked Conor. He was speechless. But he had already said too much. Way too much. "Father, I'm sorry," he sobbed. But Thomas was not listening. At the very moment when he could have soothed his father's anger, he had provoked it. He had been a fool. An idiot. An *eejit*.

"I will not hear their names in my house."

"But you must understand—"

"No, *you* must understand." Thomas glared at his son. "You'll never understand. You don't have the heart of an Irishman. Now get out."

Conor felt sick. He had failed his father and failed the memory of his mother. When he looked at his father's contorted face, he saw a man overcome with hatred; he saw viciousness he'd never known; he saw pure and utter danger. "Da, please listen to me," he begged tearfully.

"Who do you think you are?" Thomas shrieked. "You and your wretched books. You and your fucking politicians. Get out. And never come back."

Conor stood up and stepped back. He wanted to run away, to escape that ferocious stare, the torrent of vitriol, but he also wanted to stay to apologize, to beg for his father's forgiveness. He tried to speak, but there was nothing to say.

"You're no longer a son of mine. Damn you! I said, damn you and fuck off!"

He could still hear his father swearing at him after he had closed the door and left.

9

onor walked aimlessly through Lowertown, almost staggering in shame. He knew these streets by heart, but he was lost. He could hear soldiers in the George Street barracks playing cards. It sounded like fun. He assumed they were mostly Protestant soldiers longing to hunt down some Irish invaders. All he could think about was his father's story. Thomas had protected him from the full truth for so many years. He marvelled at his extraordinary restraint. He had kept the promise he had made to his dying wife. The more Conor thought about where he came from, the more he was losing a grip on where he was, and where he was going.

He wandered along Clarence Street, with its many brothels and ladies of the night. He tried not to stare, but he did notice a skulking man in a grey coat across the street, talking to a woman. A prostitute and a customer. They ignored Conor, and he looked away.

He walked in circles, up and down the squalid streets, confused and rudderless. It was now early morning and he had nowhere to go. He had no home.

He found himself pulled back to Sussex Street, toward the towering Notre Dame Cathedral. The interior was still under construction, but the magnificent structure already dwarfed the tenements.

The cathedral was more French than Irish, but it was Roman Catholic, and he stumbled into its sanctuary. He had never been inside. The golden altar glistened in the flickering light; the unfinished ceiling soared toward the heavens. He didn't expect there would be anyone there at this hour, and he was surprised when an elderly priest quietly approached him. The priest seemed to understand that he was in need but couldn't talk about it now, and left him alone, in peace. Conor kneeled in a pew, not praying, just wishing—desperately wishing—and wondering what prayer really was.

Conor had very little religious training. Thomas had not entered a church since he buried Margaret. He was determinedly Irish Catholic, but as a nationality, not a religion. Christmas was a day off at the lumber camps. Easter just meant the bars were closed. Sundays meant some free hours to nurse the wounds of the week. The priests in the camps had given Conor a smattering of religious education when Thomas was out of sight, but mostly they prayed for his eternal soul.

That's what Conor wanted to do: pray for his soul. But how?

He stared at the statue of the Virgin Mary. He felt a vague glow of contentment, or relief, or something peaceful within. The serenity in the place calmed his nerves and renewed his purpose. He had been heartless with his father; there would be a time for atonement and, maybe someday, true forgiveness. But that would take time. For now, he would not wallow in self-loathing. He had made a mistake, but his father had overreacted. He still believed that Thomas needed to move on with his life. The world outside this sanctuary—the world that, just hours before, he had embraced with passion—had not changed. The sun would rise on July 2 and there was work to do. His future was just as promising as before.

Thinking of his mother delirious and dying on a coffin ship had hardened his perspective, but not his prospects. He couldn't live his father's nightmare; he had to chase his own dreams. He breathed a determined sigh and rose from the pew. He nodded toward the altar, awkwardly genuflected to the image of suffering on the cross and left.

THE streetwalker's name was Annie; she was an eighteen-year-old orphan from County Cork. Her parents had both died of cholera when she was ten, and she had had to make her own way in the world. For a while, she begged on the streets, perfecting the needy, pitiful pout of the street urchin. It seemed a natural step to sell her body and make more money. At first, she was in demand—young, somewhat pretty and willing—and for a time she actually worked at Mrs. Campau's House. Mrs. C. ran the most established brothel on Clarence Street. It was clean, efficient and attracted a better sort. But she had recently replaced her working girls with a new selection to keep the customers interested, and Annie was back on the streets.

She rolled over in bed and looked at her customer. She was no great judge of character, but this was a troubled man. He seemed full of hate even when performing loveless sex. He had paid her well. He had been a little too rough, but he was better company than some of those drunken, vulgar lumbermen. It was getting too late now to return to the streets. The drunks had passed out and family men had gone home. Maybe she could talk this one into another go-round for the same price. "What do you say?" she whispered, breathing softly in his ear, her hand reaching teasingly below his taut stomach. "Any more money to spend?"

He didn't speak, but she could feel him respond. She smiled as he reached for his wallet in his grey coat and she lay back, bracing herself for another cold, mechanical onslaught.

There was no time for her to react when she saw the knife. She tried to scream, but his right hand tightened over her mouth. He smoothly dug the blade into her left breast. Her body quaked with pain. Her mind told her to hit him, kick him, attack him, but her arms and limbs were frozen in shock. Her murderer smiled at her helplessness as he plunged the knife deeper and slashed it across her chest.

"You might have recognized me," he whispered, almost pleasantly. "It's better this way."

He felt her muscles relax in death. Quickly, he washed off the blood and removed the money he had given her. She won't be needing it, he thought.

CONOR crossed back over Sappers Bridge into Uppertown. He retraced his steps from hours before toward Sparks Street. Where else could he go? He leaned against the imposing, closed door of the Toronto House and fell asleep. His tie was askew, his shirt soaked with sweat and his one good suit jacket rumpled, dirty and worn.

At dawn, Mary Ann Trotter opened the door, gently woke him and said, "There's an extra bed upstairs."

Happy birthday, indeed.

THAT morning, in a small upstairs room on Clarence Street, police discovered the naked body of a woman, torn to shreds by a knife. It was a room that people rented by the hour. A prostitute, probably killed over money, they deduced. The killer was long gone by now. The two policemen glanced around, looking for clues, saw none and ordered the body removed. She would be buried in a pauper's grave. There would be a perfunctory investigation, and they would close the book on a life to which no one had ever paid much attention.

The first murder in the new capital of Canada would never be solved.

PART TWO

July 1867

The fate of our land
God hath placed in your hand

Polly Ryan arrived fifteen minutes early. She sat in a tavern in LeBreton Flats, nursing cheap gin and waiting. No one paid her much attention. She knew she was still attractive to men, but she also knew that after a few drinks, most women were. She looked after herself, but there was a stifling sadness about her. She had not stopped mourning her husband. She wondered if she ever would.

She had to support herself. He would understand that. And she had her causes. They were his causes, too.

At one table, some men were playing cards, and she noticed money changing hands. At the bar, a lone patron was alternating spitting tobacco juice into a spittoon and emptying a bottle of grey-brown liquid. Whisky, she assumed. The drinker watched her with hazy lust, but made no moves toward her. It was the kind of establishment where single women looking around for strangers was quite common. But she wasn't looking at the other people; she was watching the door.

He arrived right on time, looked around the dark room as if he were searching for someone who wasn't there and left. No one seemed to notice. Except her. His face was hard to identify in the bright attack of light from the doorway, but Polly knew it was him. She finished her drink and left.

She followed him down the street and around the corner to the back of a wood-frame building. The streets were quiet. Not peaceful, just empty. She expected the building would be empty as well, and there would be no one else in the room where they would meet. Just her and him. He would give her instructions, and she would follow them. Just as she had promised.

10

====

For almost two weeks, Conor had been staying at Mrs. Trotter's Toronto House. She gave him chores to do, supposedly to pay for his room and board, but he knew he was a charity case. He had given them an edited story of what had happened with his father. Even fragments of Thomas's experiences were met with great sympathy.

He couldn't tell what his relationship was with Meg. Friend or something potentially more than that? She obviously enjoyed his company. He found himself becoming more comfortable with her, but there were doors he left shut. Especially about his past. Meg suggested he approach Thomas to try to reconcile, but Conor bristled. "Not yet!" It was the only time he had spoken sternly to her, and neither wanted it repeated.

At Mrs. Trotter's table, dinner was a treat. It was how he imagined a college seminar would be—engaged, inquisitive, challenging. She encouraged Conor to talk history and politics with Will, and asked him to tell stories he had heard from D'Arcy McGee. He loved showing how he knew the men behind the political spectacle. He even mimicked McGee's style and inflection. He recounted one night in Lapierre's when Macdonald initiated a bunfight by attacking

Liberal MPs who didn't get some joke. Will and Meg loved Conor's anecdotes. Mrs. Trotter scolded him. "I was hoping you would talk of legislation and political enterprise." But Conor knew she also loved a good story.

Conor told one story he knew Mrs. Trotter would find interesting because she admired the middle road of compromise and conciliation. In the heated days before Confederation, a Grit backbencher who always voted against Macdonald fell ill and was away for months. On his return, Macdonald crossed the floor, shook his hand and declared, "I'm delighted to see you back in good health so you can get on voting against me." The man didn't become a Macdonald supporter, but from then on was absent for many key votes.

"Hmm. Have you told Mr. McGee that story?" Mary Ann Trotter asked.

At night, Conor was in a kind of torment, just down the hall from Meg, so tantalizingly close that it drove him nearly senseless. Sometimes in the middle of the night, he would awake and yearn to knock on Meg's door, but he was certain she would be insulted by such effrontery. And so she should. He must act like a gentleman. And there was always the prying eye of Mrs. Trotter. What if she heard him? He shuddered to think of it.

MID-JULY to most Ontario Protestants meant only one thing: the Orange Parade. The brash display of Protestant power was illegal in most of the Empire, but not in Canada, and certainly not in "Loyal True Blue and Orange" Ontario. Conor had spent most Julys in Ottawa but had never gone near an Orange Parade. All he knew about the Glorious Twelfth was that it was a Protestant day and it was wise for Papists to lie low. He didn't know a single Roman

Catholic who had been to an Orange Parade. That piqued his curiosity, and his daring. "No one can keep me away from anything," he told Meg.

His father's terrible story had sparked in him a new willingness to judge British values. All his life, he had casually accepted the greatness of the Empire as a matter of course. Now he was learning that its glory came with trappings and its power came from brutality. He needed to discover what, and who, made up this country. Maybe then he could better understand his father, and himself.

For a week, he had urged Meg to join him. "I just want to peek behind the fence," he insisted. "I won't infect the crowd." He rubbed his red hair and joked, "I'll even wear a bowler hat and cover up."

Reluctantly, she agreed. "You won't like what you see," she warned. "And neither might I."

As they left the Sparks Street boarding house, Mary Ann Trotter pulled Conor aside. "Be careful," she said. "Please be careful."

CONOR O'Dea was the only Roman Catholic in the crowd as the soldiers marched on July 12, 1867. "King Billy" majestically led the parade on his gleaming white horse. Conor noticed that it was actually Matthew Lindsay, who ran a dry-goods store on Rideau Street. Mr. Lindsay was a quiet sort with simple tastes, a stalwart of the Methodist church, a teetotaller, a family man who never wore anything brighter than a grey suit. Today, he was resplendent in flowing wig and garish uniform. Today, he was William of Orange—the conqueror of Ireland.

The marchers behind him wore bowler hats and orange sashes and strutted proudly. If you failed to notice the sea of orange sashes, they sang about it, over and over again.

My father wore it as a youth
In bygone days of yore
And on the Twelfth I love to wear
The sash my father wore.

The sash. The Protestant symbol of supremacy. The Glorious Twelfth. On July 12, 1690, King William of Orange crushed the Irish by the shore of the Boyne River. To Protestant loyalists, the Battle of the Boyne solidified Britain's righteous rule over Ireland. To Irish Catholics, the Orange Parade was a heinous reminder of the day Britain strengthened its grip on Ireland's throat.

Conor tried to look into the eyes of the marchers. He saw some of Will's friends and some he thought were his. He asked Meg, "Is it true that most Protestants are members of the Orange Lodge?"

"About a third, I read somewhere." She smiled at a drummer she knew. Her smile was too friendly. It infuriated Conor.

"I know some of these marchers, too," he said. He wondered who the drummer was.

"I know lots of them," she answered, her eyes following the parade's progress. "My father was an Orangeman, you know." Her words hit Conor like the kick of a mule. He knew the power the lodges held and that every Orangeman wasn't a bigot, but still, her father! "It was the fastest way to get a job," she continued, unaware how her words were affecting him. "Especially in Toronto."

All his life, he had heard the taunts of the Protestant bullies, had listened to his father complain about the oppressive Orangemen, but he had ignored it all as idiocy and fanaticism. But these march-ers were neither idiots nor fanatics. That was the most horrifying part of it. They were businessmen, teachers, politicians and clergy—everyday people, some of stature and importance, marching in a solid line.

At the end of the parade, the youngest boys marched, perhaps the most proudly of all. The future. They chanted another catchy tune:

Titter totter, holy water
Slaughter the Catholics every one.
If that won't do
We'll cut them in two
And make them live under the Orange and Blue.

Conor's ears rang with the sound of bigotry. What was he doing, standing in the crowd, watching King Billy's soldiers parade? What was he doing with an Orangeman's daughter?

"You know that we aren't still members of the lodge," she said, reading his thoughts.

"Then what are you?" he asked, not intending to sound as cruel as his words came out.

"I'm a person, that's all."

Conor didn't answer. It wasn't that simple. People were categorized: winners and losers, good guys and bad, us and them.

The marchers started another chant:

Up the long ladder
And down the short rope,
Hurrah for King Billy
To hell with the Pope.

Meg blushed, appalled and embarrassed. "I'm sorry, Conor," she said. "I'm so ashamed." She took his arm and held it for comfort.

"It's all right," he answered, vacantly. "I understand."

But he didn't understand. And she knew it. No matter what self-styled religion her mother practised, the fact remained that Conor had fallen for an Orangeman's daughter. They were from different worlds.

He had seen the soul of British North America, and it certainly was not all right.

ON July 12, on a New Jersey field, Colonel Patrick O'Hagan watched the troops marching and smiled with satisfaction. These were experienced soldiers who had tasted battle and were eager for more. They knew a soldier's discipline and a victor's honour.

His plan was starting to take shape. Lakes Huron, Erie and Ontario would be occupied by the Fenian navy. It would be expensive, but Fenian bonds were selling well, and it wasn't as if there was such a thing as a Canadian navy. If the Great Lakes were controlled, Toronto would soon fall. Montreal was the Roman Catholic centre of Canada, and he was sure the French Canadians would prefer Fenians to Orangemen. He hoped they would actually welcome him as a liberator. He would lead the glorious march north to Montreal himself if General O'Neill agreed. At the same time, a unit from San Francisco would invade British holdings on Vancouver Island and the Fraser River country. There shouldn't be much of a fight: except for Victoria, which was hopelessly British, most of the people in British Columbia were Americans who had headed north in search of gold. They would welcome the invaders.

He saluted the soldiers as they marched past, singing the Fenian marching song:

Many battles have we won,
Along with boys in blue.
And we'll go and conquer Canada,
For we've nothing else to do.

O'Hagan laughed at the ditty. He knew the power of a marching song. It motivated the men and legitimized the cause. He had recently composed a proclamation for General O'Neill to sign, which would soon be sent to Canada. He had laboured over the wording and knew it by heart. Not a marching song, but marching orders:

A Fenian army is being equipped in the interest of Irish liberty throughout the world. It will be soon again summoned to the field in the cause of Irish nationality, and will warn its enemies that the arrogance of British power must and shall be stricken down. Fifty thousand armed patriots will march. Let every devotee of the sunburst of Erin prepare to strike for his country and God.

The President and Commander-in-Chief
The Irish Republican Army

Wordy, but you needed extravagant language to make a point. He had actually sent even more flowery proclamations north. This one was direct and to the point. It was more than a threat: it announced that the liberators were coming; it was a call to arms. And he loved the new name, the Irish Republican Army. By the time he made the proclamation public in August, Canada would be in an election and he would have had a chance to meet with politicians in Washington. It still stung that they turned back after the Battle of Ridgeway. But this time a real battalion was preparing, and he had that man laying the groundwork in Canada. They would not fail again.

At best, the United States would recognize a Fenian country, New Ireland, to their north. He would be just as happy to present President Johnson with new northern states maybe someday under his command. Those were dreams. Simply holding the country for ransom would be fine. If the Fenian army took Canada by force—

essentially kidnapping the country—they would name a free Ireland as the ransom price. The British Parliament would have to submit.

A few obstacles stood in their way. This character Macdonald was busy appeasing Canada's warring factions. He was an astute and cunning politician. Macdonald's power must be smashed. And there was D'Arcy McGee. McGee was the only person in Canada who seemed to understand the scope of Fenian ambitions. McGee was a thorn in their side. Luckily, the loudmouth had become so strident that people weren't listening to him. But that might not last.

O'Hagan wondered how the man he had hired was doing up in Canada. He prayed for his success.

HE was staying in Uppertown. He changed hotels every three days and adapted his look with each move. In his suitcase he carried costumes, wigs and make-up. Sometimes he wore the long grey coat; sometimes he didn't. It depended whether it suited his plan, to be a presence and then to disappear.

He actually liked July 12. Every time the Orangemen paraded, they created more angry Irish republicans. March, boys, he sneered. Chant your stupid rhymes. We'll win. Yes, we'll win. But he couldn't face this night without help. July 12 meant bodies lying on the banks of the River Boyne. Irish dead and Englishmen cheering. Orangemen still celebrating generations later. Thrilling to the victory. Gloating.

He pulled withered poppies out of a bag and picked out the poppy heads. He took a needle and carefully pierced the capsules, one by one, dropping them into a small crock. He lit a contained fire under the poppy heads. It was dangerous work in these wooden fire traps, but he was near a window with a steady out-draft. Eventually, a liquid emerged from the poppy heads. Like sweat. Sweet, dark, hallucinogenic sweat.

Opium.

When there was enough of the liquid, he mixed it with whisky and sugar. He could have gone to an apothecary and bought laudanum. But this was safer. It was also purer and much, much stronger.

He drank it rather daintily—he never much liked the taste—and then lay back with swirling but vivid dreams of martyrs in Dublin and murders in Ottawa. Sometimes, the drug made him mournful and despondent. Tonight, it brought him peace and purpose.

11

onor had never been much of a drinker. He knew how the bottle held people down. He'd seen it with his father and with so many others. But tonight he was determinedly drunk and trying to get drunker. He sat in an Elgin Street bar gulping beer, chasing it down with whisky and burning with anger.

"Like father, like son," he said to his glass. "Macdonald turns his drinking into a joke," he slurred. "We Irish know it is serious business."

Ottawa was a town of unhappy drunks: boisterous lumbermen with their rotgut grunts and bored civil servants seeking companionship in a bottle. There wasn't much else to do than fill the many bars.

It would soon be last call, then closing time, and he didn't know where he would go. He barely remembered how he got here.

AFTER the Orange Parade, Conor had sat through—or endured—dinner at the boarding house. Mrs. Trotter tried to navigate the conversation into waters Conor would favour: politics and business. He conversed, politely, but without enthusiasm. Yes, he thought the railway men were too influential. No, he wasn't worried about the secessionists in Nova Scotia. Yes, he would like more carrots.

Will tried to help. "When will you be going to work with Mr. McGee?" he asked.

"I might not," Conor answered.

The announcement hit those sitting at the table like a thunderbolt. D'Arcy McGee would need him in the upcoming election. That was his job: parliamentary assistant. And it was a job he loved. Everyone wanted an explanation, but no one dared ask. Not when Conor seemed so despondent.

Instead, Meg addressed the afternoon's spectacle. "Mother, that Orange Parade was terrible."

"Much of it is just silly boys acting like stupid men and stupid men acting like silly boys," Mrs. Trotter responded. But she looked at Conor and thought more deeply. "Tradition can be wonderful, but it can have true dangers."

Conor stared at his carrots without speaking.

"Customs burn deep in people's souls," she added. She'd read that somewhere.

Meg wouldn't let it go. "Is it customary to hate?"

"Yes, that's the point, dear. That's the dreadful point."

Will joined in, trying to be helpful. "Conor, didn't Mr. McGee say, 'Hate, not love, was born in blind'?"

"Something like that," Conor muttered and excused himself from the table. He didn't go upstairs to his room, or to the parlour. He walked out the front door.

CONOR roamed the streets. Metcalfe Street. Maria Street. Elgin Street. He used to find Uppertown exciting; now he found it drab and dowdy. The boardwalks seemed to creak with boredom. Maybe there was more money uptown, but it was colourless and monotonous. This was a utilitarian place, a government town. Except for the orange day lilies, which had just started to bloom in front of many Protestant homes, there were few flowers. He found himself drawn toward the great divide between Uppertown and Lowertown: the Russell House on Wellington Street. He peered into the windows. There was some kind of reception going on. He could hear the noise of revelry but couldn't quite make out any figures through the smoky glass.

"The Russell" was Ottawa's fanciest hotel. Its dining room served salmon from New Brunswick, buffalo from the North-Western Territory and venison from up the valley on silver plates over white tablecloths. Conor had dined there once with D'Arcy McGee and loved every minute of it. He had felt a little awkward, not quite knowing the etiquette of fine dining, but the lumber barons and politicians at the other tables were so loud and full of themselves that they didn't seem to notice. McGee had spilt wine all over himself as he emphasized a point by flailing his arms. But that was a year ago, before he quit drinking.

A carriage approached, and Conor stepped back. He watched the driver come into view behind the thunder of the horses. It was Patrick Buckley, Macdonald's driver. Behind, in the carriage, sat the happy couple. Conor watched with some fascination as Buckley helped them down from the carriage. Sir John A. Macdonald was elegantly dressed with a cape over his formal suit and a top hat over his curly hair. He was sporting a bright red cravat; no one could miss him. Lady Macdonald was in a flowing, dark blue hoop skirt with rows and rows of flounces. It was cut high to her neck, and she must have pulled her corset terribly tight for her waist to have become that slim. She carried a handkerchief in her gloved right hand. It was probably perfumed. Conor had never noticed how regal Agnes Macdonald could look. He was about to approach the prime minister and say hello, but he hesitated when he saw, out of the corner of his eye, a man bounding from the hotel's entrance.

John Hillyard Cameron, the grand master of the Orange Lodge, approached Macdonald, his hand extended, his orange sash glowing as he walked. Conor was keenly aware of who was important, and Cameron was one of Canada's most prestigious lawyers. Conor stayed in the shadows and watched.

Macdonald warmly took Cameron's hand. Conor couldn't believe his eyes. The cape had obscured it before, but now he could see: Macdonald wore the same sash, the Orangeman's emblem. The grand master led Sir John and Lady Macdonald into what must be the Orangeman's Ball.

He heard the prime minister declare, "I say, Cameron, did God ever make a man as distinguished as you look?"

Conor was distressed. John Macdonald may not have attended the parade, but he never missed a party. He had joined the ranks of the intolerant—and the intolerable. He was one of *them*.

Once the door was closed and the Orangemen were inside, Conor walked up to Buckley, who was tending to the lead horse and chatting with a woman. Buckley was an Irish Catholic, and Conor had sometimes seen him with Thomas.

"What do you think?" Conor said.

"I'm paid to drive. And keep my opinions to myself."

Conor thought for a second, and concluded, "I'm paid to think, and I think it's us and it's them."

Until then, Conor hadn't noticed that the woman talking with Buckley was Polly, the washerwoman.

"Have you seen your father, Conor?" she asked.

"No. Have you?"

She looked down, embarrassed. Conor turned and walked away, leaving Buckley with Polly and Macdonald with his friends.

CONOR considered going to Lapierre's to try to speak to his father, but he couldn't bear the rejection. He thought of going back to the cathedral. He had found peace there, but he didn't seek a state of grace; he wanted to suffer in his own wrath. He stayed in Uppertown and wandered into the seediest Elgin Street bar he could find. It smelled of the common man: tobacco, beer, spit and urine. No white tablecloths here.

He sat alone and kept himself company. "This is no place for a gentleman," he told his glass of whisky. "Even a fraud with one suit and one tattered pair of shoes."

It was a mixed bar. There was a group of Protestant celebrants toasting the holy day over Bushmills, not of the class to be invited to the Russell House. A few people he assumed were "regulars" were pontificating about something or other as they sucked down whisky and spit out tobacco. Of course, there were the obligatory local drunks drinking cheap yellow whisky poured from the bucket. They hung on to the bar and stared into space. And there was a vagrant with no friends or family—him—slumped in a chair. Alone. With his drinks. And his resentment.

This day had made so many things clear. Their Orange fraternity of hate held the keys to power. He was a poor Irish immigrant—a bogtrotter—and he always would be. Those who called him an upstart were dead right. He knew life's surfaces, not its depths.

How had he climbed this ladder leading nowhere? The phrase he once thought could sound clever in a political speech now rang far too true, and all about him.

Thomas O'Dea had slaved and sacrificed so that his son could get an education. Book learning was unheard of among the labourers and drifters in the lumber camps. Thomas paid the bookkeeper as much as he could manage to teach Conor sums and arithmetic. At first, Conor resisted the discipline; gradually, he embraced learning as the

93

numbers started to make magical sense. Oblate priests taught him the rudiments of reading and writing, but words on a page turned into stories when an itinerant romantic wandered into the lumber camp one January afternoon. He had a mysterious past, which enchanted Conor, and spoke with an upper-crust British accent, which inspired him. All he carried was a sack of books and plenty of tobacco for his pipe. He wore a huge Stetson hat and they nicknamed him Tex. He could spin stories of exotic adventures throughout America and as far away as Australia. Thomas paid him a small fortune to tutor his son. Tex taught Conor the basics of sentence construction, and together they read story after story. More important, he urged Conor to think for himself. Tex was helping Conor take his first steps away from Thomas's world, and Thomas encouraged it because Tex was freeing his son from the chains of illiteracy and poverty. It had never occurred to Conor how incredibly generous his father had been.

When Tex disappeared, heading deeper into the bush to work on a railway, the Oblate priests continued the lessons. Although Thomas insisted "no religion," they applied the occasional Bible story to their lessons. Conor found the stories appealing, but didn't tell his father.

Though illiterate and innumerate, Thomas O'Dea sent for books. Huge white pine logs tumbled downriver and pages of knowledge were carted back on corduroy country roads, all to supplement Conor's education and ensure his escape from this rough and dangerous life.

Sinbad. The Arabian Nights. Ivanhoe. Conor devoured the books like a wood stove eating dry wood. He shared Tom Brown's schooldays, fought alongside Rob Roy and was stranded on a desert island with Robinson Crusoe. As he got older, he turned from adventure stories to biographies of Elizabethan swashbucklers: Sir Francis Drake, Sir Walter Raleigh, Sir Humphrey Gilbert, Martin Frobisher. His father was not aware that the British librarians were sending him heroic tomes of empire builders, discoverers and conquerors. Conor travelled the Pacific with James Cook, scaled the heights to Quebec with James Wolfe and conquered Bengal with Robert Clive. He became enthralled by their dedication to empire.

He loved to read books about British society. The Brontë sisters and Jane Austen opened a world of prestige, refinement and dignity. Society luncheons, fancy-dress dances, social intrigue and mischief. That's how he had wanted to live.

When Conor reached his teens, Thomas made sure that his son never headed into the woods to do the heavy work. He worked out a deal with the cook so Conor could stay indoors as a cook's apprentice. He earned his keep in the "camboose," a square of logs in the middle of the shanty where a cooking fire was always burning. It was claustrophobic, smoky, noisy and hot as hell's kitchen, but it was safe. Conor spent hours boiling bricks of salt pork while other young men cut and hauled lumber. The others made more money, but they risked their lives.

He grew up around rowdy, coarse, lonely men. There was camaraderie among the loggers; they were proud and competitive, and strong as oxen. There was order to their lives. They settled disputes with their fists and they earned respect by proving themselves in the forest. Every year, at first snowfall, with the promise of short days and severe weather to come, some deserted. Those who stayed were a class unto themselves. Workers. Lumberjacks. Timbermen. The toughest of all men.

It amazed Conor how the men so rarely complained. He would know if they did because indoor workers didn't just feed the men, they fixed them when they were hurting. Their remedies could be worse than the pain. Pine gum to close cuts, rusting implements to pull teeth. Conor watched one cook give a skidder with indigestion a few pinches of gunpowder in boiling water. "It'll scare your problems away." The skidder survived and never came back with another medical problem. Boiled pine bark with brandy was the usual stomach-ache tonic. One cook swore that boiled beaver kidney was the best medicine. Conor became a backwoods doctor. The men started trusting him. After all, "Cookie" could boil up potions and "Bookie" could read the manuals. Of course, there were no written instructions, just traditional antidotes and balms.

Growing up in a male world, Conor viewed girls as a frightening mystery, and mothers a total unknown. The loggers would talk obsessively about women—wives, girlfriends and lovers—but never mothers or sisters. Women were something to chase in the off-season. Conquests. Prizes. Trophies. Thomas kept the off-colour stories away from his son as much as he could, but some of the men took delight in teaching him their versions of the ways of the world.

Why, he wondered now, had he not missed a mother's love or longed for a mother's comfort? Why—and this is what seemed extraordinary to him now—did he not even wonder much about his mother? Margaret. What was she like?

"You," his father had said.

Maybe he was too busy planning his own life to think about others. Maybe he was too self-centred. No, not maybe. He *was*. He took another swig of whisky.

Mothers to him were characters in novels, like Mrs. Bennett nagging her long-suffering husband, planning parties, instructing her daughters with pride and considerable prejudice. Books were his links—his only links—to the outside world of society, gentility and petticoats. No one sent him books about famine, fever ships and Irish dead along the banks of the Boyne River.

When a rogue log almost killed his father and Thomas's back gave out, they moved down the river to Ottawa full time. Conor was now free to choose his own books, or at least the ones he could afford.

He absorbed the world of politics and parliamentary democracy. He turned to practical books that might prepare him for an important future. The rise of responsible government. How a bill is passed. The role of the backbencher. If he had taken these subjects in school, he might have found them boring, but by discovering them for himself, he found them riveting. This was real adventure spiced with vested interests, big money and burning ambition.

In this small, unlikely capital, politicians were all around him. Most were puffed up and self-important, but there was something vital about them as they plotted, negotiated, schemed and occasionally actually achieved. They were devising a blueprint for a new country. And they were gentlemen. He studied their movements, practised their accents and copied their dress. He strove to become as shrewd as John Macdonald, as dogged as George Brown, as overbearing as George-Étienne Cartier, as eloquent as D'Arcy McGee—and more determined than the lot of them. If he met the right people, if he accomplished the right things, he would become as rich as a railway baron and as happy as a prince. And he would leave far behind his life in a hardscrabble lumber camp and dirt-poor Irish shanty town.

Conor began enjoying the space between his old life and the new. It was liberating, proof that he was advancing. Annoying his father was a sign of his emerging success. He went through the motions of helping his father out at the tavern, sharing the occasional meal, talking the smallest of small talk, but a coldness developed. What did they really have to say to each other anymore? Conor was preparing for a life that didn't include Thomas. He was nice to the people in the neighbourhood, but he found them more quaint than inspiring.

"I am worse than a snob," he told his emptying glass. "I'm a brat and a bully."

He rubbed smoke from his eyes and thought, The masquerade is over. No more sneaking into the halls of power, acting as if he belonged. No more saying he was a speechwriter when he was really just an assistant. No more posing.

He ordered another whisky. The liquor made him think clearly. How had he thanked his father for years of sacrifice? By taking Thomas for granted and belittling his ignorance. He had betrayed his own people. He had been . . . Come on, he thought, you're a man of words, *think* . . . He had been . . . *cavorting with the enemy*. That was it. *Cavorting with the enemy*. Macdonald was one of them; so was Meg's father. What kind of judge of character was he? These were the sorts of people he admired? He was a fool who would never amount to anything. And he didn't deserve to. He said aloud, "Jane Austen can—"

"Conor! I've finally found you." It was Meg.

He almost dropped the glass of whisky.

"Meg, you can't come in here," he slurred.

"I can go wherever I want. *You* do."

He looked around. No one seemed to notice. By now, everyone had drunk so much that they were engrossed in their own stories, telling their own lies. Drunks don't listen, they talk; they don't think, they react. He learned that at Lapierre's.

"Come." She tried to pull him out of his chair. "Let's go."

He resisted and reached for a beer to wash down the whisky.

"I'm happy here."

"You don't look that happy to me."

She let him stay seated and went over to the bartender. "How much?" she asked. She was shocked by the price. Either he had drunk an extraordinary amount or she was being cheated. She paid the barkeep, left a modest tip and dragged Conor out to the street. He was wavering unsteadily, but was able to walk the few blocks to

Parliament Hill. "Lie down," she instructed. He did as he was told, stumbling to the ground. He lay on his back and watched the sky spin madly. It was a clear night, and the stars glistened and spun like a kaleidoscope. He was afraid he might be ill.

"What do you see?" she said.

"I see stars." It came out as *shtarshs*.

"Look at them as if it's the first time you've ever seen them, and tell me what you see."

He composed himself staring at the Big Dipper. It was the only collection of stars he knew by name. "I feel I can reach up, pull the handle and grab them," he said.

"Pull them from the sky?"

He laughed. "Maybe."

She let the moment lie; let him think about this for a minute; let the other stars come into focus. Her mother had taught her to love nature, not manmade idols; to worship God's creation, not an imaginary creator; but when she looked at the stars, she felt there must be something else. Some purpose. Something greater than simple existence.

"There are things nobody can take away from us," she said.

"Is this that nature stuff you admire?" He was trying to be cruel.

She ignored him. "It's a simple truth," she said and sighed. "What's wrong, Conor? You're not a good enough actor to affect sarcasm. Tell me what's wrong."

"I lied to you by the river. I have read some Tennyson. I told you I hadn't."

She looked confused. That was just idle small talk.

"A man in one of the lumber camps had a book of poetry, but I didn't understand it. I don't understand anything. I just say things to sound impressive."

"How old were you when you read it?"

"I don't know. Ten, maybe twelve. His name was Tex. He was trying to teach me, but I couldn't follow it."

"Everything has been so hard for you," she said. "I can't imagine."

"I don't know that. All I know is . . ." He braced himself and said it: "I've been cavorting with the enemy."

"Good Lord!" she exclaimed. "Do you know how stupid that sounds?"

It did sound melodramatic. But melodrama fuels a drunk.

"Are you saying I'm the enemy?"

"You, Macdonald, the drumming marcher, your father, your—"

"People marching. So what? I thought if you didn't like something, you'd want to change it."

"Why bother?"

Why bother? Wasn't that the point: to bother to change what you don't like, to bother to get it right? "What about Mr. McGee? He's as Irish as St. Patrick, and he's not running away."

"That's different," he said. But he knew it wasn't. Somehow, McGee made sense of the contradictions and confusions of life.

She moved closer to him. "While you wallow in self-pity, there's a world out there. You wanted it so much. Don't lose it." He didn't respond, and she added, "Don't run away. Get bothered. I like you that way."

He leaned toward her, his breath reeking of cheap whisky. She gently pushed his nose up toward the heavens and they stared at the night sky together. The Milky Way looked like painter's strokes on a jet-black canvas. The North Star beckoned amid the clutter of lights. She loved the sky. It was eternal. Infinite. Mystic.

Conor closed his eyes tightly and tried to think like his father. Meg's life had been so much easier than his. Sure, her father had been killed, but off she went to London for an education. She may not be upper-crust, but she had a rich aunt who helped the family out and an understanding, deep-thinking mother. He had nobody. She was right about one thing: she couldn't imagine how hard it had been for him and how hard it was still going to be. She couldn't picture herself trying to claw her way out of poverty, working to open doors in a closed society.

"Open your eyes," she said, "and look at me." He let his eyes adjust to the sky's splendour. "You know what you need to do?" He didn't answer, and she didn't wait for a response. "Just be yourself. Quit trying to be someone you're not. You don't need to try to impress people; you are impressive." Her hair was falling in her face. She brushed it aside. "Don't forget about the Orange Parade. It happened. It'll happen again. But don't let the bigots stomp over your own ambitions."

He smiled to himself and thought, That's the kind of thing D'Arcy McGee might say.

"What happened with your father was a shame, but you won't find forgiveness in a bar. You'll find it out here, or"—she touched his left arm—"you'll find it with me." She pulled him closer, and he felt his anger dissolving. He couldn't summon his father's resentment and fury, not in the arms of this Protestant girl. They kissed cautiously.

"What's happening, Meg?" Conor was afraid she would see his eyes filling with tears. "It's all spinning too fast."

"I don't know. All I know is that you are a complicated mess of a man, and I rather like the idea of trying to sort you out."

He looked deeply into her beautiful blue eyes. "Don't ask me to speak to my father. Not yet."

"I will ask you, but no, not yet."

"What do you think I should do?"

"You will go to Montreal to work on Mr. McGee's election. You will go back to work."

"And you?"

She leaned over and kissed him softly. It was a gentle kiss—not passionate, but inviting, certainly not the kiss of a friend.

"And I will . . . " she said, "I will be waiting here."

He felt so inept, so inexperienced. "In the lumber camps, I didn't really get to know many girls."

"Shhh. Words, words, words. Can't you just be quiet?" She held him tighter.

"I need you, Meg," he muttered into her long black curls.

"I know you do."

12

It was late afternoon in Westboro, a sleepy little village west of Ottawa. Nothing much had happened here since a fox bit the Duke of Richmond and he died, far from the comforts of home. They named a rough road that ran along the valley after him. These days, farmers from "up the line" would travel that road for provisions, and the occasional logger would stop en route to Ottawa. It was not uncommon to find strangers on the tree-lined streets. A weathered sign over the door of a tiny shop read J.P. WILLARD: GUNSMITH AND GENERAL MERCHANDISE.

He had left his old grey coat in Ottawa. In a lightweight, over-sized brown jacket, he surveyed the shop, waiting patiently for the right moment. It had been a disappointing week. He had spent much of it watching Thomas O'Dea. O'Dea was drinking too much, and he seemed to be falling into that Irish pit of despair. He gave O'Dea credit, though: he wasn't filling every ear that came into that miserable bar with his lament, whatever it was. Still, O'Dea was pathetic, and he hated that. Too bad; he might have been useful. Maybe later he could be of some help.

Anyway, he had to do this job alone.

As the afternoon drifted to a lazy end, he decided the moment had come. He quickly walked into the shop. He knew the storekeeper was alone inside, and he knew no one had seen him enter.

"I'll have a Smith and Wesson revolver with six chambers and some bullets."

"Certainly," Mr. Willard answered kindly. "Are you new to these parts?"

The man in the large brown jacket ignored him.

"You're a logger, then?" Mr. Willard searched for eye contact with the customer.

Again, no answer.

Unfriendly chap, the shopkeeper thought, as he opened the back cupboard and fetched the goods. He presented the gun and the ammunition to the stranger.

"Nice weapon, here," he said. "Very popular in the United States, I'm told."

The customer simply took the handgun from him, looked it over carefully and started loading bullets into the cartridge. It was as if Mr. Willard wasn't even there.

"Impatient, aren't you?" the storekeeper remarked. Perhaps he should have started to feel uneasy by now—maybe he should have called for help—but his mind was on other things. "Well, me too, I guess. I'm a bit impatient myself. I want to get home and see the grandchildren." He didn't expect a response from this unfriendly man, so he stuck to business. "That will be a dollar, unless you would rather pay in sterling?" It had been a slow afternoon. It would be nice to see some money in the till.

The stranger continued to act as if he were alone in the room and Willard didn't exist.

"I said, that will be a dollar."

He finished loading the gun and, for the first time, looked straight into the mortal face of James P. Willard. But a memory caught him off guard. A flash of humanity. This man and his own grandfather were so much alike: the same rosy cheeks, full white hair and kind eyes. He could picture his grandfather weaving stories of Irish heroes: the Wexford Martyrs, Mary Doyle, Wolfe Tone. He remembered his boyhood before his father's imprisonment, before the rot set in. If no one had seen him come in here, there was no need to kill this man. He took the money from his back pocket, put the dollar on the table and, as politely as he could, muttered, "Thank you."

He started for the door. As he reached for the doorknob, he stopped. What was he thinking? Had he gone mad? He turned to Willard and said, almost sympathetically, "I can't go soft."

Two shots exploded. The force of the bullets threw the old man back to the wall. He still had a look of shock on his face as he hit the ground, dead. It had happened so fast that Mr. Willard had not had time to scream.

His murderer quickly collected more ammunition and another revolver, stuffed them in his pockets and casually walked out into the late-afternoon sun.

No one had seen him. And no one seemed to have been startled by the noise. With children shooting squirrels and farmers hunting gophers, gunshots were common in country towns. By the time James Willard's granddaughter found his body, his murderer had thrown away the brown jacket, retrieved his long grey coat and was far away. Not up the river, where the police would assume, but back to Ottawa.

He had spent a relatively quiet July. He planned a busier August.

LADY Macdonald wasn't snooping. She was putting away a pair of shoes in a closet in her husband's office when she stumbled across a little rocking horse. It was perched at the back of the closet, covered in dust.

"It was little Johnny's," he said that night. "My son who died."

She could see that his eyes were watering, but she pressed on, carefully. "You never talk of those years. Your children . . . your . . . wife."

"It's an old story. Isabella got sick in the first year of our marriage and never recovered. She basically lay in bed for twelve years, comforted by an increasing amount of patent medicine and laudanum."

"And you worked."

"I worked and tried my best to help."

"And your sons?"

"Well, you've met Hugh. He's a chip off the old block. A little stubborn, but a promising Tory, I would think. Louisa really brought him up. I was too busy with . . ."

"With your work," she said for him.

"Yes, thank God for dutiful sisters."

She was learning to accept his selfishness. She knew countless political battles had left their scars, but they were flesh wounds. His pain was deeper. He was famously charming, cute with quips and stories, but there was a cunningness behind it all. If he couldn't make the rules himself, he looked for ways to circumvent them.

Where did the politician end and the person begin? Who was he, really? A family man wounded by premature death, or a career politician who would not let anything thwart his ambitions? Had she married someone desperately in need of love, or a man with a cold heart?

She watched as he reached for a glass on a side table.

The facts spoke for themselves. He used people like his "dutiful" sister and ignored his only living son; he destroyed political enemies without a thought and discarded friends when their purpose was served. But here, with a child's toy secretly stashed away, he looked so vulnerable, so forgivable, so worth all the effort it took to be with him. She might never reach into his heart and really know him, but she could try. That was her job. She looked at the rocking horse. And then at her husband.

"I couldn't part with it when little John died," he said. "He was just two years old when he fell."

She dared ask the question that haunted her. "John, is that why you drink so much?" She knew she probably should not have asked the question so directly. He ignored it anyway.

"You know my younger brother James died, too. Right in front of me. He was struck down by a man who was supposed to be caring for us." She thought he might put down his drink and seek comfort in her arms. Instead, he took a small sip. "I was seven years old. James was only five."

The pain in his voice was deep, naked, honest. This was the real John Macdonald: not a strutting statesman, but a vulnerable man chased by demons; not a hardened political actor, but a suffering brother, father and husband. *Her* suffering husband. And she loved him for that.

"Tell me: Why do I live and the others don't?"

How could she answer? What could she say? She was a new wife; this was a new start. "John," she said tentatively, "let's have a child of our own. I want us to be a family."

He looked at her blankly, then a slow nod and a trace of a smile. He put down his drink and moved closer to his young wife. Much closer.

THE entire Trotter family saw Conor off at the railway station. Mary Ann Trotter was like a mother hen with her flock. "Say hello to Mr. McGee for me," she commanded. "Tell him I have some stories for him." The Widow Trotter was becoming the mother Conor never had—or never remembered.

Conor smiled back at her. "If I can get a word in, I will."

Will gave him an awkward punch in the arm. Meg allowed a peck on the cheek and squeezed his hand. Very proper and reserved, he thought, but suggestive, just as Jane Austen might have written. Conor thought he saw some of the boys who had marched in the Orange Parade watching them, but he ignored them. Meg pulled him slightly toward her, whispering, "I need you too."

He shuddered, mumbled something back and boarded the train.

Conor brought along a book to occupy himself on the journey: a collection of poetry by Thomas D'Arcy McGee.

IN the first-class section of the train, another man was reading a book by D'Arcy McGee. The dense but very popular *History of Ireland* obscured the reader's face. A grey coat lay on his lap, covering one of the guns he had acquired from the late James Willard of Westboro.

He too was going to Montreal to meet D'Arcy McGee.

PART THREE

August 1867

The fate of our land
God hath placed in your hand;
He hath made you to know
The heart of your foe

Thomas D'Arcy McGee—poet, author, journalist, member of Parliament for Montreal West and Father of Confederation—sprung from his bed in hysterics. Clutching his sheets, his eyes wide with fear, he was screaming something about a waterfall.

"Jesus, no!" he yelled. "For the love of Jesus, no!"

Mary McGee reached out in the darkness. "What in the world is the matter?"

He didn't answer. Or couldn't answer. His eyes darted around the room, red and blurry with panic, until suddenly Mary spun into focus. "I had a dream," he said, clutching her close to him. "A nightmare."

"I know that," she answered gently. "But that's no reason to wake the dead with your shrieking." He smiled, barely. Recently, he had been prone to nightmares. His swollen leg hurt him so much at night, and he was under such intense political pressure, that his muscles rarely relaxed. But this nightmare was different: it was so real.

"I dreamed," he began haltingly, "that I was running along the bank of a river, calling to a boat in the water. It was heading toward a waterfall. The boat was out of control, drifting to certain disaster, and no one would pay attention to my warnings." He looked at his wife for understanding. "They were doomed. But I couldn't get anybody's attention."

"And you do hate to be ignored," Mary joked feebly.

He didn't respond. His eyes just grew wilder. "And then, I was pulled into the water, too. It was terrible. The boat floated safely to shore. No one on board knew how close they had come to disaster. And no one cared."

Mary McGee could hear noise outside. She assumed it was just men coming home from the tavern. D'Arcy was too deep in his nightmare to hear anything.

"Now I was caught in the rushing water. The current held me and I was heading toward the waterfall."

"D'Arcy," Mary whispered, "it was just a dream."

He gazed beyond her as if watching the nightmare again on the wall. "I was grabbing for something, anything, calling for help. But I was alone, all alone, and being pulled to my death by the current's force."

"But you survived," Mary reminded him.

"Yes, I survived. In dreams, you always survive. It's only in life you go over the edge."

Mary didn't say another word. She watched as her husband closed his eyes and fell back to sleep. But she couldn't sleep. Not again that night. She lay awake, thinking about his dream. Wondering. And worrying. There was trouble seething in Montreal, and as always, D'Arcy was at the centre of it.

13

====

Conor, where are you, you overpaid, overwhiskered boy?"

"I'm at my desk, sir."

"Well, I need that list of—"

"Here it is," Conor said, handing D'Arcy McGee a piece of paper.

"That's better."

Conor was back in Montreal, riding the tidal wave of McGee's bombast. McGee had just read a proclamation written by General O'Neill, the Fenian commander-in-chief in New York, and he was furious. "'Fifty thousand are ready'—what nonsense," he bellowed. "I'd ignore the blather, but this talk of liberation can incite the people, the irresponsible meddlers."

McGee was barely five foot three, but when on a rant, he seemed to tower over everyone—even Conor, who stood at least six inches taller. McGee was quick-tempered and fiery. Volcanic. He was constantly dishevelled, in his baggy suits, stained shirts and undone ties. His black hair was persistently askew and his beard in dire need of trimming. His dirty fingernails often sifted through his curly hair. His wife, Mary, told him he looked like an unmade bed. In fact, when once asked if she worried about him away from home so often with many single women about, she answered, "I take great comfort in his ugliness."

McGee was running for re-election in Montreal West. Part of the riding was St. Ann's parish in the Irish community of Griffintown, clustered between the railway tracks and the Lachine Canal. It was Montreal's version of Ottawa's Lowertown, but with more people, more spirit, more energy—and more tragedy. Typhus and cholera built up in the open sewers and spread through the crowded homes. In 1852 a fire destroyed half the buildings and left five hundred families homeless. Griffintown sat on low-lying land and was prone to flooding. The worst flood was in 1857, the year D'Arcy McGee moved to Montreal. McGee told his friend Father Dowd that God seemed to watch over Griffintown with Old Testament fury.

Men from Griffintown dug the canals, built the bridges and laid the railways. They worked terribly long days, raised strong families, kept the breweries and distilleries alive on Saturday nights and went to mass on Sunday mornings. They were D'Arcy McGee's people. They welcomed him into their midst. They supported and encouraged him, and what was most important, voted for him with rare consistency. McGee had never lost an election in Griffintown. In fact, he had won a few by acclamation. But during the first election of the new Dominion, something was going dreadfully wrong. Griffintown was in turmoil, the people rebellious, and the little Irishman was in the campaign battle of his life. Conor noticed it as soon as he arrived from Ottawa. The city was tense, the people in Griffintown edgy.

"Think nothing of it, my bucko," McGee told him. "It's the weather. It's so hot here that even the streets seethe with anger."

Conor knew the problem was much deeper than that. By constantly attacking the Fenian movement, not only had McGee infuriated many in Griffintown, but he had given his opponent, Bernard Devlin, an election issue. "D'Arcy McGee works with Orangemen," Devlin told the crowds. "He is anti-Ireland and anti-Catholic."

McGee relished a good fight and revelled in the rough and tumble of an election, but the intensity of the Montreal campaign left him depressed. "Why do Irishmen have to fight each other with the fire of the devil?"

Conor knew it was a rhetorical question. He was learning when to listen and not answer—which with D'Arcy McGee was most of the time. Still, he thought he would try a line on him. "Sir, why not say that Fenianism is a rung on a ladder leading nowhere?"

McGee thought for a moment. "Change it to 'intolerance' and make it the first rung, and I'll use it." He smiled. "'Intolerance is the first rung on a ladder leading nowhere.' Have you been thinking of that one for a while?"

Conor tried to act nonchalant. McGee liked his sentence. He might even use it!

"Well done, boyo," he said. "Well done."

"Sir, I would prefer that you not call me that."

McGee looked stunned. "I call you every name under the sun."

"But not 'boy' or 'boyo.' And could you save 'my bucko' for your opponents?"

"Toughening, are we? Or getting more sensitive?"

"I went through some changes in Ottawa."

There was a softening in the air. "How's your da?" McGee asked.

"Fine, I guess," Conor answered rather sheepishly.

"That's not what I hear."

"What do you know?" Conor asked tentatively.

"If you think he's fine, I obviously know more than you."

Conor just nodded.

"Listen to me, son. He deserves better."

Better than what? Conor thought. Me? He felt like saying that Thomas hated McGee with particular passion, but he supposed he knew that. "We had a talk," he said simply. "A fight, actually."

"I heard it was more than a fight."

"That's true, I guess, but now I know more about what he went through."

"You do, eh? No one can really know what an immigrant has been through. What pain. What sacrifices. Once you remember that, the better."

He held his gaze on Conor so that the word "sacrifices" would not be missed. Then he was the old McGee again. He brandished a piece of paper with Conor's writing on it. "Now get back to work. I'll call you no names, but I swear it's a wonder I keep you around. Your spelling is atrocious and your grammar worse."

DURING the Montreal election, Conor stayed at Scanlon's Hotel. Charles Scanlon was a McGee supporter, and he provided the room for a pittance. On free evenings, Conor pored over books and articles. He was reading Jules Verne's *Journey to the Centre of the Earth*. He liked the story, but most of all he liked that Verne was the most popular writer this year and that this was the book people were talking about. When he read, he also practised the language. McGee was right: he had much to learn about spelling and grammar. But it was mispronunciation that he worried about the most. He worked on this as he worked on everything else: with resourceful, and sometimes painful, diligence. In the privacy of his room, he would read each word out loud to ensure he said it properly. If he wasn't sure of a word's pronunciation, he would ask Mr. McGee.

A year ago, he called someone a "retrobate" trying to use a D'Arcy McGee–type word. "It's 'reprobate,' you young fool," McGee corrected him. And he called Conor a reprobate for a week. He was a tough teacher, but Conor was learning.

While D'Arcy McGee could help Conor with words, he was

little help with etiquette. His table manners were atrocious. McGee ate with the same bluster as he conversed: elbows flapping like birds' wings and his mouth overflowing with food. Conor was determined to learn the ways of the table. Sometimes he was invited to important dinners, but he would be seated at a table in the back with other assistants or with the press. He always watched John A. Macdonald. Macdonald seemed comfortable at the table. He was somewhat studied, but graceful and polished. But his good behaviour had its limits. By the dessert course, he often shocked the ladies with his stories and questionable jokes.

A mother might have taught Conor the niceties of manners and deportment. He pictured Margaret O'Dea hovering over her young son, sternly pointing at his elbows on the table as he sipped a root vegetable soup she had just prepared. The room would be tidy, with feminine touches: lace curtains, cut glass and maybe even figurines. He would obediently take his elbows off the table, and she would smile proudly. He imagined her reading to him at night. Could she read? Probably not. But she would have told him stories, nurtured him, comforted him—loved him. Instead, Margaret O'Dea lay on Grosse Isle in the middle of the St. Lawrence River. He had to teach himself.

Once a week when he was in Montreal, Conor walked along St. Catherine Street to dine at the St. Lawrence Hotel. In a freshly pressed suit, starched shirt and perfectly tied cravat, he was the picture of sophistication. He even sported a new walking stick. He would often bring a newspaper to give himself cover while he watched others. He studied the placement of the cutlery and when and how it should be used.

The hotel had a large American clientele. During the Civil War, many prominent Southerners stayed there. It was apparently the only bar in Montreal that served mint juleps. John Wilkes Booth had been a guest just before heading to Washington's Ford's Theatre to assassinate Abraham Lincoln. Conor was no Southern sympathizer, but he admired the table manners of Southern gentlemen.

Conor watched a man in a white linen suit sniff the cork of a red Bordeaux—claret, the English said. The waiter poured an inch. The customer held the glass up, rolled the liquid in the glass and studied it in the light. He ate a small piece of bread. Then, finally, he took a sip. He seemed to savour his performance as much as he did the wine. He nodded at the waiter, who then poured the wine. This was hardly the way you served a grunt at Lapierre's. Lesson for the night: choosing a wine is a ritual as much as a task. He would have to learn more about this. He studied how Americans cut their meat and then transferred their fork to their right hand to eat. The English would keep the fork in their left hand. He adopted the English system.

The waiter was a friend of his, a French Canadian who pretended to know the bayou when he addressed the Southerners. It was good for tips. He told Conor that the special tonight was beefsteak and onions.

"What's special about it?"

"The price. I can get you an extra piece. No one will notice. The chef is already into the cooking wine."

Lesson number two: it's not just what you know, it's who you know. But Conor already knew that.

14

Jolicoeur's Saloon was a popular drinking spot at the crossroads between English-speaking and French-speaking Montreal, on the corner of St. Catherine Street and St. Lawrence—"the Main." It was a kind of no-man's-land, neutral ground for a series of all-candidates meetings over the August 1 weekend. Just before the meeting started, Conor stood off to the side of the stage, alone. He examined the sweltering crowd through the smoke and rising sweat. He listened to the accents of old Europe dance across a New World hall, and saw a people divided. The French Canadians huddled together in a group; they didn't mix with the English, and the English certainly didn't mix with them. The Irish immigrants clustered together with their own songs and customs. The rich clung to each other for protection. And so did the poor. Ulster Protestants looked at the Irish Catholics with disgust. The look was returned with pity as the Catholics thought hell awaited their Protestant neighbours. The Scottish Presbyterians scowled at the Methodists. The Church of England looked down on everybody. The Americans were supposed to have created a melting pot, but their union had been torn apart in a horribly vicious civil war. Canada was a country of factions that rarely met together, let alone mixed. What future could it have?

Conor could taste the harsh whisky in the Elgin Street bar again—it was the flavour of defeat. There was no point. McGee and Macdonald, and all their talk of a new land and new ideas . . . it was an impossible dream. Over the loud din of differing, disagreeing people, Conor could hear his father's defeated voice: "Confederation is a waste of energy. Canada is a waste of time." It sounded sensible, logical, even liberating—there was no point.

Just then, D'Arcy McGee touched his elbow. Conor jumped with surprise. "It would be easy to give up, wouldn't it?" McGee whispered. Conor was dumbfounded. "But it would be wrong, Conor. Dead wrong." McGee held his arm a little tighter. "My generation will never bring them all together, but yours might, if you care enough and try to understand each other."

McGee's words amazed Conor. Why did he always seem to be able to read his thoughts?

Conor noticed Barney Devlin entering the room with aplomb. McGee watched his exuberant entrance as well. "He has all the wit and perspective of a temper tantrum," McGee said under his breath.

"Do you really think it's worth it?" Conor asked, watching Devlin wave to a group of his supporters at the bar. A well-dressed man with a bushy red beard waved back and gave a cheer.

"I've never been so sure," McGee answered. "Never."

A rather distinguished man gracefully walked up to them. Conor noted how he carried his walking stick with flair and ease. He would have to work on that.

"Mr. McGee, a word, if I might."

McGee reached out and took the gentleman's hand. "Joseph Faulkner," he said. "How nice to see you."

Faulkner returned the handshake formally. Even in the heat, his tie was firmly tied, his collar severely starched and his jacket tightly done up. Very dapper; Conor was impressed. He would have been more impressed had McGee introduced him. But he was preoccupied.

"Did you get my letter?" Faulkner asked.

"Yes, but I cannot agree with you, Joe. The Fenians have to be stopped. This fanaticism must be cured."

Joseph Faulkner had supported McGee in the past, but had broken with him because of his attack on the Fenians. He felt McGee was unnecessarily stirring up trouble and should let the issue die down naturally.

"I hope you're not going to be too inflammatory tonight."

"I'll bore them all to sleep. You know me."

"Yes, I do. All too well," Faulkner muttered—rather rudely, Conor thought—and walked off.

McGee turned to Conor, trying to keep a brave face. "Just another of my friends," he said.

Friends, family, Conor thought, who can you turn to? Who can you trust? D'Arcy McGee saw the pain in Conor's face and patted him on the shoulder. "So how are you, young man? Truly?"

Conor heard himself say, "I went to an Orange Parade." He knew it was bad form to talk like this just before a speech, but it was too late now.

"They play a fine fife," McGee responded with a wry smile, but he saw that Conor was in no mood for a joke. "Look, Conor, don't let the fools cloud your mind. There isn't anybody prouder of his Irish-Catholic heritage than I am, but you can't be outraged about the Orange Lodge without being ashamed of the Fenians. It's a secret organization just like the Orangemen, only it's on our side, so we're not supposed to object. Well, I object. I'm on neither side. They both have their own bigots and blockheads."

"And they both hate you."

"Yes, they both hate me. Still, we are becoming better friends,

Catholic and Protestant. We rarely cut each other's throat in the name of God anymore." They both watched a crowd at the bar drinking and whooping it up, and Conor marvelled at McGee's enthusiasm under pressure. "Now go and join my wife, lad. She's got some foolish idea that I'm getting sick or something. Tell her that what I'm doing—no, what *we're* doing—is worth every bead of sweat and every bloody insult."

Conor smiled at his short, scruffy employer. In the heat, McGee looked sloppier than usual. Yet he stood tall; taller than anyone in the crowd.

"I believe you have a speech to make, sir."

McGee took Conor's hand, firmly shook it and headed for the stage.

IT was so hot in Jolicoeur's Saloon that the man in the smoky shadows draped his grey coat over his shoulder. He had brought it because he needed the pockets. He drifted through the crowd on a prowl. He had changed his look; simply shaving off his moustache and growing longer sideburns had altered the shape of his face. But the sneer was the same and a hellish fire was still in his eyes. He continually pushed back his hair or rubbed his eyes, covering his features as often as possible. When he was afraid he might be too conspicuous, he used his coat as a shield, blocking his face. Stir it up, he thought, and soon the pot would boil over. A word here, a complaint there, a nasty rumour launched—it was actually rather fun. The Fenians were in town, and they were in business. There was no army—not yet—just him. But then, it took only a spark to start a fire.

D'ARCY McGee always preferred to speak last, to have the final say, but tonight he had picked the shortest straw and would be the first speaker. Walking to the podium, he tried not to limp, but he clearly favoured his sore leg, leaning on his walking stick. Conor thought he was greeted with more cheers than boos. Confederation and its architects were still popular; the problem was that those who yelled in derision always made more noise.

Conor's attention was focused on McGee. He didn't notice the man in the well-tailored suit, sporting a bushy red beard, booing particularly loudly. He didn't see another man quietly approach him at the bar. He didn't hear the exchange.

"You don't much like that fellow McGee, I see."

"I'd just as soon see him dead."

While McGee took his place on the makeshift stage, the man with the grey coat took a careful look at the sloppy little man. He looked tired. Well, he *should* be tired. He's worn out, spent and just about finished. He kept his eyes on McGee as he pulled a tomato from his coat pocket and gave it to the red-bearded heckler beside him. "Here, take this. There may be some fun later."

McGee stood at the podium and waved to the crowd. "Greetings, my friends, and good evening to all of you privileged to vote in this free and glorious Dominion." He knew his opening words were banal. They lacked spirit and artistry. Mary was right; he wasn't feeling well. He was sweating under his waistcoat and jacket. His leg had been hurting him for days, and tonight, in this oppressive heat, the throbbing was like a blacksmith's hammer.

Conor knew the next words from the speech. McGee had practised, or tested, them on him. "Canada," he declared, "has already played an important part in the history of civil and religious liberty, in the emancipation of the Catholics, in the enfranchisement of the Jews, in the interests of the Negroes."

A voice called out from the back, "Sit down, traitor, before you fall down."

Why "traitor"? Conor thought. His enemies called him a turn-coat because he worked so well with Protestants, but he fought for Catholic schools, worked for Irish causes. He was hardly a traitor. But the word had power, and his opponents knew it hurt.

Another voice yelled, "You look like you're drunk."

Conor wanted to shout back, "He hasn't touched a drink in months." But McGee *was* wavering like a drunken man.

"If we are a generation worthy to organize a nation, assuredly the materials are abundant and are at hand." McGee was ad-libbing and losing the moment.

The voice that first yelled "traitor" now started a chant: "Trai-tor, trai-tor, trai-tor . . ."

Barney Devlin's boys quickly picked it up: "Trai-tor, trai-tor, trai-tor . . ."

The heckling seemed to give McGee strength. He tried to speak above the chanting. "I am a man of peace," he yelled. "And peace has her victories, no less than war."

The same voice that started the chanting yelled, "Sit down, you're finished!"

McGee wondered who it was, but he could hardly take a second to reflect. He responded with an old retort: "It's a comfort to be attacked by you, my bucko." He was trying to lighten the air, but there was no lightness to be found. Still, McGee desperately tried to gain some control of the meeting. He searched for Conor in the crowd. And Mary—poor Mary, why did she have to watch this? She deserved better. But then, so did he. He felt a sharp shot of pain in his leg, and the blood rushed from his face. He clutched his walking stick and somehow gained his composure, smiling at a friend in the crowd to hide his distress. He explored the darkness at the back of the room, searching for the voice of the man who had started this ruckus.

"What about the Fenians?" That voice again; the same Irish accent. "Why do you attack your own people?"

"I'll answer you, sir," McGee responded, "whoever you are." The crowd hushed for a moment. "You're right. I'm against the Fenians. Old World prejudice has no place here. I strangled the notion of Fenianism when I came to Montreal, and I'm not going to be annoyed by its carcass."

The crowd started to still. McGee's bravery was winning people over.

"I will not allow firebrands to take over this election campaign, or foreign schemers to wreck this great country." He was speaking directly to the hidden shape at the back of the room, the man who had started the trouble. "You and your type will not destroy this government. You . . . you . . ." He looked over at Conor, summoning strength, and smiled. "You reprobate."

Conor actually laughed. But Barney Devlin's boys weren't laughing. "Start throwing, boys," the voice yelled, and an egg came flying toward the stage. It just missed McGee. A second egg came from the left. A tomato hit him on his shoulder. That same voice renewed the chant. "Trai-tor, trai-tor . . ." It was gaining momentum. "Trai-tor, trai-tor . . ."

McGee held his ground. "Some say I should leave the Fenians alone," he yelled over the noise. "Well, I won't leave extremists of any sort alone." He saw a man at the bar take aim and throw a tomato directly at him. He ducked. The tomato splattered behind him. "Some say my cause isn't worth it," he continued. "At moments like this, I know more than ever that it is."

McGee's voice was now drowned out by chants. "Trai-tor, trai-tor, trai-tor . . ." He stood defiant and unafraid, but he looked dazed. The Irish faction had destroyed the meeting. But worse, this display made them all look like fools in the eyes of others at the meeting. It would just add to prejudices.

"Trai-tor, trai-tor, trai-tor . . ."

It was stupid and shameful. Montreal was polarized between Irish and English. French and British. Catholic and Protestant. And he stood in the middle, battling the radical extremes. The target for everybody's scorn.

"Trai-tor, trai-tor, trai-tor . . ."

He felt that sharp pain again, but this time it continued rising up his leg. The blisteringly hot room started spinning. He was becoming light-headed.

"Trai-tor, trai-tor, trai-tor . . ."

His reached for his walking stick, but it fell cruelly to the ground. He was helpless and rapidly losing control.

"Trai-tor, trai . . ."

A cool wave engulfed him. It was blissful. Refreshing. Peaceful. The noise was fading out. Disappearing. Slowly. Gently. Like a cool northern wind blowing . . . blowing . . . blowing him off his feet . . .

Conor and Mary ran to the stage. Conor caught McGee just as he fell. At first, it looked as if one of the objects thrown at him had knocked him down, but McGee had simply collapsed from exhaustion. Mary whispered in her husband's unhearing ear, "Now you'll go to bed, love. Now you'll rest."

A policeman rushed to the stage. A doctor quickly followed. All eyes were on the podium, watching McGee, amazed at the spectacle. Nobody noticed a man leaving the hall with a grey coat slung over his shoulder and a look of pure satisfaction on his face.

Yes, he thought, the pot has been pleasantly stirred.

15

D r. O'Brien was firm. "D'Arcy, the ulcer in your leg is worsening.
Under no circumstance are you to leave your house for at least a
week." Mary McGee stood by the doctor like a co-conspirator.
She would make sure his instructions were followed. If D'Arcy lost
the election, so be it.

"But I have to go to Ontario. I'm needed," McGee protested.

"Just a week, dear," Mary insisted. His adventure in Ontario was
nothing but foolishness as far as she was concerned. Imagine, while
running for his life in the federal election in Montreal, he was also
running for the provincial legislature in Ontario, a province he'd
never lived in. Didn't he have enough on his plate?

"There's work to be done. You'll not put me in prison."

"In a week, you can go back to your meetings and be insulted,"
Mary said. "For now, fight your battles in bed. I'm your enemy."

Conor snickered. He thought of offering up some lumber camp
remedies. Perhaps a pinch of gunpowder with that potion, sir, or beaver kidney extract. No one seemed in the mood for a joke, so he kept
it to himself. It would be his job to keep his employer off his feet for
seven long days. McGee the wild animal corralled, and he the hired
hand trying to keep him penned. But Conor had his own designs on
this week. The instant Mary McGee and the doctor left, he pulled a

chair over to the side of the bed. "Are you tired, sir?" he asked. "May we talk a bit?"

"Of course I'm not tired," McGee lied. "It was a simple fall."

"I want to speak to you about my father."

D'Arcy McGee's face grew serious. "Yes, Thomas O'Dea. He's a good man, but very bitter, far too bitter."

"He thinks you're a . . ." He tried not to use the word in the chant from Jolicoeur's, but he could think of no other. "He thinks that you're a traitor."

"I daresay he's not alone."

"And I guess he thinks I'm something far worse."

McGee ran his hand through his messy hair and sighed.

"He told me about Ireland and the famine," Conor said. "He described the ship over here."

McGee sadly nodded. "Fever ships. Coffin ships. I know them well."

"He told me about my mother," Conor continued. "Her name was Margaret. She died in the crossing."

McGee bit his tongue as the pain rushed through his leg. "Conor, it's hard for you to understand what your father has been through."

"He says you don't understand."

McGee considered the accusation. "An immigrant—no, a *refugee*—will always be an outsider, and that's what your father is. No one can live inside your father's skin and really know what he feels, but I think I have some sense of his anger. I was a refugee, too. In fact, I think I understand the people who shouted me down last night, even that man at the back of the room."

"What?" Conor exclaimed. "How?"

"Listen, tomorrow a reporter from Cincinnati is coming here to interview me." Conor knew about the interview, but he had assumed it would be cancelled now that McGee was in a sickbed. McGee anticipated his reaction and continued. "Mary can't object. We can do it from my room here. I want you to listen in. He wants to hear about the old days—the days of Young Ireland. Rebellion. Insurrection." His tired voice seemed to fill the room. "You see, I once stood with them. We didn't use the word then, but it's fair to say that I was . . ." He paused, as if daring himself to use the word "Fenian," and chose instead to say, "I was just like them."

MARY McGee marched into the room without knocking and dismissed Conor. He was not—"I repeat, *not*"—to return until the next day at noon. "D'Arcy needs his sleep."

McGee smiled. "You're right, Mary. Tomorrow at noon. Because at two o'clock I have an interview with some American reporter. It can't be moved." He held up his arm as if deflecting an attack. "Conor will be here to keep it short. No problem."

She cast an angry look at Conor, as if he was part of some plot with her husband.

"It's not his fault. The interview was set up last week and we don't know where the reporter is staying. I can rest in the morning, and surely I'll have the strength to talk a bit in the afternoon."

"I don't have the strength to stop you," she said softly. And he knew he had won.

"Now, Conor, go and find out more about that mysterious troublemaker last night. Then, Mary, we'll burn him in a pot of boiling Guinness and be done with him."

She didn't smile.

CONOR went to Irish bars throughout the parish and simply hung around, drinking a few pints and asking a lot of questions. He heard great stories of conspiracies hatching throughout Griffintown, of Fenians on the border, of a free Ireland on the horizon, but nothing specific—nothing clear about whoever had started the trouble at Jolicoeur's. Nobody, it seemed, had seen his face. Those who had, or thought they might have, could not remember any distinguishing features.

"Was he tall?"

"No, medium height."

"Did he have a beard?"

"No. I don't think so.

"What was the colour of his hair?"

"Hard to say. He wore a hat, and I never got a good look at his face."

"Would you recognize him again?"

"No, I doubt it."

Conor felt like the world's worst detective. But then, there was probably nothing to worry about. He was just another of Barney Devlin's boys.

CONOR wrote to Meg daily. He struggled timidly over each word. He could write complicated political treatises and solidly argue a point of privilege, but he'd never written a love letter. So he hid behind reportage: reports on his day, reports on the election, reports on the latest book he was reading.

He had been slowly composing a real love letter for days, and stumbling over every sentence. He discovered he had to write about someone else first. Another woman. Even if she was from his own imagination. Encouraged by his talk earlier in the day with D'Arcy McGee, and fuelled by a few pints, he took out his pen and began writing.

Dear Meg,
I want to tell you about my mother . . .

SOMETIMES he told people to call him Patrick, but usually he avoided trading names. He had stored a box of clothes at the St. Lawrence Hotel when he first came up from New York State. Picking it up was easy. A few dollars and a Southern accent, and the boy behind the counter paid him little attention. His bag of tricks stored a make-up kit, hair dye, wigs and false facial hair.

He had taken a room above Barney's Tavern in the guise of a workman: overalls, open-necked shirt and tweed jacket. From his dirty window, he watched McGee's assistant arrive and then leave an hour later. Meddling son of a bitch. He'd be dead if he weren't potentially useful. He would have to go down to the bar later to find out what he had been up to.

He considered his options for tomorrow. He should wear a suit, but not too expensive. He'd sport a rather garish tie. He was American, after all, not a boring British subject. A touch of grey on the temples, a thick moustache, maybe a distinguishing scar on his right cheek. He looked in the mirror. Not bad. Maybe add to the moustache and make it a salt-and-pepper beard. That was better. He was a new man: Jasper Green from Cincinnati.

16

It was a typically dreary evening at Lapierre's when Polly Ryan walked in.

"This is no place for you," Thomas O'Dea told her from behind the bar.

"Oh, don't you worry about me," she said casually.

Thomas liked Polly. He felt a kinship. She washed clothes and cleaned other people's houses; he washed mugs and filled other people's glasses. They were about the same age. Both had lost spouses; both were alone and terribly lonely.

"How's your son?" she asked. "And I will have a beer."

"You've heard, I suppose, that he's in Montreal with McGee." He made no move to get her a drink. Her accent was County Clare, his was Galway.

"I've also heard that there is no ladies' section in this bar, and I still want that beer."

Thomas almost smiled.

"I saw your son about town after your fight. He was looking sad."

"Aren't we all?"

There was something mysterious about this washerwoman, but also a sense of strength and resolve. "Don't lose him, Thomas," she said. "You've already lost so much else."

"Is that why you came in here? To meddle in my business? I don't intrude in yours."

She looked around the bar and then at Thomas. "Forget the beer, but remember what I said. You're a good man. Be nice."

MEG was thrilled each time she received one of Conor's letters. She carried the latest one wherever she went. It was about his mother. She had lost her own father and understood Conor's longing to know more about this unknown, gentle person named Margaret. The stories of Ireland particularly moved her, especially the unimaginable trip across the ocean. Her family had come to Canada from New York State during the American War of Independence. They were United Empire Loyalists: conservatives who didn't support the Yankee rebels.

She walked along Metcalfe Street, on the way to the market to buy the evening meal for the boarders. It had been raining for the past two days; the streets were muddy and she stayed on the boardwalk. She stepped away from a carriage hurling filth as its wheels passed. She pictured Conor's mother sitting up all night with a dying woman . . . feeling the fevers slowly boil inside her . . . trying to stay strong in front of her husband and child. She wondered if she could ever be that brave.

"So if it isn't Meg Trotter," someone called from behind her.

Another added, "Are you a Papist now, Meg?"

She knew these people from school, sons of Orangemen who had marched in the parade. Quickly, they surrounded her.

"Leave me alone," she ordered.

"No, you leave *him* alone," the largest of the group responded. The others laughed. She recognized the drummer she had waved at during the parade. She had never thought of him as a bully. She searched for his name. Dave? Dan? Doug? Something like that. She looked at him for some sympathy, and he responded solemnly, "Stick to your own kind, Meg. It's better that way." It was as if he were reciting a lesson in church.

Meg was terrified but didn't want them to see her fear. She shoved one of them. He gave ground. She stared at the drummer. He recoiled.

They left as quickly as they had arrived. And she ran down the boardwalk, clutching her letter from Conor.

"MCMICKEN, is there no end to your reports?" The prime minister was sitting in the Rideau Club, sipping on a glass of champagne, reading the *Ottawa Citizen* and considering buying a new suit he saw advertised. Cartier buys his suits in London, he mused. I am a true Canadian, buying locally when it's all I can afford. He didn't really care about affairs of the state on this gloomy August day.

"I have a brief report from the Mother Country, sir."

"Derby and Disraeli's problems. Probably Gladstone's soon. Not mine, so it sounds good to me, already." He turned the newspaper's page and nursed his drink. "Carry on, I'm listening as best I can."

Macdonald loved the Old World pretentions of the Rideau Club. It felt so very British. As the club's founding president, he enjoyed holding court in his favourite overstuffed chair in the large sitting room. It was strategically placed so he could both watch what was going on and be seen by those who mattered. Occasionally, he would smile at friends or frown at enemies. Gilbert McMicken sat beside him, focusing only on the prime minister.

"As you know, there were Fenian uprisings in Ireland last March," McMicken declared.

"And as *you* know, the Royal Irish Constabulary quelled them," Macdonald responded. He loved to have the facts at his fingertips and didn't conceal his delight in reporting back to McMicken. "Three men were hanged in Manchester, I do believe."

"That's right, sir, but it's more complicated. The ringleader, a man called Tom Kelly, was being taken from court to Manchester jail when his Fenian colleagues intercepted the van, and in the process, a policeman was killed."

"'Fenian colleagues'? You mean murderers." He held up the advertisement. "Do you like the look of this tie?"

McMicken ignored the diversion. "They were caught, convicted of murder and hanged."

"As I just told you." Macdonald went back to the newspaper, muttering, "I may have too many red ties."

"In retaliation, a bomb has just exploded in London's Clerkenwell Prison. I don't know how many are dead yet. We just got the dispatch."

Now he had the prime minister's attention, although Macdonald was determined not to let him know it. He put the newspaper down, but held on to his champagne glass. "A bomb? In London?"

"They are taking the battle for Irish independence out of Ireland and into Britain."

Macdonald didn't know what to say. McMicken filled the void. "Tom Kelly is an American. It seems he developed some of these tactics in the Civil War."

"Is there any connection to what's happening here?"

"I don't know. We will try to find out."

"I fear the Irish fight can only get worse there," Macdonald sighed. "But here, it's just a bunch of hotheads getting us worked up for nothing. I know you disagree, and Mr. McGee goes on and on about it, but that's my view."

McMicken sensed that Macdonald did appreciate the dangers in this new world of conspiracy and terrorism; he just wished they would go away.

17

He arrived at two exactly and introduced himself to Mary McGee as Jasper Green. He had a perfect Southern drawl, not a hint of Irish in his voice. She was polite but distant as he made small talk about the weather and took in the downstairs room. Very Irish, he thought, with clichéd shamrocks and sickening green paint. A little womanish. This was her house, clearly. The front door had a cheap lock—he could break it in seconds—but the house was on a busy street and it might be reckless to try to break in. The back windows led to an alley, so there was a means of escape, but it was an active place. McGee's family littered the house, and there was that ever-present assistant.

"I do hope your husband is feeling better," he said. Obsequious. Caring. Thoughtful. But she didn't seem to buy his act.

"You are not to keep him long," she instructed. "He is still very tired."

Conor was upstairs in the bedroom, reporting his failure to discover anything about the troublemaker at Jolicoeur's. He was delighted to be called downstairs to avoid accusations of ineptitude. He led the reporter upstairs.

McGee was propped up in his bed with his bad leg elevated on pillows. He still looked weak, but there was eagerness in his eyes as he met Jasper Green. He enjoyed talking to reporters. He loved talking about himself.

"I gather it's Young Ireland that interests you," McGee said. He felt they had better get right to it because Mary and Dr. O'Brien could interrupt them at any time.

"Yes, I'm doing a piece on the roots of Fenianism, and I'm told you are the man to talk to." The bedroom had a large window. He couldn't tell if there was a way down—an escape route.

"I know a thing or two about Irish history. Have you read my book?"

The reporter nodded. He saw that McGee had a sharp letter opener within easy reach on his bedside table. His meddlesome assistant was probably unarmed. "You've been a part of some Irish history yourself, I understand." Flatter the bastard, egg him on and push a bruise. "Could I say you were a Fenian?"

Conor cocked an eye. Interesting. The big question right away. It was well known that D'Arcy McGee had stood against the British in Ireland back in the 1840s. His political foes in Ottawa loved to taunt him about it. He always claimed he was a propagandist, not a warrior. And he was hardly alone in having a rebellious past. George-Étienne Cartier, the very picture of the establishment, had fought the Château Clique in the 1837 rebellion. In fact, he had barely escaped the gallows. William Lyon Mackenzie, the famous leader of the rebellion in Toronto, was later elected to the Legislative Assembly, where his voice was still heard but the roar had gone. But what of McGee? He certainly avoided calling himself a Fenian yesterday.

"I would not put it that way, sir." McGee clearly disliked the question being put so bluntly—Conor could tell by the way he made the word "sir" sound like a slur. "It was at the height—or the depth—of the famine, and I joined up with a group under the illustrious name of Young Ireland. We were rebels, no question about it. We decried the famine and hurled abuse at injustice. We were a good lot: idealistic, but not as extreme and certainly not as violent as these dimwits today. We felt Ireland should belong to the Irish, and I think that still."

Conor did not say a word. He just watched and listened. The reporter took notes, as if he cared.

"Back then, I was angry—no, I was furious—and with good cause. The famine was so terrible, it cannot be exaggerated. The English landlords stayed in their green and pleasant land while hopelessness and despair stared us straight in the face. My heart grew sick at the daily scenes of misery. Nothing green, nothing noble, could grow on our land."

"But what happened?" Conor asked. It wasn't his interview, but he had to know. If he learned more about McGee's days in Ireland, then maybe he could better understand his father—and himself.

"Well, I never fired a gun, if that's what you want to know, Conor." McGee thought for a few seconds and chuckled. "But I did cause more than my share of trouble—as always, with my pen and with my mouth. I made speeches, damned good ones, attacking the English for this and blasting them for that. And I wrote articles urging people to send us money and arms."

The reporter picked up on the last word. "Arms?"

"Have you ever been to Ireland, Mr. Green?"

"No, I've never left this continent," he lied.

"Put yourself back in those times, in that place, if you can. Irish towns had become poorhouses, farms were fever sheds, the country one great graveyard. One-quarter of the population had died of disease or famine. And there was a mass exodus to the New World. A population of eight million cut in half in just a few years. Yes, I admit I was a fool. I remember once writing, 'Farewell, sickle; welcome, sword,' and actually thinking it was a noble phrase." He sat up quickly in bed. "But I would not go along with what some of the others wanted: an open declaration of war with England. I was inflammatory and imprudent, but I had some common sense." He lay down again. "We would have been destroyed, anyway. Read your history. It's in my book. The great Tudor queen, Elizabeth, sent her pirates into Ireland for plunder, the parliamentarian Oliver Cromwell massacred us, and you've seen what your fellow citizens think of William of Orange. King Billy's heirs still march as if they're on the banks of the River Boyne. Yes, English statesmen and soldiers have had a taste for Irish massacres."

He abruptly stopped talking. He could feel the fury within him and he wanted to calm it. "But I would never want to be defined by hatred. Learn about the past, remember it, but use that knowledge to prevent hatred from continuing."

The reporter looked up from his notes. What a pile of shite, he thought. I should kill the bastard right now. "What happened to you next?" he asked politely.

"Ah, the plot thickens. I went to Scotland, raising money for Young Ireland. I had a list of nearly four hundred men ready to take the risk. Yes, those were heady days." A spasm of pain in his leg reminded McGee that these were different days, a different country, and he a far different man. "One day, I went into a reading room in Paisley. I'll never forget it. I picked up a government magazine called *Hue and Cry*, and written there in bold letters was a police notice for the arrest of one Thomas D'Arcy McGee. I was twenty-three years old, with a three-hundred-guinea price on my head."

"My God," Conor blurted out. "You were a wanted man!"

"Sounds exciting, doesn't it? Well, it scared the devil out of me. I was warned that the English army knew I was in Scotland. I had to get away. I took the guise of a sickly Dublin student on holiday and fled to the north of England. From there, I was secreted by boat to Belfast. The ship was filled with Orangemen cheering the defeat of the young Irelanders. And defeat it was. My friends either had been rounded up or, like me, were on the run. We were finished before we had even begun."

Conor wondered if he saw a tear forming in McGee's eye.

"Poor Mary," he continued. "She was in Dublin, fretting though all of this. We had been married only a short time, and she was with child. It must have been terrible for her. I saw her for about an hour by the River Foyle in Derry. We had just enough time to say goodbye. The English were, as they say, hot on my trail."

He could probably slip some poison in his medicine. But that wouldn't be dramatic enough. That letter opener was certainly inviting. There was a lull in the conversation; he had to fill it. What would a reporter want to know? Facts. Names. Dates. "When exactly was this?" he asked.

"It was September of '48," McGee answered, reciting the day he knew so well. "On September 1, I boarded a ship called the *Shamrock* off the coast of Derry. I sailed alone to America, bursting with hatred for the English and longing for my wife and country." Then he slowly smiled and said to Conor, "You're looking at a man who once appeared destined for the priesthood." Conor looked shocked. Jasper Green stared at McGee blankly. "Yes, I was disguised as a seminary student for the trip across the Atlantic, Lord preserve my soul."

"There's something I don't understand," the reporter said. "Why did you eventually come to British North America?" He said "British" with a slight sneer.

McGee was prepared for the question. "When I went to America, I quickly got a job writing anti-British articles in newspapers. I started as a reporter—like you, I suppose." There was no response, so McGee continued. "Then I began publishing newspapers myself. My main concern was the plight of the Irish immigrant. We were pouring into the slums of New York and Boston like rainwater into a sewer. If we found work, it was for the lowest of wages. If an Irish worker complained, he was replaceable. The next ship would dock any day.

"We were farmers, people from the land, but when we came to America, we settled in cities. It was wrong. I tried to get people to move west, to stay close to the earth, where their values were, but the farthest most got was the Erie Canal. Irish sweat and muscle dug that canal, and Irish graves litter its shore. You've heard of the expression 'low Irish,' haven't you?"

Conor nodded. The reporter said simply, "Yes, I've heard the phrase."

"There were signs everywhere in this so-called land of the free forbidding us to work. 'No Irish Need Apply.' It was outrageous. Let me ask you a question. What is worse: being evicted from farms in Ireland, or living in an American shantytown, digging a canal? Living and starving in Ireland, or rotting in a New York tenement, dreaming of your homeland?"

Jasper Green from Cincinnati looked up from his notebook. He could hear noise downstairs. Someone was at the door. Was it the special delivery letter? No, too early.

McGee continued, "They call me a hypocrite because I was once a rebel, or they say I'm a turncoat because I settled in a British country, but the Fenians are the true hypocrites. Those treacherous, self-declared Irish leaders—they could have promoted a better life in America for Irish immigrants, but chose instead to attack the peaceful British colonies to the north. Canada hadn't done them any harm."

"What about the Orangemen?" Conor asked, expecting a torrent for a response. It was not his place to interrupt an interview.

"Good question, Conor," McGee roared. "To hear Devlin talk, you would think Protestant extremists flourished only in the shadow of the Union Jack. The fact is, the New England states are so zealously Puritan they could make a Toronto Orangeman look like the Pope's uncle." Conor smiled, but McGee was serious. "Many Americans despise our poverty, ridicule our accent and scorn our religion." McGee looked at the man called Jasper Green. "Where are you from, sir?

"Cincinnati."

"Did you know that in 1855 no Roman Catholic was permitted to parade on the fourth of July in Cincinnati?" He did not. He'd never even been to Ohio. McGee was on a roll and didn't expect an answer anyway. "Do you know the average Irish labourer in America lives less than ten years after moving there? Do you have any idea how many of us died in the front lines in your Civil War?" McGee stopped to catch his breath, again not expecting a reply, and carried on. "Yes, the war. That too helped change my mind. I wanted slavery abolished as much as any thinking man, but Irishmen fought to free the slaves in the cotton fields while their brothers were enslaved in northern factories. It was all wrong. I remember saying to Macdonald at the Charlottetown Conference, 'The difference between us and the American Founding Fathers is that we aren't writing words of liberty while we whip our slaves.'"

A good pistol-whipping would serve you right, the man thought, but he said, "Peace, order and good government isn't so uplifting." He didn't plan to be provocative, but he could not resist puncturing this balloon of nonsense.

"It's a pretty good start for a country," McGee responded. "One, I admit, that was born in compromise and political chicanery." He turned to Conor and winked. "But you'd have to ask Mr. Macdonald about that."

He could hear talking downstairs. McGee's wife and someone else. Maybe a doctor. He could poison McGee and his precious assistant and implicate the doctor. He'd done that before.

142

"Most important, we have our Catholic schools. I helped ensure that. But I thought you wanted to hear how the Irish rebel became a Canadian patriot?"

"Yes, please, do tell." The reporter readied his pen. Might as well let the political diatribe continue.

"When I came to Canada in 1856, I was struck with a thought: I wasn't leaving a land of liberty and entering British tyranny, I was actually following the route slaves were taking to freedom. I saw them. Black men and women risking their lives along the Underground Railroad to come to this British territory—a territory, mind you, which had abolished slavery back in the last century. Think about it: servitude in the United States or liberty on British soil? I began to question which offered true freedom and democracy. This country is alive with hope. Canada is a place of space and open land. People can settle here and stay close to their roots. They can buy land for practically nothing and work it, not for absentee landlords who could evict them at a whim, but for themselves."

"That's *my* question," Conor interrupted. "The landlords. How could you forget what they had done? How can you forgive?"

The assassin looked at him with surprised admiration.

"Just look at the politics of it, Conor. If we had the kind of government in Ireland that we have built here in Canada, there would never have been a need for Young Ireland—a strong national government, yes, but robust provincial governments as well, representing particular interests. Ontario has its own government for the likes of George Brown, Nova Scotia for the likes of Joe Howe and Charles Tupper, and Quebec for the likes of Cartier." He laughed, enjoying his trivializations. "And we have the freedom and openness of Canadian democracy—for the likes of McGee," he bellowed, still laughing.

"I don't know those names. I'm an American," Jasper Green from Cincinnati stated bluntly.

McGee looked at him sternly. "Write this in your newspaper, sir: 'We are building a northern country of compromise, good faith and fair play.'"

The assassin was squirming in his chair. What drivel. He could stab him with a pen. That would be wondrously fitting. He pretended to be taking McGee's sickening dictation.

"The one thing needed for making Canada the happiest of homes is to rub down all sharp angles, to get rid of old quarrels. We Irishmen—Protestant and Catholic—born and bred in a land of religious controversy, should never forget that we now live in a land of religious freedom." Again he turned to Conor and looked him straight in the eye. "Certainly, we have a long way to go, a terribly long way, but I would live nowhere else."

There was a knock on the door. The reporter looked startled and reached into his pocket. It was Dr. O'Brien. "Your interview is over, D'Arcy. I'll have a look at you and then you should rest."

Conor walked the American reporter to the door. A strange fellow, he thought. There was something distant about the man. Most reporters he knew were gregarious and rather fun to be with. Most were brimming with questions, on and off the record. This man was thoughtful, but barely inquisitive. He was almost blank and forgettable behind his cold eyes and greying beard.

He didn't even say goodbye.

18

Downstairs, Mary McGee sat alone, lost in thought. Four years ago, her husband's political supporters had presented him with a house on St. Catherine Street. He needed to be a land-owner to hold political office. Their home was so dignified, so refined, so unlike D'Arcy. Few of the mementoes and gifts that overfilled the drawing room were of much value, except, perhaps, some of D'Arcy's books. It was an Irish-Canadian room through and through. The heavy curtains had shamrocks woven into them, and there was an abundance of Irish colour: green upholstery, green carpet, green cushions. It was a lovely room, she thought, with a comforting fire-place and warm atmosphere. After years of barely making ends meet, her family finally had a real home.

The rebel lived—if he didn't always act—like a gentleman.

She glanced down at the newspaper she was holding. On the front page was an account of the trouble at Jolicoeur's Saloon. At the bottom of the page was a glowing article about John Macdonald joking that, as a professional cabinetmaker, he wished he had better wood to work with. John plays politics while D'Arcy wages war, she thought. She felt old and weary; her skin had weathered, her hair was greying and her smile had grown melancholy. It was all just getting too much for her. John Macdonald had a young, ambitious wife urging him on. D'Arcy, she thought, was not so lucky.

She scanned the article about her husband and realized she had been reading the first paragraph over and over, scarcely taking in a word. She looked up at the picture of the Holy Mother on the wall and uttered her deepest wish: that D'Arcy would give up fighting and settle down. He had stopped drinking, that was a blessing, but politics was just as intoxicating and just as lethal. For twenty years, he had served his passion for one cause after another. Without his fervent speeches, Confederation would never have come about—even Macdonald admitted as much. He had climbed his way up the pedestal, and now he stood on his tiptoes, tottering. In the newspaper article, he was called a firebrand. She wondered how many people had called him that over the years. A stubborn reformer. A renegade rebel. A hero. And now his own people in Griffintown were calling him a traitor. A traitor to what? Many of his colleagues were outspoken; his problem was his absolute faith in his convictions. He was obstinate and inflexible, bull-headed and unyielding, highstrung and . . . also the sweetest, most kind-hearted man she had ever known. That so many people failed to see that always amazed her. Maybe because they never saw him play with Frasa and young Peggy, or shared her grief when they mourned the deaths of their children.

Even agonizing memories were soothed by his words. She mouthed her favourite poem, written in those terrible days of exile:

My Irish wife has clear blue eyes
My heaven by day, my stars by night.

For she to me is dearer
Than castles strong, or lands, or life.

An outlaw—so I'm near her
To love to death my Irish wife.

Such strong love and such deep emotion; such pride and such persistence. This crusade he was leading against secret societies was something she respected, but it was so dangerous. Fenians, Orangemen, why couldn't he leave them to squabble among themselves? Why couldn't he leave well enough alone? For his sake. For his family's sake. And hers.

Well, she had a secret of her own—one she dared not tell anyone. She wished more than anything that her husband would lose this infernal election. She would nurse him through the humiliation and help steer him through a change of careers. Surely, one of his admirers would help him get a respectable job.

Conor O'Dea was an amiable young man, but she resented the time her husband spent with him. In many ways, Conor reminded her of D'Arcy as a young man: full of ideas and bursting with promise. She knew that each time D'Arcy berated Conor, he was trying to build his character. Years before, D'Arcy had looked up to the great Irish politician Daniel O'Connell in much the same way Conor looked up to him. Perhaps Conor rekindled the flame of those naive days, and that was why D'Arcy gave him so much of his time; precious time he could be spending with her and with his family.

While all eyes focused on him, who paid attention to her? It was always *his* mess of curls, *his* beautiful voice, *his* effortless prose, *his* causes; each cause more important than her.

She knew that D'Arcy had been talking about the old days with that reporter. Young Ireland. Famine. Rebellion. Exile. The memory haunted her, a nightmare she never wanted to live again: abandoned as her husband took on the role of Irish folk hero. They love their rebels in Ireland. They tell glorious tales about them and write plaintive ballads about them. But they leech their stories of blood and agony, and they forget about those left at home.

Yes, the old days. He escaped to the United States to become a famous newspaperman while she stayed at home, practically penniless, bringing up their daughter. He wrote her beautiful letters of love, but they only made her yearn for him more. Eventually, he earned enough money to pay for their passage over to America, and they joined him in Brooklyn. Finally, they could try to build a life together.

Mary was startled out of her thoughts by a knock on the door. She groaned as she pulled herself out of the chair. What is it this time? An angry constituent? A man in search of a job for his son? A friend in need of money? A postman handed her a special delivery letter. Probably an invitation to make another speech, she thought, so he can get into even more trouble. She smiled at her little witticism as she opened the envelope. She looked at the letter and let out a silent, hollow gasp. Then, as if she suddenly found her lost vocal cords, a horrifying wail gathered in her throat and her screaming echoed through the house.

CONOR had lingered in McGee's library, looking up passages on Young Ireland. He came rushing into the front room when he heard her scream. D'Arcy McGee struggled out of bed as fast as his swollen leg would allow. Dr. O'Brien followed, confused and out of place. Mary stood like a statue, transfixed by the words on the paper. Conor took the letter from her stiff hands. The short letter was printed in simple, childlike block letters: "If you say any more against Fenians, you will die." It was unsigned. Instead, at the bottom of the page was a crude drawing of a gallows and a coffin.

By now, D'Arcy McGee had hobbled down the stairs. Conor was about to hide the letter from him, but he knew better. Without comment, he handed it to him. McGee read it grimly, showing no emotion at all. He looked at Mary and rubbed his hand through his hair, then, like a military commander, turned to Conor and issued an order: "Get down to *The Gazette* and have this letter published immediately. Tell the editor I will spend the rest of the week preparing an article for the paper, called . . ." He stopped to think. "'The Attempts to Establish Fenianism in Montreal.' Tell him I will pull no punches. I will name names. And damn the guilty."

In his bedclothes, leaning against the wall for support, he looked frail and vulnerable, but his eyes were alive with rage. "No more stories of the past, Conor. We've got a fight on our hands." He turned toward the stairs and bellowed, "I won't stand for this. I can't."

Mary watched her husband limp upstairs. She was still shivering with cold dread. No one had paid her any attention. Old words kept swirling in her mind: "To love . . . to love to death . . . to love to death my Irish wife."

19

In Ottawa, Meg Trotter was helping her mother prepare ice cream. The day before, in the back kitchen of the Toronto House, they had made a hot custard of milk, sugar, eggs and vanilla. They had let it cool overnight. Now, Mary Ann Trotter was adding ice and salt while her daughter steadily turned the machine's handle. Meg kept her hair tied back to keep it out of her eyes.

"Do you know that people in town call you the Widow Trotter?" Meg asked her mother.

"Of course, and I don't mind. I loved your father very much."

"But can't you be known for who you are now, not who you married?"

"What do you mean, Meg?" Mary Ann Trotter knew there was something else on her daughter's mind.

"Why does everyone judge a woman by her companion?"

"Are you thinking of Conor?"

"People have been treating me strangely. You know, different religions, different backgrounds."

Her mother nodded. She had worried about this.

"People are condemning me, but you don't mind, Mother. You haven't told me not to see Conor."

"Well, the Widow Trotter has some modern views," her mother

answered, smiling, adding more ice. "But I will tell you something plainly, Meg: I will not allow anyone to hurt you. Not anyone. We will go back to Toronto—or wherever—if there is even the hint of trouble."

Meg turned the handle with extra determination. She knew her mother meant it. She had always admired her mother's strong will. She made her own judgments, set her own course in life—and always put her family first.

Watching the custard turn to ice cream, Mary Ann Trotter reflected on her life in Toronto. Her husband had been a blacksmith. To her surprise, he had proven to be a particularly good businessman, expanding his shop and investing in others. He was popular and gregarious, and handsome in a rugged, athletic way, if you didn't mind the smell of dirt and horses about him. Mary Ann almost laughed to herself as she conjured up his image. Meg had inherited his thick black hair. Sometimes when she looked at her daughter, she could see him—just a fragment, a loving trace.

His death was so senseless. He had been struck by a stray bullet in a barroom fight. Two drunks—one a Protestant, the other a Catholic—fighting over some ancient and petty grievance, killing someone else by mistake.

"Being called the Widow Trotter reminds me of your father."

"It reminds me of death. Everywhere I turn, people talk of hatred and death."

MEG had been to the Byward Market many times, but she had rarely stopped to take in the tenement houses nearby. Some of the stone buildings had character and could be cleaned up, but the wooden houses looked like fire traps. She was amazed at how dirty Lowertown was: sewage in gutters by the wretched shacks; emaciated pigs wandering the streets, sniffing at the ever-present excrement. Her family had a milking cow in the back of the boarding house, so she was used to animals—but not in front. It was disgraceful. Was this the way these people wanted to live? No, of course not; this was the way they were forced to live. These homes were probably owned by her neighbours uptown, who came by only to collect the rent. She admired Conor all the more, thinking how hard he was working to escape the imprisonment of poverty.

Polly Ryan saw her coming. She had been keeping an eye on Conor O'Dea's girlfriend, the Protestant from Sparks Street. There weren't very many mixed relationships in Ottawa. If this one grew, there could be trouble. Her responsibility was to look out for trouble. She made sure the young girl didn't notice her, but watched closely as Meg knocked on Thomas O'Dea's door and he opened it.

"Who are you and what do you want?" he barked.

"My name is Meg Trotter," she said, holding back her fear. "I would like to talk to you about Conor."

Thomas stared at her, hardly believing her impudence. He could tell by her accent that she was of English stock and by her dress that she had come from Uppertown.

"May I come in?" she asked politely.

"What is your business?"

"Mr. O'Dea, Conor has told me about you. You must have worked dreadfully hard to have your son educated. You must love him very much."

"So?"

She wanted to declare, "I think I love him, too," but she dared not. She said, simply, "I just wanted to meet you."

"Well, you've met me." He tried to slam the door, but she boldly put her foot out and stopped it.

"Will you let me come in?"

So Conor was now with a Protestant girl, Thomas thought. He might as well be if he associated with Macdonald and McGee.

"I am hoping I can help you reconcile with Conor."

He looked at her with fire in his eyes. "I have no son," he said. "Now move your foot."

Meg had never seen such intense anger. She recoiled, and Thomas O'Dea slammed the door in her face.

POLLY Ryan watched the pretty girl run up Sussex Street crying, her black hair flying behind her. She looked terrified. Polly wondered what had happened. How it might play in the wide picture. She would have to find out. He might want to know.

20

Conor O'Dea arrived at D'Arcy McGee's bedroom door armed with a tray of salt fish, fried pork rinds and beans, a concoction that delighted the feisty Irishman.

"My God, Conor, you are a good cook."

"I got a lot of practice in the lumber camps. I can boil you up a barley soup if you want, and I do wonders with molasses."

"I suspect your backcountry soup was thin as water and molasses was all there was for taste." He didn't know how true that was. Just don't start calling me Cookie, Conor thought.

McGee attacked the food with vigour. Lying in bed, blankets up to his neck, his unruly hair almost filling the pillow, he looked rather comical, but he was intent on his article about the Fenians and still upset about the trouble at Jolicoeur's. With his mouth full, he demanded, "Tell me about the mystery man. Should I challenge him to a duel?"

"You would have to find him first. No one seems to know him. I still can't find out anything. Strange, isn't it?"

"Very strange. If he were from around here, I would know him."

D'Arcy McGee had spent the week he was supposed to be convalescing propped up in bed, his leg suspended to ease the pain, furiously writing his article for *The Gazette*. Although his health was gradually improving, his temper was not. He harangued Dr. O'Brien for overreacting; he howled at Mary, complaining that he was chained to his bed; and, of course, he bellowed orders to Conor. Where were the statistics to embellish his arguments? He needed dates checked, names clarified. Why did everything take so long? Hurry up, damn you!

After the meal, McGee wiped his face with his sleeve and showed the finished article to Conor. He had charged that the Fenians dominated Montreal's Irish societies and claimed that they had actually infiltrated the Montreal police force. In sharp and unyielding language, he accused Barney Devlin of financing his campaign with Fenian money from New York.

"Are you sure you want this published, sir?" Conor asked. "It may make matters worse for you."

"I was denied the right to free speech, and then my life was threatened. Even if I wanted to, I couldn't back down."

Conor studied the list of people McGee had called Fenian supporters. "Devlin's name is not on the list."

"No, because he's not a Fenian. Devlin's a damn fool and a dupe, that's all. They're using him to get at me."

Conor knew the fuss the newspaper article would cause, but he also knew it was easier to float upstream on the Niagara than to try to stop D'Arcy McGee once he had set his mind on something. "I'll take this right down to *The Gazette*," he said.

"No, you won't." McGee dragged himself out of bed. "We'll both go. It's been a week since I've smelled the streets and tasted the sights. I'm ready for a walk. Tomorrow I'll be fit to finish off this campaign, and that imbecile Devlin along the way. Come on, help me on with my clothes."

AFTER the stale atmosphere of his sick room, even the thick city air was invigorating. Leaning heavily on Conor's arm, McGee cheerfully waved his cane at people passing by. He soaked in the summer radiance. During the past week, McGee had been so preoccupied with present-day problems that Conor had not asked more questions about the past, but this walk, and this summer afternoon, gave him a fresh opportunity.

"Are you, in any way, embarrassed by your rebel past?" he asked cautiously.

"No man needs blush at forty for the follies of one and twenty," McGee answered. "In fact, you could use a little adventure yourself." And he chuckled. "Look, we were reacting to the famine. We were young and angry. But we kept our struggle to Ireland. Not like these Fenians here."

A constituent came up to them and shook McGee's hand. "It's a delight to see you up and about, Mr. McGee. Good health to you, sir."

McGee beamed. "And good health to you, my friend."

Something else had been concerning Conor. "What did you think of that reporter?"

"Rather a cold fish, I would say. But we have to get the message out in America that our Confederation is strong."

Conor dropped the thought. Something troubled him about the reporter, but it wasn't important.

"I don't want to make everything look perfect up here," McGee continued. "There's much still to do. But I resent American indifference to our nation-building and their interference in our affairs."

Conor was pleased that McGee was walking with a little more ease. Perhaps the exercise was stretching his sore leg. McGee waved to another constituent across the street. The man did not return the gesture. He pretended the insult had not happened and again took

Conor's arm for support. "Soon we are going to have to get back to the campaign. I've lost ground while lying in bed."

"How do you think you are going to do?"

"I've never lost an election yet," McGee answered, evasively. "I don't know about my venture into Ontario, but here, in Montreal, yes, I'll win. It's just a few who have been causing all the trouble. But it doesn't take many voices to sing a loud song."

Conor noticed the man who would not return McGee's wave still scowling at them from across the street. One of the few, he thought. They walked in silence

Then the attack came.

In the corner of his eye, Conor caught a rustling in the bushes. He thought he heard someone yell, "All right, boys, that's him." It happened so fast that he wasn't sure of the details. About ten people jumped out of the bushes. They started throwing—not tomatoes or eggs this time, but rocks and gravel. A rock hit McGee's shoulder, and he faltered. Conor grabbed him. Together they tumbled to the ground. Conor screamed at the attackers, picked up the rock that had hit McGee and uselessly hurled it back. With D'Arcy McGee helpless and humiliated on the ground, and Conor trying to shelter him from attack, the mob ran away laughing and cheering.

It was not until later—after they dropped off McGee's damning article at the newspaper office, after they hailed a hackney carriage to take them home, after McGee refused to go to the police, after they both suffered Mary McGee's furious recrimination—that Conor had time to carefully reconstruct the attack. Someone had yelled from the bushes. He remembered the voice. An Irish accent. Was it the same voice as at the back of the hall at Jolicoeur's? He thought so, but he wasn't sure. During the attack, he thought he saw someone sneak away. Was that the person who started it? Maybe. It was hard to say. But he was familiar. And he wore a long grey coat.

157

21

=

n Ottawa, Sir John A. Macdonald was in a playful mood. He had handily won his seat in Kingston. His nemesis, George Brown, had been defeated in Toronto. "Go back to printing drivel, George," he murmured merrily. "In your stuffed shirt with your rich wife, your earnest obsessions and your endless prattle about reform." He avoided reading George Brown's newspaper, *The Globe*, whenever possible.

God was indeed in his heaven, and he was in the premier's chair. His position of power and prominence secure. Yes, his desk was still laden with problems, but they could wait until tomorrow. The rains were over and the muddy streets were now baking in sunlight. It was a splendid late-summer afternoon. He summoned Patrick Buckley to prepare the horse and carriage, and pulled Lady Macdonald away from her book.

The treeless Sandy Hill offered little shade during the dreadfully hot summer. "How overactive those loggers have been," Agnes once remarked, to her husband's great amusement. "The houses are built on sand, dear; hence the name. We're plain-spoken here in Canada." Sir John took her hand and escorted her into the carriage and they set off through the dusty, dry streets of the trussed-up lumber town.

Sir John was content to sit back and enjoy the ride, perhaps head out into the countryside, but Lady Macdonald had other matters on her mind. "What's happening in Montreal is vile, don't you think?" she asked.

"Yes," he sighed, afraid of where her inquiry might lead. He knew she liked D'Arcy McGee more than most of the self-obsessed politicians she met in Ottawa. She and D'Arcy could talk for hours about poetry, books, even flowers. He had actually supported one of her chief causes, the new St. Alban's Church on Daly Street. Imagine a Romanist donating five dollars toward the Church of England! Yes, he was a good sort in her view, especially now that he was off the bottle.

"Why don't you help D'Arcy?"

"My dear, I've been busy in Kingston."

"You know that isn't an excuse. I understand you haven't even written him a letter of support."

Macdonald didn't want to talk about this. Agnes could be worse than the hounds in the Opposition. He knew the embattled Irishman could use his help, but he simply couldn't offer it. McGee was forever getting himself into these messes because he used his mouth like a Gatling gun. Weapons sometimes backfired, and Macdonald didn't want to get wounded. Still, he cherished the times he and D'Arcy had shared on the floor in Parliament, in the parlour at the Russell House and in the back rooms at Lapierre's. They had actually begun as political rivals. Initially, he had dismissed McGee as an unbecoming Irish runt, little more than a dilettante and an adventurer. But he would never forget McGee's maiden speech in the legislature. The power of his words, the lilt in his voice, the sheer brilliance of his oratory. It was certainly not easy being attacked by D'Arcy McGee. Macdonald could remember his words by heart. "This is a government of corruption," McGee proclaimed. "Their faith is in corruption. Their hope is in corruption. Their creed is in corruption." A bit strong, Macdonald thought, but they were the words of a man who cared, not those of a dilettante. He decided to try to get this eloquent Irishman on his side.

George-Étienne Cartier was not as easily impressed. McGee had actually defeated Macdonald's political partner in a Montreal campaign. Cartier had to run again in a constituency in the Laurentian hills. It was a humiliation Cartier would never forget. He declared that the Irish electors in Montreal "could be bought for a barrel of flour apiece and some salt fish thrown in for the leaders." McGee never said an angry word in response, but he could never seem to remember the name of Cartier's new riding. He kept calling him "The Honourable Member from . . . ah . . . some country constituency."

Politics, thought Macdonald. What sport!

Along the bumpy road to Confederation, it was clear to Macdonald that McGee had the passion to inspire the people, and it was clear to McGee that Macdonald had the political sense to turn his words into a reality. So they became colleagues, and as Agnes was reminding him, they became friends.

"So why," she asked again, "won't you help him?"

How could he explain it to her? He had survived as a politician because he knew how to fit the message to the audience. He knew when to speak up and when to keep his head down. McGee must have been away from school the day discretion was taught—or did they ever teach that in Ireland? Macdonald was by nature a cautious man (already he was called "Old Tomorrow" because he put off difficult decisions), and the row in Montreal was a fight he couldn't win. Besides, it was an Irish fight, and he had no business entering it. D'Arcy would have to endure this one alone. It wasn't practical to defend him now.

"Let's say I know D'Arcy can handle it himself," he finally declared, aware that that would not satisfy her.

160

"He has no choice," she answered with a distinct tone of disgust. Agnes always got the last word. That was fine with Sir John, as long as it was the end of the subject.

With delight, he spotted a diversion. "Look. Speaking of McGee, there's his assistant's father." It never ceased to astound Agnes what a wizard her husband was with faces and names. He ordered Buckley to stop the carriage as they came alongside Thomas O'Dea, who was shuffling along the boardwalk.

"Good afternoon to you, sir," proclaimed the prime minister.

Thomas looked up, nodded at Buckley and scowled at Macdonald.

Sir John, oblivious to the slight, was always willing to talk to a potential voting man. "My good man, did God ever make a man as solemn as you look?" Thomas O'Dea continued to scowl and Macdonald continued to talk. "I just want to tell you that your son is doing marvellous work for the new Dominion. He's an able worker for D'Arcy McGee and a credit to the British nation."

Macdonald was in danger of making a speech, and Thomas O'Dea cut off his rhetoric with a brisk "Good day to you" and walked off rudely.

"What a sullen man," Agnes said, watching Thomas walk away. She noticed that he was propping the small of his back with his right hand.

"Aye, he's not too friendly a chap," answered Sir John. "But he does pour a decent glass of whisky." He was so used to insults dealing with the Liberals in Parliament that he had barely taken notice of Thomas's attitude. "Still, he has every reason to be proud of that son of his. I like his spunk and spirit."

A twinkle came to Macdonald's eye. "Carry on," he instructed Buckley. "Let's go to the Russell House." He looked at his wife with a mischievous grin. "For tea, dear. Only for tea."

As the carriage churned ahead, it kicked up a cloud of dust that blew in Thomas O'Dea's face. Standing in a veil of filth, watching the grand carriage drive away, he spit dirt and swore aloud. What right does that Orangeman have telling me to be proud? My son "an able worker for McGee . . . a credit to the British nation." Well, damn them all, he thought, rubbing dust from his eyes. Damn Macdonald and damn McGee! And damn this British nation!

THE Russell House Hotel was the height of elegance, at least by Ottawa's standards. It was made of sturdy stone, not rotting wood. It towered four storeys, if you counted the attic. Inside this bit of Piccadilly on the Ottawa River, gentlemen chatted in large overstuffed chairs while smoking or chewing tobacco. Each chair had well-used ashtrays and spittoons handy. Lady Macdonald was pleased that chewing tobacco was one vice her husband hadn't embraced. They were heading into the parlour when Macdonald spotted George-Étienne Cartier in the hallway.

"Cartier," he bellowed, "why aren't you fighting the good fight in Quebec?"

"Railway meetings, John. Business doesn't stop during elections."

Macdonald had taken note that Cartier, his Quebec lieutenant and political partner, rarely called him *Sir* John. Cartier was still peeved that he hadn't received the same honour on July 1. Your day will come, Macdonald thought. Be patient.

"I would ask you to join us, but I think the talk of business would bore you, Lady Macdonald," Cartier said. He was a master of condescension. Macdonald hoped his young wife would ignore the insult. She didn't.

"What do you think about the situation Mr. McGee faces in Montreal, Mr. Cartier?" she asked, sternly.

"A rambunctious rebel fighting off his rebellious countrymen, I suppose."

She had expected a dismissive answer and was ready. "Strange coming from you, sir—one who rebelled against the Crown in '37 and was lucky to have been pardoned."

"Agnes," Macdonald jumped in, "that was a long time ago, and we must be moving on." He smiled at Cartier, thinking that it served him right. "On with your business, George. I'll drop by if I can."

Macdonald escorted his wife into the parlour and excused himself quickly. He wanted to see what Cartier was up to.

In the bar, the industrialist Hugh Allan held court, his long white beard glistening in the window light. The best seat in the house. Allan was the richest man in Canada: a financier, a shipping magnate and a railway baron. He ruled Montreal commerce from his mansion on the hill. Cartier had joined Allan and two others at the table, but Macdonald didn't know the other two men. They must be concocting something. Not business of the state, or he would know about it. Or was he being left in the dark?

A foursome was playing cards at one table, a man was asleep with the Montreal *Gazette* draped on his chest at another and a heated conversation raged in the corner. Macdonald ignored them all and headed for the seat of power. "Hugh, how good to see you. What brings you to our humble Westminster?"

"Just trying to keep the wheels turning, Prime Minister," he answered.

"You know, I don't think we can print enough money for you to spend."

Allan laughed, but without humour. Macdonald waited for a fuller explanation. None was offered. He looked at the two other men at the table. Functionaries, he assumed. And he ignored them.

Cartier broke the uncomfortable silence. "You make the promises, John; we try to see them realized."

Another man joined the table. He was tall and stately, with

163

long, well-groomed whiskers. "Prime Minister, how nice to see you," Casimir Gzowski declared in a thick Polish accent. Macdonald smiled. He admired Colonel Gzowski. He combined the grace of the nobility and the initiative of a self-made man. His firm engineered bridges and surveyed railways, and he was even vying to pave Toronto's Yonge Street.

Gzowski was welcomed to the table while Macdonald was left standing. The prime minister was starting to feel like a courtier in the presence of greater powers. He had better flex some muscle. He aimed at a target he could hit. "I'll see you in cabinet, George," signalling that he was about to leave their presence, that he had somewhere else to go.

"I'm still not pleased with our defences, Sir John," Colonel Gzowski declared, surprising Macdonald with his bluntness. "You must establish a true military presence in this country."

Macdonald had heard it all before. An army cost money, and there were better uses of the country's limited resources. At least Gzowski had put his money where his mouth was and had started a volunteer regiment in Toronto.

"Working on it, Casimir. I can't just snap my fingers and get things done."

"No, you can't," Hugh Allan said, entering the discussion. "But you can put your hand up and be counted."

That's what money gives you: the power to tell anybody to go to hell, even the prime minister of Canada. Cartier seemed mildly amused, although in cabinet, Macdonald had never heard him advocate a stronger military presence. He would have to apologize to Cartier for what Agnes had said. It was true Cartier had fled Canada after the Rebellion of 1837. He could have faced the gallows for his part in the rebellion—others had—but Cartier was from a wealthy family, and his pleas for forgiveness and a change of heart were accepted. It was the right thing to do. He had served his province and country extraordinarily well since.

Casimir Gzowski was a former rebel, too. He had been part of a major uprising against the Russians in his youth, and then escaped to North America, where he had learned English and earned a fortune.

Two rebels forming the very picture of the establishment, sitting like bookends beside the pillar of power from Montreal. Gzowski, the imposing son of a Polish nobleman, and George Cartier, the diminutive Quebec lawyer. Cartier might fiercely defend Quebec's interests, but he looked as British as a bulldog with shirts from Jermyn Street, suits from Bond Street and a burning desire for a knighthood. Cartier also had a mistress he escorted about society, much to Agnes's horror. Perhaps that was another reason for her jab at him. Macdonald actually pitied Cartier, locked in a loveless marriage, reaching out for attention and recognition.

He would rather the comfort of a glass of sherry, but his wife had already ordered tea and scones. He had better join her.

"I'VE been given your name and am told you're with us." Those were the only words the stranger uttered when Jimmy Brennan opened his front door. It was evening on the backstreets of Montreal's Griffintown. Brennan, a young man barely out of his teens, was startled and scared.

"Who are you?" He tried to catch a view of the person's face in the flickering gas light, but the man stayed in the shadows.

"Are you alone?" the stranger responded, ignoring his question.

"Yes," Jimmy blurted out. "I'm alone." That was his first mistake. The stranger brushed him aside and marched into his room. He already knew all about Jimmy Brennan: an aimless, unemployed young man, one of Barney Devlin's more exuberant "boys." Not the best man in a thoughtful discussion, but a good partner in a fight.

"Are you from the States? From the brotherhood?" Brennan asked.

The stranger stared at Jimmy. He wanted to study this creature. Did he have the stuff of a revolutionary? Could he be useful?

"I may need your help," he whispered, barely moving his lips.

"So you *are* from the brotherhood." Jimmy Brennan felt the beginnings of a nervous twitch.

The visitor took off his old grey coat and sat down, never taking his eyes off the anxious young man. He moved out of the shadows. It didn't matter whether he was seen now. He had gone too far.

For a while, he just sat there. He enjoyed the silence. He hated talking. Even as a boy, he had always been known as the quiet one. He never had any friends, but no one ever bullied him. Unlike the other loners, he had been respected—and feared. "I'm here on a mission," he eventually said. "I may need your help. You might have to assist me in the field, or give me a place to stay." He stared at Jimmy with his intense, dark eyes. "I need to know if you're loyal, if you're a true soldier."

"I'm loyal," Jimmy said, probably a bit too quickly. He didn't know what to do. He was all for a bit of fun, like heckling McGee, picking a fight with a Protestant, breaking a window or two, but this man was . . . well, he was frightening. One night, someone had asked him if he was Fenian and he had said, "Yeah." He wanted to teach the Orangemen a lesson. Why the hell not? Jimmy Brennan's political philosophy was about as well developed as the scanty moustache he was trying to grow.

"Can I depend on you?" the stranger muttered, already knowing the answer.

Jimmy was now twitching incessantly. "I'm not sure." He fumbled for words. "I'm . . . I don't know what . . . I don't want to get into any trouble." Jimmy Brennan was flustered. That was his second mistake.

The stranger nodded. He stood and picked up his coat. Jimmy breathed a sigh of relief. Great, he thought, he's going to go and find someone else. But Jimmy didn't notice him put his hand in one of his coat pockets. That was his third, and final, mistake.

"Too bad, Jimmy. You just can't be trusted." He pulled a knife from the pocket. "And you saw my face."

Jimmy Brennan was speechless, but then, he had already stumbled over his last words. The man grabbed him by his hair, yanked his head back and, with the precision of a surgeon, sliced his exposed throat. Jimmy Brennan died as he had lived: bewildered and belittled.

The stranger watched impassively as the lifeblood poured out of Jimmy's arteries. It never ceased to amaze him how much blood there was in the human body—even one with no spine. He put on his coat and closed the door behind him. What a nuisance, he thought. He would have to enlist someone else. His business was finished in Montreal. It was time to get back to Ottawa. He would look for more recruits there.

22

The vote in Prescott was discouraging. D'Arcy McGee had spent very little time campaigning in the Ontario town, and though comfortable with the issues, he was unfamiliar with the local turf. His opponent chose "No Outsiders" as his campaign slogan. McGee, ever the outsider, fell to defeat.

"You know, Conor, if I had been able to spend more time there, I bet you I would have won," he said. And maybe it was true. The heated battle against Barney Devlin had sapped his energy, and his poor health had restricted his travel, but the fact remained that he had suffered his first electoral defeat and could no longer claim invincibility. D'Arcy McGee now knew the acrid taste of losing, and he didn't much like it.

Montreal was next. The two-day vote was held a week after the Prescott election. Barney Devlin was running like a man half his age—or, as McGee told Conor, "like a man with half a brain." At Cutler's Tavern, he called McGee a turncoat; in Victoria Square, he said he was a troublemaker; in front of the post office, he had a chance to condemn McGee to his face. It was really just a coincidence—McGee was there to post a letter and found himself face to face with his adversary. For a second, they looked at each other like prizefighters in a ring, then McGee tipped his hat with a simple, friendly gesture of greeting. Devlin spat in his face and stormed off.

That was the mood in post-Confederation Montreal.

McGee tried to keep a brave face in front of Conor and his family, but he was clearly nervous. He joked, "Devlin's got the spit, but I've got the polish."

On the first day of voting, McGee's margin was tight, but he was ahead. The bad news, though, was that Devlin was leading in Griffintown. If McGee were to lose this election, it would be the Irish-Catholic voters who threw him out.

The final vote was counted the next day. The wait for the results was excruciating. Finally, the news came: McGee had won, but by fewer than two hundred votes. The little Irishman fell into his chair, exhausted and relieved. The vote was clearly a slap in the face, but it was not a knockout punch. There would be time later to evaluate the problems and assess the reasons for the drop in his support.

"Mary, we should go to the Mechanics' Hall and thank the workers," he said, adding uncharacteristically, "but we mustn't stay too long." In times past, he would have been the life of the party, leading everyone in song and dance. But there was no joy this night. He was suffering far too much pain in his leg—and in his heart—for celebration.

Conor was the first person to meet the McGees at the Mechanics' Hall door. This had been their campaign headquarters, and he had been helping organize the party. He firmly grasped McGee's hand. "Congratulations, sir. You won again." He noticed McGee's grip was not as strong as usual. A rousing chorus of "For He's a Jolly Good Fellow" drowned out McGee's response. With Mary firmly supporting him, McGee limped to the stage, shaking hands along the way.

D'Arcy McGee scrutinized the crowd of friendly, admiring faces and winked at his wife, standing by his side. "Isn't it nice, Mary," he began his acceptance speech, "to be among friends and not to be heckled and booed when I start to speak?"

Someone yelled, "We're with you, D'Arcy!"

Over the applause, McGee ran his fingers through his tousled hair. He felt weak and leaned more heavily on Mary. "I am here to tell you that I will not give in, either to Fenians or to their agents. Free speech is more important than one man's election. I will defend it on the streets of Montreal and in the rows of Parliament."

Mary whispered in his ear, "That's enough for tonight, dear."

He knew she was right, but he added one more sentence: "We are fighting in Griffintown the battle for Irish equality—equality among everyone in Canada." Mary nudged him again. "We've enough fights ahead, my friends," he concluded. "Drink heartily and have a great time; you've earned it. Thank you all, and God bless."

Conor helped guide them out of the hall. "Let's leave through the back door," he advised them. "It will be faster." That was only half the truth. While McGee was speaking, Conor noticed that a crowd was gathering outside the front door. Barney Devlin's boys were still spoiling for a fight.

D'Arcy and Mary McGee were safely travelling homeward in a carriage when trouble broke out. With a crash, all the windows of the hall were shattered by a barrage of rocks. The people inside were terrified. It was like a siege. The door started to creak as the mob pushed to get in. Barney Devlin's boys wanted blood. "Bring us McGee!" the voices yelled through the door. A thud. A crash of a foot striking wood. And the front door flew open. Within a second, the mob had poured into the hall. The siege turned into a barroom brawl. Fists flying. Furniture thrown. Some people fleeing. Others cowering. Someone smashed a chair over a man's head. A knife blade flashed. A slingshot. Then, like a thunderbolt, a gun blast echoed through the room and a man fell. The mob turned and ran scared. The body on the ground lay motionless.

Conor had watched it all from the back of the hall, horrified and helpless. What was happening to this country? It was falling apart right before his eyes.

If he had still been here, they would have killed him, he thought. They meant to kill D'Arcy McGee.

COLONEL Patrick O'Hagan walked sprightly along the boardwalk. He and General John O'Neill were headed to the White House. In his pocket, he proudly carried a week-old *New York Herald*. Its editorial urged the takeover of Canada. In his heart, he carried the conviction that he was about to lead a holy war against the English. He was certain that everything was falling into place.

Doors had opened for O'Neill and him throughout the northern states. After all, O'Neill was a war hero, and he was a veteran, too. America owed them a debt, and O'Hagan was cashing in. All along the eastern seaboard, new Irish immigrants were cheering the plans to invade Canada. They had spent the day in Washington with three senators and two congressmen, all of whom supported the Fenian cause. And now they were about to meet William Seward, the powerful secretary of state. O'Hagan was sure that if they played their cards right, they would get Seward's blessing. Seward had been one of Abraham Lincoln's leading cabinet members during the Civil War. He proudly called himself an "expansionist." Recently, he had looked north at the British provinces and declared, "You are building excellent states soon to be admitted into the Union."

It was only common sense.

Lincoln was dead now and Seward held even more power under the new president, Andrew Johnson. Seward's dreams of the Stars and Stripes flying from the equator to the North Pole merged with Fenian dreams of revenge. Under Seward's leadership, the United

States had just bought Alaska from the Russians for seven million dollars. Canada was not for sale, but it was ripe for annexation.

It was Manifest Destiny.

O'Hagan and O'Neill stood on the steps of the president's mansion. The British had burned down the house in 1814. It was time for retaliation.

Entering the White House, O'Hagan felt a glow of excitement, the same sensation he had experienced on the battlefield: the expectation of something momentous, something glorious or something terrible. They were quickly ushered into a waiting room, where they sat for barely a minute before Seward himself came out of an adjoining office to greet them.

"Good evening, gentlemen," the secretary of state declared, reaching out to shake O'Neill's hand first. "I have a little surprise for you."

He ushered them through the door. Sitting behind the tidy mahogany desk, smiling broadly, was President Johnson. O'Neill had met him in 1862, when Andrew Johnson was the military governor of Tennessee, but they had not seen each other since. O'Hagan stayed a step behind, clearly the lesser officer.

Johnson enjoyed watching their surprised reactions. "Did you not think I support your cause?" he asked.

"Well," O'Neill stammered, "I hoped. But I thought, after the Ridgeway battle—"

"I waited as long as I could," Johnson interrupted. "Five days before denouncing your invasion. What in God's name more did you want?"

"We are better organized now."

"I've heard."

"And we have a few surprises in the works up in Canada," O'Hagan couldn't resist adding.

"Probably we had better read about that after the fact," Seward jumped in.

The president agreed. "Yes, this issue is delicate."

Colonel O'Hagan smiled.

"I will get to the point quickly," the president continued. "The United States cannot openly support your aims. It would be against the Neutrality Laws."

"But not against your interests," O'Neill declared.

"We realize that. That's why my message is not one that should anger you. Continue going about your business here without too much brashness, and you won't be stopped; we'll allow your cause to flourish without interference."

"Have you heard what's happening to the government in Canada?" O'Hagan interjected. He knew he should defer to General O'Neill, but this was too important. Could they count on American support?

"Yes, I've been staying in touch. It seems the country is running scared before it has even learned how to walk."

"Well said, sir." O'Hagan smiled, choosing his next words carefully: "If this new country shows it cannot take care of itself, that it can barely run an election, that it is close to anarchy"—he paused for effect—"if the voters have lost respect for Canadian laws and its leaders, what would the United States government do then?"

"I never answer questions that begin with the word 'if,'" the president said. A standard answer. He glanced at Seward as if wondering how many cards he should play. Seward silently nodded. O'Hagan wondered if the secretary of state was really in charge, and Seward, watching O'Hagan lead the questioning, wondered who was really in charge of the Fenians. President Johnson walked over to the window and looked out on Pennsylvania Avenue. "Let me answer your inquiry this way: I personally will not court war with Britain, but it is not in the interest of the United States to have anarchy to our north." He paused before continuing: "That said, the government of Great Britain has never acted as our friend; I see no reason why we should act as theirs."

Seward added pointedly, "Especially if the Canadians can't keep their house in order."

The answer was convoluted. Johnson wanted the Irish vote and liked the idea of more land, but after the Civil War he wanted no more American casualties. Seward was more hawkish—or was he?

General O'Neill surprised O'Hagan by asking a direct question of the president: "Sir, do you want Canada?"

The president of the United States hesitated, but his secretary of state did not. Seward looked O'Neill straight in the eye and declared, "We will recognize accomplished fact."

O'Hagan smiled broadly. The people in the Irish neighbourhoods wanted revenge, and the government wanted Canada. He just had to deliver. The work of the man he had sent north was so important. He prayed he would accomplish his noble mission.

Britain would pay for centuries of injustice.

23

ir John A. Macdonald sat in his ornate Parliament Hill office and glanced around him. He didn't much care for the floral wallpaper, but he loved the blue marble fireplace and kept a fire burning in it all winter. The office was decorated to impress, but also to deceive. There was a hidden compartment in the bottom left drawer of his large desk, where he kept an extra bottle of whisky. To the left of his desk was a concealed door, an escape route from pressing business. The desk, a gift like most of his possessions, came with an inscription that delighted him: "Dominion Secretory."

He pondered the future of this land called Canada.

He had just heard about D'Arcy McGee's narrow victory and the battle at his campaign headquarters. Someone had actually been killed. It had been a violent election across the land.

In Ontario, the Liberal frontbencher and former stonemason, Alexander Mackenzie, was regularly shouted down. "His opponents showed good judgment," Macdonald mumbled. "He's as cold as block of granite." But that wasn't the point. This was supposed to be a peaceful, law-abiding nation, and it was behaving like an out-of-control child.

In Nova Scotia, candidates opposing Confederation won every seat in Parliament except Charles Tupper's. Thank God for the good doctor, Macdonald thought. I wonder what he'll want in return? He glanced at the bottom drawer. Apparently, a mob had gathered in front of Tupper's house and burned him in effigy. Macdonald reached into the drawer. He had been sent a newspaper clipping from Nova Scotia. The editorial regretted the incident in front of Tupper's home, not because it happened, but because "he was not set afire himself!" Macdonald drank directly from the bottle. One swig. He looked at the secret exit, longing to escape. He put the bottle away and sighed. Now that he was thoroughly depressed, he felt in just the right mood to face Gilbert McMicken and hear the latest from the world of espionage.

Macdonald showed no hint of concern when McMicken marched into his office. He greeted him warmly. "Are you here to cheer me up?" he asked.

"I'm here to report to you, sir."

How could poor Gilbert ever have thought he had the personality for politics? the prime minster wondered. He is a man absolutely devoid of humour, much better suited as a spymaster. "Well, sit down and tell me about the Fenians," Macdonald said. "I presume this time you will be talking about Canada."

"I understand you know what happened in Montreal," McMicken began.

"Yes, and I wonder whether D'Arcy caused a lot of it by working everybody into a frenzy."

"In part," admitted McMicken. "I suppose he might have handled it better, but he was trying to make people like you pay more attention."

Macdonald caught the remark's implication and decided to let it drop. "You have my attention, so give me some information."

"The first thing is that Mr. McGee was right. We are convinced that the centre of Fenian activity has moved from Toronto to Montreal."

Macdonald did not respond. If he were a Fenian, he too would want to get out of Protestant Toronto, with its King and Queen Streets and rising army of busybody teetotallers.

"It looked as if the Fenian movement was going to collapse. They went through a bitter leadership struggle and seemed to be coming apart over petty issues. Instead, they are rebuilding. Remember I told you that there was new leadership in the United States?"

Macdonald nodded.

"There are a few former Yankee officers going around the northern states, canvassing for donations and lobbying sympathetic politicians. They have breathed new life into what we hoped was a carcass."

"What I've seen from the Americans," Macdonald exclaimed, "is nothing but encouragement for this sedition."

"The American authorities are turning a blind eye, to be sure. Our spies tell us the government is not actually helping the Fenians; it is simply allowing them to shake the tree."

"What do you mean?"

"The *New York Herald* coined the expression. 'There is no need for the government to shake the tree,' the paper wrote. 'Canada will fall like a ripe fruit into the American garden.'"

Macdonald winced and said, almost under his breath, "Seward wants to free Canadians from British tyranny so brothers can feel free to kill each other in their next civil war."

McMicken listened politely and continued his prepared report. "Meanwhile, the Fenians continue to gather a militia. Mainly out-of-work soldiers looking for a bit of adventure."

"Back to what you said about Montreal," Macdonald interrupted. "I thought you had a man on the inside there?"

"We had, but he died."

Sir John just stared at his spymaster, his expression hardening.

"I was going to get to that, sir," McMicken explained. "You see, he was the person killed that night at McGee's headquarters. Our man must have been exposed, and he was killed in the melee."

Sir John A. Macdonald's eyes widened. He knew that when McMicken left, he would finish the bottle.

MEG was about to post her letter to Conor when a hand reached out and grabbed her from behind. "It's a letter to the Papist, isn't it?" It was one of the boys who had earlier threatened her. She struggled, trying to pull her hand away, but he held tight. Two others appeared beside him. Three more lurked nearby.

"We told you, Meg," the one holding her arm said. "Forget Conor O'Dea, or there will be trouble."

He released her hand, and Conor's letter fell to the ground.

It was the same group as before. The leader of the pack was the son of a well-known Orangeman. She didn't know any of them very well, except the drummer from the parade. He looked a little ashamed to be there. She was sure of his name now: Daniel. Aware of the power she had over boys, she turned directly to him. "Daniel, what right do you have to threaten me?"

He cowered, but the one who had grabbed her answered, "We're not threatening you, Meg. We're just giving you some advice: stick to your own kind."

She felt a rush of bravery surge up her spine. It stabilized her and focused her mind. No one was going to hurt her just because she was seeing Conor. This was a civilized country. They would just call her names—but so what? She stood her ground. "Leave me alone," she ordered, defiantly.

The ringleader reached out and touched her hair. "You're very beautiful, Meg. I don't want to see you hurt." He released her hair slowly, strand by strand. "Come on, lads, she's got the message." He started to walk away, casually, as if it had just been a friendly chat. The others followed.

She called out to the one named Daniel, who lagged behind. "What do you think you are doing?" She knew she sounded like her mother, and she liked the sound of it.

"Meg, people are really angry," he said, sincerely. "We're only trying to help. If you stay with him, you'll . . . you'll go to hell."

He turned and ran to catch up to the others. Those fools, Meg thought. Those stupid, bigoted fools! She bent over to pick up Conor's letter and her hair fell in her eyes. As she pushed it back, she realized that her hand was shaking—in anger, and in fear.

THOMAS O'Dea lay sprawled on an old hard-backed chair. He wondered what his childhood friends were doing in Ireland and how his family was getting on. He missed the patchwork fields of Connemara and the streets of Galway. Was it Ireland he longed for? Or those youthful days with his wife? It hardly mattered. He was now a wreck of a man, crushed by life and defeated by his adopted British country.

Conor had asked him how his mother would have reacted. Thomas had to concede that was a good question. Maybe Margaret would have loved it here, found the newness of everything exciting, the harsh, untamed wilderness enchanting. But he knew better. There was nothing new about another British nation, and there was nothing enchanting about the tall white pines that towered up the Ottawa Valley—wood for ships' masts and fine British homes. There was nothing good about the cheap wooden stakes he had hammered together to mark her grave.

If she had lived, maybe they would have homesteaded; built a house, farmed some land, made a life. Instead, he had applied as a teamster upriver, hauling sleighs piled with timber from the cutting section to the river. He was a good worker, and that impressed the bosses. At times, he liked the challenge, piling as many as fifty huge white pine logs on one sleigh, and he admired the strength and stamina of the big Clydesdales. But it was perilous work trudging along icy skid roads, carefully balancing the logs, sitting on top of the precarious pyramid. Every day, he risked his neck up and down hills, in weather so cold he saw men cry in agony. It was winter work, and it kept him employed half a year. In the summers, while the raftsmen guided the logs downriver, he went downriver himself and tended bar. He would help his fellow lumbermen literally drink away their earnings.

At first, he had to beg the bosses to let him keep Conor in the camp. Thomas was a good enough worker for them to accept his son as long as he didn't eat too much or keep the men up at night. He never indulged Conor, but he did protect and shelter him. A sympathetic cook helped Thomas care for the growing boy, and he was soon put to work boiling salt pork, stirring thin, greasy soup, fetching hemlock to add some flavour to the tea. Conor worked hard, getting up without complaint at four o'clock every morning, and people liked him. If they didn't they would have to face Thomas. One skidder, "Cockeye" George McNee from Arnprior, had it in for him. "There's something high and mighty about that boy of yours," he complained to Thomas. "Who does he think he is?" He said it only once, though. Thomas O'Dea was a hard man, too.

Tex wandered into the camp when Conor was maybe twelve, an educated man from a wealthy family experiencing life by working as a labourer. He was slumming, as far as Thomas was concerned, and that was demeaning. But Conor adored him. Thomas considered keeping Conor away from him, but he knew he would be acting out of jealousy, so he paid Tex to work with his son on his reading and writing.

What would Margaret think of that? She might think Thomas was brave and selfless. And a damn good father. What did Conor think? Thomas suspected he thought his father was an imbecile and not worthy to share a shanty with the likes of Tex.

Then, one season, a widow-maker—a stray branch as thick as any tree he'd seen in Ireland—skidded off the sleigh and sent Thomas tumbling into six feet of snow. He almost suffocated. He couldn't move; his leg was broken, his back wrenched and his usefulness to the logging company over. The cook couldn't properly set his leg, and whatever the fall did to his back, the pain never left him.

In Ottawa, any pride he had left was drowning in whisky. He watched his son slipping away from him, steadily and cruelly. Until the final break. Anger and bitterness now consumed him: he could feel it, taste it, smell it, even see it, until it nearly blinded him.

He looked up at the gun he kept on the shelf under a cloth. It would be easy just to end it. Relief from the pain. Escape.

And then his senses sharpened. He felt another presence in the room. In the dark corner, someone was standing there, silently staring at him. He hadn't heard him enter.

"Who are you?" he gasped. "What are you doing here?"

"I am an Irish patriot with a question for you, Thomas O'Dea: Do you love Ireland?"

Thomas's mind raced. The accent was city-Irish, from Dublin, but was this a British trick?

"I understand you're a man loyal to our cause," the stranger continued. "And you've good reason for hating Canada."

"Perhaps I have," Thomas responded, suspiciously. "But this is my room and you are uninvited, so I ask you again, who the hell are you?"

"I am a soldier. From the brotherhood."

Thomas's heart missed a beat. A soldier. An Irish soldier. He asked, "What do you want of me?"

The stranger took off his coat and placed it on a chair. He still had not moved from the dark corner, so Thomas had yet to get a good look at his face.

"I just need some friends in Ottawa," he said faintly. "I need someone to assist me if I require it, to give me shelter if I ask for it."

"How?"

"You'll find out."

"Why?"

The question was met with steely silence. *He* was to ask the questions, not Thomas O'Dea. He said simply, "Are you with me?"

Thomas wasn't sure. Was this man offering him a chance to do something with his shattered life? Or the opposite?

"Your son works for McGee—"

"I have no son," Thomas interrupted. "Not anymore."

The mysterious man in the shadows grinned openly. Thomas caught a flash of yellowing teeth behind a half-grown beard.

The mention of Conor had enraged him, and Thomas felt a surge of defiance. He and this man might have much in common. "Will you have a cup of tea?" Thomas asked, his Irish brogue sounding more pronounced than usual. "Or a whisky?"

"No. I've work to do," the stranger answered, throwing his coat back over his shoulders. But he added, "I'll see you later . . . my friend."

This time when he closed the door, Thomas O'Dea heard the sound.

WALKING along gaslit Sussex Street, the man in the grey coat allowed himself to relax. He was pleased, almost content. The election in Montreal had been a fiasco. McGee was faltering. Macdonald was scared. He had people in place in Montreal and Ottawa. And now he had a potential accomplice: Thomas O'Dea in his pathetic little room. It was perfect. Not only would O'Dea go along with everything he needed, but he was the ideal person to take the fall. After all, he had a motive: that wretched son of his. He smiled. Conor O'Dea. What an insignificant blunderer he was, going around asking anyone who knew the difference between a Jamesons and a Bushmills who was causing trouble in Montreal, and sitting there beside his darling McGee while he "interviewed" the turncoat. Well done, young Mr. O'Dea. What a detective you are. I may just give you more cases to investigate.

He laughed out loud.

IT was just a chance meeting, and it could easily have resulted in a quick, merciless death. The assassin had done the unthinkable: he had let his defences down and allowed his mind to wander. A few blocks from Thomas O'Dea's room, he heard a sound from behind. "Hey, I know you. We met in Montreal."

His back stiffened like that of an alert dog. Who was this? Who knew him? He walked a bit faster, trying not to attract attention and pretending not to have heard the fool.

"It's me . . . Jim Whelan."

His fingers tightened around the knife in his coat pocket. The man was alongside him now.

"We met in Jolicoeur's, remember? We sure gave that bastard McGee a good run for his money."

He stopped and slowly turned to see who this babbling idiot was. The Irish accent was unmistakable, and yes, he did recognize the face. He was one of Barney Devlin's boys. A pretty good tomato thrower, as he recalled.

"Patrick James Whelan's my name," he said, extending his hand in greeting. "Most people call me Jim."

The assassin shook his right hand, still clutching the knife in his pocket with his left.

"I see you're growing a beard."

He answered Whelan's friendly chatter with a simple grunt.

"What are you doing in Ottawa?" Whelan persisted.

"Business," the man in the grey coat muttered.

He stared at this friendly man as a jaguar might study its prey. Whelan's was not one of the names on the list the tedious colonel had given him, so he was not officially a Fenian, but he had taken note of this man when he was in Montreal. Whelan spent a lot of time with Irish patriots and seemed to seek people's approval. That was interesting. He remembered that he had also said something at Jolicoeur's Saloon about wanting to see McGee dead. That was useful.

Whelan was of medium height and dressed rather well for this backwoods town. A bushy red beard took up much of his face. He looked at the world through eager but confused eyes. Still, all in all, he carried himself well. In the right light, under the proper conditions, it could be said that he and Whelan almost looked alike.

"Why are you in Ottawa?" he finally asked.

"I work here now." Whelan was relieved to be asked a question. "I left the wife in Montreal so I could make some money when Parliament's in session. The politicians will be coming back soon." Whelan remembered that this man was not much of a talker, and he rather regretted stopping him, but he was lonely in Ottawa and it was nice to see a familiar face. "I'm a tailor, you see," Whelan continued, "and there's lots of work here with those politicians always trying to look their best." He chuckled at his own joke while the man in the grey coat studied him. A friendly creature, he thought. Friendly to a fault.

"I don't think I caught your name," Whelan prodded.

"Marshall," he responded. And he smiled. Incredibly, this was the second time he had smiled in one night.

He could use a backup, and this tailor would do nicely. A Barney Devlin boy here in Ottawa—one who was never too shy, or too quiet, about his hatred of McGee. Yes, it was a perfect fit. Maybe better than Thomas O'Dea.

He released the knife from his grip and tapped him on the shoulder. "Mr. Whelan, let me buy you a drink."

SHE didn't want him to go. He was still too weak and he needed time to rest and heal, but Mary McGee could not control her husband. If Parliament was in session, he had to be there. She knew she was no match against the pull of duty and the attraction of Parliament's theatre. They were standing on the platform, waiting for the train to be called.

As the train to Ottawa rumbled into the station, he whispered in her ear, "One year. That's all I want. I will resign my seat in a year."

She looked at him in disbelief.

"I just want to make sure this Confederation adventure stays on track."

"Should I believe you, D'Arcy?"

"Do you?"

"Yes. Yes, I do. I really think I do."

He squeezed her right arm softly, kissed her more politely than passionately, then called out, "Conor, you whiskered dawdler, let's go."

Conor, who had been hovering a few yards away to give husband and wife private time together, looked at Mary McGee sympathetically, as if to say, "Going to Ottawa . . . It's not my fault."

And he left with D'Arcy McGee.

PART FOUR

September 1867–April 1868

The fate of our land
God hath placed in your hand;
He hath made you to know
The heart of your foe,
And the schemes he hath plann'd

Sir John A. Macdonald sat in the audience, sunning himself, ostensibly enjoying the visiting classics professor's speech. It was a lovely summer's day in Kingston, so the lecture was held outside on Queen's University's new campus. Half-constructed limestone buildings surrounded them, blossoming with promise. The professor from Oxford University felt trapped in the provincial backwoods and longed for civilization, but Macdonald glowed with pride. Kingston was growing into a sophisticated centre of learning. Maybe, he thought, his constituency could become the Athens of Canada.

Occasionally, the prime minister glanced across the lake to the United States, where the guns had not long ended their fury. There were so many urgent problems today, and this tedious professor droned on and on about problems people had faced long before the birth of Christ. About Sparta. Or was it Crete? About Pericles. Or was it Horodites? Or maybe Herodotus? Macdonald didn't have the faintest idea. The entire speech was in ancient Greek.

Lady Macdonald, harking back to her classical education, could follow fairly well; still, she occasionally drifted off, unable to keep up with the rhetoric. But Sir John appeared to listen intently. He laughed at some clever witticism and nodded appropriately at a particularly wise observation—not understanding a single word. At the end of the speech, Sir John was one of the first to congratulate the Oxford professor. "Well done, sir," he said, shaking his hand and quickly retreating before an involved discussion could begin.

The prime minister strolled over to the gathering of newspapermen. "Didn't you think the professor was brilliant? I particularly admired the bit about the development of Athenian culture. Kind of reminds one of Kingston, don't you think?" None of the reporters had understood the speech, but each took note of Sir John's comparison: Kingston, a burgeoning

academic centre comparable to ancient Athens—that could make interest-
ing copy.

As Sir John moved through the crowd, shaking hands and back-
slapping, Agnes whispered in his ear. "I didn't know you understood
Greek."

"I don't," he answered. "But I understand politics."

24

The train rumbled along the track, leaving Montreal behind. Their second-class compartment was luxurious enough, and D'Arcy McGee was content there, but Conor longed for first class. McGee kept his papers securely in front of him as he wrote furiously. He was always writing, as if he felt there wasn't enough time in the day to get all his thoughts on paper.

McGee stopped working and looked out the window, taking in the small farms and patches of fields passing by. He held on to the paper he had been writing on as the train shook. Conor thought he was contemplating a turn of phrase, or thinking of his family, and was surprised when he asked, "Still no word on the troublemaker?"

"No," Conor answered, "but it's been quiet since the election."

McGee turned his attention back to the window. The farms were getting smaller and the seemingly endless forest was taking over. Conor knew never to bother McGee when he was writing, but he wanted to take advantage of this quiet moment. "You know how you tell me in a debate to put myself in the shoes of the other man? Imagine how he would argue his point, and prepare accordingly?"

"Yes, of course."

"Even address his arguments before he gets a chance to make them?"

"Anticipatory rebuttal, yes." McGee was still gazing out the train window.

"Well, I keep trying to guess this man's actions, anticipate them, but I can't figure him out."

"You know his motive. He's a Fenian. He wants to discredit me."

"Yes, but the attack at the Mechanics' Hall—"

"Unrelated. It won't happen again," McGee interrupted sternly.

Conor felt McGee was in denial about the attack and its tragic outcome, but he knew he could not say so.

McGee shifted his attention from the window to Conor. "Let me give you the best advice I can offer: look inside your own heart; know yourself first, and then try . . ." He paused, to make sure he had Conor's full attention. "Try to understand the heart of your foe."

Conor considered that for a moment. "But what," he asked, "if he has no heart?"

D'Arcy McGee was about to say something, but instead went back to work.

CONOR saw her from a distance as the train sputtered into the station. Meg Trotter waiting for the Montreal train. She was wearing a light-green silk dress, pulled tight at the waist, expanding to a wide hoop at the ankles. And it was cut a little lower at the neck than anything he'd seen her in before. He rushed down the train steps toward her, but he didn't dare give her a hug in public. He held back awkwardly. She laughed, reached out and kissed him. "Stop being so proper," she teased.

Conor realized he had left D'Arcy McGee behind and went back to help him down the steps to the platform. McGee feigned astonishment when he saw Meg. "You didn't inform me of this," he said. Conor smiled bashfully. McGee added, "But of course, I knew."

192

Conor and Meg walked arm in arm to her mother's boarding house. McGee kept pace; he was walking better, but still depending on his cane. "So what am I to think?" McGee asked, sounding amused but strangely parental.

"Whatever you like," Meg responded. "Mr. McGee, you will have your regular room, and, Conor, you can move in with Will."

"That's a relief," D'Arcy McGee said under his breath.

Conor loved how playful she could be with McGee. And how she seemed to tame him.

Conor had agonized over this reunion. Would they feel awkward in each other's presence? Would Meg finally see him as he was: callow and unworthy? Was this a passing infatuation for her? A flirtation? But she seemed as happy to see him as he was to see her. He touched her hair, that wild mass of black curls. He felt at home. Almost at home. Walking along Sparks Street toward the Toronto House, Conor was painfully aware that he had turned his back on his own neighbourhood and his father's tiny basement flat in Lowertown.

THE Toronto House was not the preferred Ottawa address, but D'Arcy McGee had started staying with Mary Ann Trotter when he quit drinking because she limited the liquor on the premises. He also loved the spirited conversation at her dinner table and her inquiring mind.

Tonight, McGee was the only guest at dinner. Hector Langevin had led a group of Quebec politicians to George-Étienne Cartier's house around the corner on Maria Street. A few junior members of Parliament had just said their goodbyes and were probably already ensconced in the Russell's bar, hoping to be seen and heard.

As always, Mrs. Trotter was full of questions. She wanted to know chapter and verse about the Montreal election. McGee edited out much of the detail, saying barely a word about Jolicoeur's or the Mechanics' Hall incident. Meg pushed for information, and he admitted a man had been killed. "But after we had left," Conor clarified.

Will added his share of meaningless information. He was still quite fascinated with this game of base ball; Conor wasn't. Meg talked about the latest series of essays she had read by Ralph Emerson. "Do you know he studies Buddhist and Hindu religions?" Conor didn't, and he didn't much care. He just wanted the everlasting meal to end so he could be alone with Meg.

After dinner, McGee retired to his room to read and Conor offered to help Meg and her mother with the dishes. Anything to hurry them along. When they could finally steal a moment, Conor said, loudly enough for her mother to hear, "Meg, would you like to go for a walk? The stars should be spectacular tonight." He didn't want to be accused of an impropriety.

As they walked along Sparks Street, she took Conor's arm. "About a month ago, the Offord House shut down," Meg said. "Mother simply runs a better hotel. I think we are starting to do quite well." Without discussing where they were going, they turned toward the river.

Conor noticed that Meg often looked over her shoulder.

"I remember you from when I was a younger, you know," he said. "But I didn't think you ever saw me."

"I saw you, always with your face in a book. Afraid to look up."

"Winters in the lumber camps can make you rather shy, especially with someone much more worldly."

Worldly? In Ottawa? The thought made her laugh. And she added, "Conor, you don't sound like the other Irish boys, or people from up the valley. How did you lose your accent?"

"Work, practice and more practice." Then he broke into a lumberjack's sing-song speech: "I'll be goin' up the line this winter. I knows the pay is to be good, by jeezes."

"Is that why you were so quiet? You didn't want to sound like that?"

"I never wanted to sound like that. And I guess I just wasn't ready to talk."

They passed the East Block and continued west along the path on the river's ridge. Lovers' Walk. There were still scatterings of logs left in the water from the spring and summer log drive. Meg shivered, imagining the work the loggers did and, not for the first time, thinking that Conor had never really had a childhood.

"Tell me about the logging camps," she urged softly.

"What's there to tell? My father kept me away from the dangerous work, and I learned how to cook and wash the dishes. A skill I employed tonight, you might have noticed."

She smiled. He hated to talk about his youth.

"My main memory is smoke and sweat and darkness. I'm not really complaining, because I wasn't outside felling trees in the freezing cold. But the camboose was its own kind of hell."

"Camboose?"

"The men lived in shanties, in lines of bunks, surrounding an inside cooking fire. That was the camboose—a square of logs where we cooked. The only ventilation was the hole in the roof where some of the smoke went. The cooks and I manned the kettles and pots and kept the fire going." He left the nickname he hated out of his description. "It was a world of extremes, frigid outside and swelteringly hot inside. I worked in a pit of dried sweat, boiling pots and choking smoke. That's what I remember."

There was someone following them. She sensed it. But he hadn't noticed. "Did you learn how to shoot a gun?" she asked, trying to hide the fear in her voice.

"Sure. The cooks and I would go out and hunt for rabbits, grouse, any creature stupid enough to come nearby and tasty enough to add to a soup."

She took another look over her shoulder.

Meg had decided not to tell Conor that she had been threatened, or "warned," by the Orange gang. He might want to retaliate. She didn't want to start a spiral of futile violence. But she did want protection.

"Will you teach me?" she asked. She took another look over her shoulder. "Will you teach me to shoot?"

"WILL you teach me to shoot?"

That night, Conor couldn't get Meg's words out of his mind. He had answered, "Yes, I guess," but he hadn't meant it. He was proficient with a rifle. He had learned from loggers who would throw an axe at a hapless squirrel just for fun and thought nothing of gunning down an angry bear. As a cook's assistant, he had been relegated to chasing down smaller animals, and he actually became a very good shot. He just didn't like it. He took no delight in killing and saw no sport in the hunt. Some men felt power when they held a gun; Conor felt afraid of the weapon's power. And anyway, women shouldn't be firing guns. What was Meg asking this for?

He had let the matter drop, but something had happened to make her skittish. Right after the shooting remark, she asked him to walk her home. She held on to his hand tightly, almost desperately. When they entered the house, she said simply, "I'm sorry. I'll see you tomorrow." And rushed to her room.

"Will you teach me to shoot?" It went against everything she stood for. He didn't fully understand her talk of humanism and transcendentalism, but he knew it didn't involve guns and shooting. She was scared. Why? He fell asleep wondering.

THE news from Kingston shocked Sir John A. Macdonald. If he paid more attention to his finances, maybe he wouldn't have been surprised, but that was never his style. He went from day to day, expecting the sun to shine. If it didn't, he blamed the Opposition.

There was no sun shining on his bank account. The Commercial Bank of Canada had collapsed, leaving hundreds of people in dire financial straits. No one was affected more than the prime minister. The Kingston-based bank was his law practice's main client. Although he had long ago let his practice fritter away, he was still one of the bank's directors. Now he was $80,000 in debt. He would have to borrow to pay his bills that month. His only income was his salary as prime minister, and he wasn't certain that would last for long.

The prime minister of Canada was nearly bankrupt. And he was drunk. He sat in his upstairs study, his head covering a mass of bills and correspondence, murmuring despair about life, money and politics. He would have to pull himself together for the next session of Parliament. But not yet. Blindly, he reached for the bottle and knocked it over.

Agnes heard the noise and peered into the office. She called these episodes his "attacks" or said that he "disappeared into the shadows." It sounded romantic. Like Coleridge or Byron. But she hated these attacks; she dreaded the shadows. She stood at the doorway for a second, looking in on him sadly. She closed the door, said a quiet prayer and left him alone with his shattered bottle, his fears and his demons.

THE man named Marshall handed Jim Whelan another drink. A thick liquid in a small glass. Whelan gagged at the taste of it, but it made him light-headed. "What is this?" he asked.

"Think of it as a chaser to go with the whisky."

"It's that, to be sure," Whelan giggled. He was having fun, even though there was something strange about Marshall. He was quiet and sullen, but he knew how to show him a good time in the burlesque theatres and back rooms on Clarence Street. Whelan didn't really miss his wife in Montreal; in fact, it was nice to be away from her stern and sober ways. He was having a great time in Ottawa and making pretty good money. Marshall was actually his best customer, asking him to make up a variety of different jackets and waistcoats.

"Drink up. It's medicine I take when I get a headache. It works well with a dram of Jamesons." He watched as Whelan sipped the liquid opium. "We've got so many reasons to hate them."

"What? Hate who?" Whelan was finding that the mix of whisky and opiate actually made him feel good about the world.

"Hate the English bastards," he said. "Remember Oliver Cromwell? Killing Catholics by the score. And King Billy? Never forget King William of Orange."

Whelan wanted to please Marshall, to impress him. Marshall was giving him slogans to chew on, and he heartily ate them up: "Don't forget our heroes." "Sing praise on our martyrs." "We can never forget."

With burning intensity, Marshall asked, "Do you understand?"

Whelan nodded. The room was spinning pleasantly. He understood. At least, he thought he did.

25

==

onor, you oversized drink of water get in here," McGee sang out. "My St. Patrick's Day speech is ready."

"Another great oration?"

McGee smiled, feigning modesty. "Perhaps. Let's just say it is enhanced with invincible logic and incredible artistry. Do you want to read it?"

"If I can be of help."

McGee thoughtfully toyed with his walking stick and said, "Actually, no, you can't. You'll be there tonight. You can hear it with the others."

Conor was a little insulted.

"You've better things to do," McGee said. "I'm going to have a nap. Spend some time with your raven-haired friend. I hear there's a pretty good parade in town today."

Conor smiled.

"Have some fun," D'Arcy McGee said. "Life's too short."

ST. Patrick's Day. Now it was the Irish Catholics' turn to parade along the slushy Ottawa streets. When Conor was young and still upriver in March, every St. Patrick's Day someone would magically produce a bottle, or ten, and a toast to Saint Paddy would become a drunken frenzy. He would hide away during those hours. When he returned to Ottawa to live year-round, he turned his back on Irish festivities, but now he wanted to share the spectacle, to take in the excitement—to belong. He also wanted to show Meg the difference between celebration and condemnation. This was a parade they could watch without venom.

He wondered whether his father would be there. He hoped so.

Conor had pinned a green ribbon on his jacket. A touch of Ireland. He was thinking he might soon be able to afford a better jacket. He'd heard there was a new Irish tailor in town. Maybe he could get a deal.

WHEN Conor and Meg left the boarding house, he didn't sense a threat in the group of boys hovering nearby, nor did he notice that they followed them. But Meg did, and she clung to his arm.

PATRICK Buckley was the parade's grand marshal this year. Macdonald's driver had a stable full of horses, and he provided them for the parade. The week before, a man named James Whelan had approached Buckley and asked if he could help. Buckley didn't know him, but Whelan's red beard and heavy accent were good Irish calling cards. He needed someone to ride a horse at the back of the parade, so he welcomed the help. He even named Whelan a parade marshal and invited him to the banquet that night.

A parade marshal—it made Whelan proud. And it made him think of his new friend. Marshall—he never said what his first name was—had begged off. He said he was too busy to attend the parade, but he urged the tailor to participate.

THE St. Patrick's Day Parade was certainly less earnest than the Orange victory march. More of a quick Irish jaunt and off to the pub, thought Conor. Mid-March was still chilly in the "arctic lumber village." It seemed the gentlemanly thing to do to put his arm around Meg to keep her warm.

He nodded to Buckley leading the parade, and Buckley nodded back proudly. It was a real honour to be grand marshal. Conor greeted a few people he knew. But there was no sign of Thomas. He noticed Polly the washerwoman, though, dressed in a bright green dress—a little too flamboyant for Conor's taste. She had been staring at Meg, taking her in, as if memorizing her.

Polly walked over to them. "Your father's not here. He has to work."

"Thanks," Conor said and quickly looked away. Polly moved on.

"That was rude of you," Meg protested.

"I don't like her. I think she's"—he searched for the phrase—"a fallen woman."

"I'm sure it's of great comfort to her that you care so much about her virtue."

"There's something weird about her. She's a busybody. And she's too close to my father."

Meg let the matter drop. They watched the parade pass them by, taking little note of the man with the red beard proudly riding a horse at the back, sitting tall in a long grey coat.

THAT evening, D'Arcy McGee was the keynote speaker at the St. Patrick's Day banquet. Sir John and Lady Macdonald were seated at the head table, blending his slight Scottish accent with the room's symphony of Irish chatter. It made Conor think that maybe he had been too harsh in condemning Macdonald for attending the Orange celebration in July. Macdonald just never missed a large party and an open bar.

The prime minister called over to Patrick Buckley, feigning an Irish accent, "Praise be to the saints, Buckley, did God ever make a man as Irish as you look?" Buckley glowed with pride.

Conor had asked Meg to join him, but she said she had to help her mother. Maybe, he thought, she'd had enough Irish for one day. Conor sat at the back of the room with members of the press. He liked sitting with the newspapermen. He didn't have to worry about his table manners—they certainly didn't worry about theirs—and by and large they were a convivial lot. Their conversation was irreverent and salty, and their clothes were as old as his. Conor could relax.

He watched McGee and Macdonald sitting politely together and wondered what they were talking about. McGee was sipping on a glass of water, while Macdonald was gulping down the wine. The prime minister ignored the intricate rituals of checking the wine in the light and savouring the complexities of the grape. His procedure was to fill the glass, drink the contents and fill it again. Their conversation seemed almost businesslike, not like the songs and toasts at Lapierre's, when they both drank and talked with gusto.

Conor asked for a refill of wine. A few of the reporters were almost keeping up with the prime minister's drinking. It was St. Patrick's Day, after all. He told his tablemates stories of McGee and Macdonald at Lapierre's, and recited some drinking songs McGee had written.

McGee looked down at the press table with interest. Conor O'Dea was the life of the table. Good for him.

Macdonald rose to speak and surprised Conor by saying, "I share the regret that Mr. McGee is not a minister of the Crown. Yet never was he greater or more esteemed in the affections of the public than at the present day." That's probably what they had been talking about at the table, Conor thought—McGee making some subtle yet clear jab about his seat in the back benches. Conor thought Macdonald spoke rather awkwardly. This really wasn't his crowd. After a few more forgettable words, he handed the podium over to McGee.

D'Arcy McGee rose to speak confidently. "May I thank you," he began, "for allowing me to say a word on behalf of that ancient and illustrious island."

"Darn right," someone yelled.

McGee smiled. It was encouragement, not heckling. And it gave him a cue to deliver his message. "For those of us who dwell in Canada," he declared, "there is no better way to serve Ireland than by burying out of sight our old feuds and factions. That will be worth all the revolvers that were ever stolen from a Cork gun shop and all the republican chemicals that were ever smuggled out of New York."

Conor thought the speech went well. The former rebel stated his case against Fenians without saying the word. Macdonald thought it was too inflammatory, but he kept his opinion to himself. Among parade marshals the response was mixed. Patrick Buckley paid more attention to the admiring glances Sir John A. Macdonald passed his way. James Whelan thought the references to Cork and New York were insulting. He wondered what Marshall would think. But Marshall wasn't there.

MARSHALL—he was getting used to being called that—found the starched, ministerial collar uncomfortable. He was taking more precautions these days not to be recognized. Today, he had covered his head in a top hat, dyed his beard blond and looked the very picture of an upright, ardent young Methodist preacher. He considered his little army in Ottawa. Some would help him willingly; others would help him unknowingly.

He stiffly walked into the telegraph office and sent a message to New York. One word: "Soon."

AT the Fenian Brotherhood's New York headquarters, Colonel Patrick O'Hagan received the message and smiled. He dipped his pen in the inkwell and wrote General O'Neill,

I suggest that we should get our men in readiness. If we delay, then we are guilty of neglect.

Yours fraternally,
Patrick O'Hagan

26

April 6, 1868. The Dominion of Canada was two hundred and seventy-nine days old. It was a cloudless early-spring night, and the full moon shone so brightly that the city fathers decided to save money and not light the gas lamps. There was still a winter chill in the air, though, and some snow patches on the ground. Inside the Parliament Buildings, a large crowd had gathered long before the late sitting began. There was always a good turnout for a D'Arcy McGee speech. Conor proudly walked past the people who had lined up.

Nova Scotia was the problem this April night. A delegation led by Joseph Howe was in England, trying to take the province out of the union. "Confederation is artificial," Howe was arguing. "It is like a child trying to walk on stilts. What Nova Scotia needs is to come back down to earth." With the possible exception of Charles Tupper, whom Howe hated with burning passion, Joseph Howe was the greatest Nova Scotian politician of his day. Before July 1, he called Confederation the "Botheration Scheme." Afterward, he worked diligently to see its repeal. His ardent opposition was serious indeed.

McGee liked Joe Howe and always thought the Nova Scotian's real problem with Confederation was that it was someone else's idea.

McGee felt it was important for him to speak to this issue. National unity was too fragile, and Canada had too many enemies for its friends to remain silent. Joseph Howe wouldn't be there to hear him, but he would get reports.

Thomas D'Arcy McGee rose in the House of Commons with great purpose and considerable pride. He loved the cut and thrust of debate here and knew he had more friends than enemies in this chamber. He gently leaned his bad leg on a chair for comfort and support, and instinctively ran his fingers through his maze of tangled hair. He looked over the assemblage and silently thanked God that Barney Devlin's boys were back in Montreal's taverns. In this forum, a man could speak his mind freely.

"What we need above everything else is the healing influence of time," he told the House. He was speaking of Nova Scotia, but also thinking about the Irish in Montreal. "Time will mellow. Its hands will heal. So let us give this enterprise a chance to grow. Let us give it time."

McGee noticed Conor standing with Will Trotter and a few other pageboys. Conor shouldn't be down there, McGee thought; he should be in the gallery. He certainly had a knack for getting close to the action.

McGee's voice rose as he continued, "Our friends have nothing to fear but that Confederation will be administered with serious and even-handed justice. Its single action has to be fairness to each person and each province." It was clear that the members of Parliament and the people in the gallery hung on McGee's every word.

Conor smiled proudly. This was a vision of Canada he wished his father could appreciate.

Sir John A. Macdonald appeared to be listening intently, but his mind was actually wandering. He was thinking how much older D'Arcy looked: his hair slightly greyer, his voice not so strident, and he looked in pain. Still, he thought, McGee is a magician with words. It made him rather jealous. On St. Patrick's Day, Macdonald thought McGee had delivered his remarks with bombast and exaggeration, but tonight he had the clarity of political purpose. His defence of Confederation was powerful and profound. McGee declared, "If we are a generation worthy to organize a nation, assuredly the materials are abundant and at hand." And the prime minister thought, Well put, D'Arcy. Well put, indeed.

In the east gallery, a man watched D'Arcy McGee with contempt. Patrick James Whelan clasped his hand into a fist as McGee spoke of fairness and nation-building. Just listening to that Irish traitor infuriated him. Marshall had suggested he go to the House of Commons and watch McGee speak. Marshall had special plans for tonight. He had given Whelan a set of instructions but said it was best that he not know too much. It was clear that mischief was in the air. Perhaps some good sport, like at Jolicoeur's.

"I call it a northern nation," McGee continued. "For such it must become if all of us do our duty to the last."

Whelan had stopped listening. Yes, he was up for some amusement, or whatever Marshall wanted, especially at McGee's expense. Marshall had become a good friend—a comfort in this lonely city of pompous politicians. He was a strange but pleasant fellow, quiet and moody, and quite generous. He had even given him a new coat to wear. It was grey and long—just like his.

McGee ended with a flourish. "And I, who have been, and still am, Confederation's warmest advocate, speak here not as a representative of any race or of any province, but as thoroughly and emphatically a Canadian."

The House erupted in applause as McGee sat down, exhausted but beaming with pride. It was after midnight. The members continued pounding their desks in approval. When McGee spoke, it was like a reconfirmation of Canada; it made people feel a little more secure. McGee glanced over at Sir John, who winked and pretended to toast him with a glass of something that looked like water.

27

Sir John A. Macdonald scurried up to McGee outside the chamber. He wanted to be the first to congratulate him. "D'Arcy, I'd sell my soul to the devil to be able to speak like you."

"My friend, I can get them to listen; you get them to do what you want."

"Did God ever make a man—"

"I think you can put that cliché to rest now, Sir John," McGee interrupted.

Macdonald looked hurt but chuckled. "Agnes says the same thing."

They lit each other's cigars and, through a cloud of smoke, shared a rare peaceful moment. Somehow it was hard for McGee to stay mad at Macdonald for very long. He would cast a spell with those sad, beguiling eyes, begging for understanding, and before McGee knew it, he was sympathizing with Macdonald for enduring such burdens of office.

In times past, they might have lingered at the House of Commons bar for a nightcap, but McGee was tired and his leg was sore. He suppressed a yawn and instructed the prime minister to go home to his wife. Macdonald said he would oblige him soon. He knew that Agnes would be waiting up for him. She could never understand why Parliament had to sit so late. "What in the world do you have to talk about for so long?" she would ask. And he would be hard pressed for an answer.

McGee waved goodbye to Macdonald somewhat wistfully. He called out for Conor, who was hovering nearby. "Come, you rascal," he ordered. "Help me on with my coat."

As Conor held his rather tattered overcoat for him, he whispered, "I think your speech impressed the prime minister, sir."

McGee placed a white silk hat over his black curls and smiled. "Thanks, Conor. And don't dawdle—it's still an early start tomorrow."

Normally, Conor would have walked home with D'Arcy McGee. After all, they were staying at the same boarding house. But he had promised to wait for Will, who was taking longer than usual changing out of his pageboy uniform. So Conor watched as McGee limped away, leaning heavily on his bamboo walking stick. Even under his shining white hat, Conor thought McGee could never look elegant. He would always be the renegade Irish immigrant in the halls of the mighty.

Conor called out to him, "Good night, sir."

"It's not night, it's morning," McGee called back.

Conor watched as McGee said a few words to Robert McFarland, the member from Perth, and they walked out of his sight together. McGee walked along Metcalfe Street with McFarland. They parted on Sparks Street. McFarland turned left toward Sappers Bridge. McGee turned right along Sparks. The Toronto House was about halfway along the south side of the street, in the Desbarats Block. The boarding house would be locked at this late hour, but the Widow Trotter usually waited up for her son. At the door, D'Arcy McGee removed his right glove and fumbled in his pocket for his key. He took a long, hard drag on his cigar and inserted the key in the lock. He bent down to ensure that the key entered the door smoothly.

Then the bullet shattered the back of his head.

CONOR and Will were around the corner on Metcalfe Street when they heard the sound. At first, Conor thought someone was shooting squirrels—but at this hour? For an instant, he and Will looked at each other in horror. Then they both started running toward the sound of the gun blast. As he rounded the corner of Sparks Street, Conor saw McGee's white hat lying in front of Mrs. Trotter's door. And a body lying on the ground.

No, not McGee! Conor gasped in disbelief and ran wildly toward the doorway. He knelt beside the body, sobbing and screaming. It was an appalling sight. McGee had died instantly. The bullet had torn apart the back of his head. His face was bloodied almost beyond recognition; there were gunpowder burns in his hair, and his teeth lay on the boardwalk in front of him. Conor took him in his arms and hugged him.

Will ran down the street to the office of the *Ottawa Times*. The pressmen were still at work. "Mr. McGee is dead!" he yelled through the window. "D'Arcy McGee has been murdered."

Conor clung to McGee as if trying to comfort him. The street was silent, but the full moon cast a bright light. Conor looked around ferociously. Where was the killer? How had he escaped? Or had he? His mind raced. Why hadn't he seen the murderer running away when he turned the corner? How did he get away? Unless . . . unless . . . unless he was still on Sparks Street. Hiding nearby. Watching him.

Conor thought he saw a shadow move. A shape down the street by the liquor store. A silhouette defined by moonlight. There were boxes stacked outside the door; it was an ideal place to hide. Gently, he eased McGee's shattered head to the ground. There was someone there. He was sure of it. Again, the silhouette by the boxes moved. And like a wildcat, Conor attacked. He darted toward the liquor store with speed he didn't know he had. The shadow burst out from behind the boxes and sped into an alley.

211

Conor ran as fast as he could, but the shadow was faster and he lost him. All Conor saw was his long grey coat.

LADY Macdonald had been restless all night. She hated it when Parliament sat late, and the April night's full moon filled her with a strange dread. She wanted her husband home, safe in her arms. When she heard the carriage wheels, she practically flew downstairs to open the door. She greeted Sir John with an earnest kiss.

"What a speech," he announced, somewhat taken aback. "You should have heard it. McGee was in top form."

"Come upstairs where it's cosy and tell me about it." She couldn't care less about parliamentary matters, especially when they took her husband away from her most of the night; she cared about him, keeping him happy and free from worries, but she would listen to him recount the night's events if only to hear the reassuring sound of his voice.

She nestled in his arms by the fireplace in their bedroom, ignoring the smell of gin and cigars on his breath. She felt her eyes grow heavy and her mind relax. And then her peaceful world exploded. There was furious knocking on the outside door. Sir John jumped up and flung open the window. "What on earth is it?" he called out. Agnes would never forget the answer. Each word felt like the blow of an iron bar against her heart. "D'Arcy McGee is murdered. He's lying on Sparks Street. Shot in the head."

CONOR raced through the alleys, screaming like a madman. "Where are you?" He heard a noise to his right. "Who are you?" He twirled to his right. There was a distant sound behind him. He turned desperately. And then silence. Somewhere in the night, the murderer had escaped.

Think. What would you do? What might he *do?*

He looked back across Sparks Street. He remembered that the Offord House, the boarding house next door to McKenna's Tavern, was vacant. A perfect place to hide. He checked the front door. It was unlocked. He peeked in, but he couldn't see anything in the dark. There was no furniture; even the carpets had been taken up. It was as still as death. Then he heard a slight crackling sound—scuffling—in the back. He considered darting toward it. But it might be a trick. A sudden chill rushed through him. He hesitated.

Take your time. Don't be reckless.

He crept through the hall, slowly, carefully, checking each doorway. The back door was open. He peered out the open door. There was no one there. Nothing. Still, he felt a presence. He stepped into the back alley. There were fresh footprints in the snow. And then he heard a sound. A human noise? He stood, rigid and aware, as if tracking an animal in the north woods.

Listen. Try to be invisible.

He heard a scurrying sound, a cruel laugh, and then a man on a horse rode away. Conor stood there, covered in D'Arcy McGee's drying blood, helpless and miserable. He should have run through the building. He had delayed and let McGee's murderer get away.

He shrieked at the disappearing rider, "Remember my name: Conor O'Dea. I swear I'll find you. I'll get you." But he knew his words were hollow. He had failed.

MEG was fast asleep when she heard the gunshot. In an instant, she dressed and ran downstairs. Her mother stopped her in the hallway. "Mr. McGee has been murdered. There's nothing you can do. Stay in here."

"Conor!" Meg's eyes scanned about, looking for him. "Where's

Conor?" Ignoring her mother, she ran out the door, pushing through the crowd that had gathered. She saw that the door at the Offord House was swinging open, and with no regard for how dangerous it could be, she entered. The back door was also open. In the alley she saw Conor standing alone, sobbing. At this moment of despair, she knew her mother was right. Later, she would try to comfort him, but for now there was nothing she could do. She quietly left.

BY the time the prime minister arrived at the Toronto House's doorstep, Dr. McGillvray had pronounced D'Arcy McGee dead. Sir John helped lift the corpse from the cold sidewalk and carried it into Mrs. Trotter's parlour. Macdonald couldn't bear to look at the once-vigorous man now slumped in death, grotesque and motionless. He had noticed that on the blood-drenched boardwalk, a half-smoked cigar still smouldered. He had lit it for his friend a little over an hour before.

Someone must contact Mary, he thought.

FATHER Dowd, the parish priest at St. Ann's Church in Griffintown, had known the McGee family since they arrived in Montreal a decade before. He had supported D'Arcy McGee's politics, helped him to turn away from the bottle, comforted the family when they mourned their dead children; he had grown to love the rambunctious politician and his gentle, kind wife. Sir John himself telegraphed Father Dowd and asked him to tell Mary.

The priest arrived at Mary McGee's door before the sun rose. When Mary, dazed from sleep, came to the door, Father Dowd stood there for a minute, unable to speak. Finally, he whispered softly, "Mary, I've terrible news. D'Arcy has been murdered."

She heard the words but tried to push them aside, ignore them, make them go away. This could not be true. It must not be true. Father Dowd reached out to comfort her. She shied away. "Go away!" she yelled. "It's a lie." Yet he stayed. Even though he was not an old man, he had already seen much suffering in the poor Irish parish, but never had he felt such pain as he did now, watching this grand woman suffer.

Mary's mind spun. It was a dream, after all . . . a nightmare . . . what had D'Arcy himself dreamt? . . . swimming away from the shore . . . but he woke up . . . you always wake up . . . and she . . . the Irish wife . . . to love . . . to love to death . . .

She collapsed in the priest's arms.

SIR John A. Macdonald sent the word out immediately. "Arrest all suspicious-looking persons." By "suspicious" he meant "Irish." Irish Catholics. Papists. Romanists. He was known as a man of goodwill and compromise, but all that was lost in his hysterical reaction. "Just start arresting the bastards," he ordered.

POLLY Ryan had gone to bed early. She had expected to hear from him during the day, or if not from him directly, at least from an emissary. After all, a D'Arcy McGee speech and a full moon made a dramatic combination. When she heard nothing, she went to bed. As she fell asleep, she considered the twists and turns her life had taken. Tragedy, a terrible struggle to survive and, perhaps now, redemption. She felt proud, almost content. She was doing her duty.

A flurry of activity on the streets awakened her. Outside, in Lowertown, the streets were alive with police and commotion. Something terrible must have happened. She could see uniformed men pounding on doors, searching door to door. She moved away from the window, pulling her blankets up tight; her gas lantern remained unlit, her door firmly locked.

THOMAS O'Dea answered the pounding on his door. "You're under arrest," a policeman barked. And another took him by the arm.

"For what?"

"Suspicion. Now don't try running."

Stupid ass, thought Thomas. Where could he run? He didn't resist, letting them roughly escort him into a wagon and off to the jail. The cells were almost filled. He couldn't make out everyone as he was led to his cell, but they all seemed to be Irishmen.

"It's like St. Patrick's Day all over again in here," a jovial prisoner called out to him. Thomas knew the voice from the bar at Lapierre's.

Thomas called out, "Who is in here?"

The headwaiter from the Russell House answered, "I am. Johnny Doyle."

"What are you doing here?" Thomas asked.

"Damned if I know."

Patrick Buckley called out, "I'm here, too."

"What's this about?"

"Someone murdered McGee. They're arresting us all. Just in case."

"That's illegal."

"You going to fight it?"

If John Macdonald's favourite driver was arrested under suspicion, Thomas knew he was powerless.

"It's a sin and shame to mix me up with his murder," Buckley said.

"How many people are in here?" Thomas asked.

Buckley answered, "All the cells are filled but one."

PATRICK James Whelan sat in Michael Starr's tavern on Clarence Street, waiting for Marshall. At closing time, he went upstairs to his room. What a night it had been! What excitement! His body trembled as he thought about it. McGee, the traitor, was dead, a casualty in the war for Irish independence, and he, James Whelan, was a soldier in the glorious battle. A few months ago, he had been just another Irish tailor stumbling through a boring, uneventful existence. Now there was a mission in his life: a free Ireland and the end of British North America.

The sun rose fully into view. It was a new day.

He was glad McGee was dead. He had stood in the way of their dreams of nationhood, and his assassination would serve as a warning. That's what Marshall had said, and Marshall knew so much. He might have killed McGee himself if Marshall had wanted him to. But at least he had done his part. It made him proud that Marshall had used him.

The morning sun was already bright and strong, but it had yet to burn the harsh chill out of the air. It would be a pleasant spring day in Ottawa. The politicians will be jumpy, he thought. Marshall had really put a scare into them. That was good.

When he heard the knock on the door, he thought it was Marshall. But he always knocked softly; this was loud, angry pounding. The instant he opened the door, a giant hand reached in and grabbed him. It was a policeman.

"Are you Patrick James Whelan?" the voice behind the uniform demanded.

Whelan nodded and felt a quiver of fear. The policeman's grasp on his arm tightened. It hurt. But what could he do? He needed Marshall.

"You are under arrest for the murder of D'Arcy McGee."

He heard the words, but they didn't make sense. He tried to gain command of his thoughts. This was a time to be brave, to hold his own, to pretend he was in control. But he wasn't. Before they led him away, James Whelan was allowed to put on the grey coat Marshall had given him and the boots he had lent him. He glanced at the morning sun shining freely through his window as they led him away.

28

A cross the country, Canadians were in mourning. The new nation was in a state of shock—and panic. It was just too horrible to be believed: Thomas D'Arcy McGee assassinated a block away from Parliament Hill, gunned down in the moonlight. Rumours spread like brushfire. If the Fenians were that powerful, surely they were going to strike again. Who could stop them? Could the country last a year?

Guards were increased around all government buildings. There was a rumour that Fenians were going to blow up the Parliament Buildings. In Kingston, it was reported that Irish revolutionaries planned to free all the prisoners. What was true and what wasn't? No one was really sure. The only certainty was that the Ottawa police had done their job; the murderer was behind bars. The *Montreal Herald* summed it up with the headline "No Doubt Whelan Guilty."

The evidence against Whelan seemed conclusive. Police found a Smith and Wesson revolver in his coat—a six-shooter, the same kind of gun used to kill McGee. One of its chambers was empty and a bullet had recently been fired. Whelan had a motive: he was a well-known Fenian supporter, one of the infamous Barney Devlin boys during the Montreal election. He even had a Fenian newspaper in his coat pocket. After the election, he had left his wife in

Montreal and come to Ottawa. Surely he was following McGee. He had watched McGee's speech from the visitors' gallery and had been seen clenching his fist in anger.

Conor O'Dea was a main witness. He had told police about the footprints in the snow, and they matched Whelan's boots. And there was that coat. Although there were no eyewitnesses to the murder, people including Conor—actually, *especially* Conor—saw a man in a grey coat nearby. It was a coat just like Whelan's.

Any trial was seen as a simple formality before the inevitable hanging.

But Conor wasn't sure. "I know everything points to his guilt," he told Meg. "But it seems too cut-and-dried, too convenient. Maybe he seems too guilty."

"GOOD God, man, what are we going to do?" Sir John was practically shouting at Gilbert McMicken. Usually, McMicken stood up to the prime minister, but not tonight. He knew he had better not antagonize Macdonald while he was under such pressure. He answered plainly, "We think we have the man."

"Well, I damn well hope so," Macdonald exclaimed, clutching his glass of port for dear life. "Did Whelan act alone?"

"I don't know," McMicken sighed. "If I had to guess, I would guess not."

Macdonald took a deep breath and walked over to his desk, slowly exhaling. He pulled a piece of paper from his top drawer and handed it to the policeman. "Here's why I sent for you. Read this."

The letter's handwriting was childlike, and the ink was a brownish-red colour. It looked like blood.

Your life is in our hands. You can save it only if you leave town within ten days.

No British spy will live in our midst.

Let the bloody fate of D'Arcy McGee warn you.

The hour draws nigh. Be it the knife or the pistol.

Be warned.

It was signed, "Many Fenians."

McMicken looked up from the letter and closed his eyes in thought. All he could think to say was, "We can increase the guard around you."

"Don't be daft. There are already enough police around me to throw a party, and still the letter got through."

McMicken became businesslike. "There is no doubt, sir, that the Fenians felt Mr. McGee was their worst enemy. However, they know they won't make any headway in Canada until you are put out of the way, too."

"Well, no one can accuse you of trying to spare my feelings."

Macdonald gulped down some dark port. Fortified wine. I can use some fortification, he thought. He was not a particularly brave man, but he was practical. Canada did not have the army to withstand an invasion. More important, he was not sure the country had yet developed the kind of collective spirit to pull together and defend itself. If he panicked, it would play right into the extremists' hands. He must stand up to these madmen. He had no other choice.

"Any more word on this man who was causing the trouble in Montreal?"

"No. It might have been Whelan. But we're not sure."

"What, pray tell, *are* you sure of?" Macdonald roared.

McMicken ignored the prime minister's outburst. "In Irish bars in the States, they are toasting the man who killed McGee," he said.

"And there is even talk of another raid before July the first if the American government doesn't act vigorously."

"Act vigorously! Why, they're not acting at all. Sniffing around for the Irish vote while we endure—what did you call it?—'a reign of terror.' It sounds like the French Revolution, for God's sake." Macdonald took the threatening piece of paper and crumpled it into a ball. "Without D'Arcy, I'm not sure we would even have a Canada. He was the heart of it. And now he lies in a closed casket with the back of his head blown off." He threw the letter in the wastepaper basket.

McMicken stood upright.

"Listen," Macdonald continued, gaining his composure. "No one is to know about this letter. No one. I'll go around Ottawa pretending there's no danger. I'll put on a brave face. I'm a good actor. But let me tell you: I'm scared. I'm damned scared."

LADY Macdonald leaned against the door. Her head spun and she steadied herself on the door frame. Sir John would be furious if he knew that she had been listening in on the conversation, but she knew something awful was happening and she wanted to discover what. Since D'Arcy's murder, he had become so sullen and distant. She was afraid he would descend into the shadows again. All this talk of spying and intrigue, and now she was a part of it, eavesdropping on his private conversations. She didn't have the stomach for it. These Fenians made her blood run cold. The logic was clear to her: if the fanatics were really determined to win, they had to kill her husband. They needed another dramatic death. A Protestant death. This was no idle threat.

She had come to hear the conversation innocently enough, almost bursting into John's office to give him her news. She had seen the doctor in the morning. She was going to have—her eyes filled with tears—a baby. This should be such a joyous time. The beginning of life. Instead, her family was consumed by death. She felt cheated and betrayed, and terrified for her husband. She ran to her room in tears.

29

t was an epic funeral. Montreal had never seen anything like it. The procession started at the McGee house on St. Catherine Street. There were two stops—St. Patrick's Church and Notre Dame Cathedral—before the journey's end at Notre-Dame-des-Neiges cemetery.

The police led off the procession, their band playing Handel's solemn Dead March. The hearse, fifteen feet long and sixteen feet high, was pulled by six grey horses. Inside, D'Arcy McGee lay in a tentlike canopy held up by pillars, his coffin adorned with feathers. He probably would have been amused that in death he was treated like such a fancy, distinguished gentleman. He would have been more impressed with the crowd. Eighty thousand people lined the streets of Montreal to share his final journey. Irish, English, Scottish, French—religion, language and background didn't matter today; the mourners gathered as Canadians.

Mary and the children rode in the carriage directly behind the hearse. She looked out on the huge crowd, still disbelieving. It was almost a curiosity, a macabre party. A few months earlier, D'Arcy McGee had been humiliated in this city. Now he was hailed as a fallen hero.

Conor stood in the crowd, alone, tears streaming down his

face. Meg and her mother had begged him not to go to Montreal, but he felt he had to be there. As the mourning coach passed him, he thought Mary McGee recognized him, but he wasn't sure. She looked bewildered and lost. She seemed so far away.

It was Easter Monday. It would have been D'Arcy McGee's forty-third birthday.

"**DEAD** and buried," he said to himself. "Just where he belongs." The assassin also stood in the crowd as D'Arcy McGee's coffin passed by. He admired his work and considered his next steps. First, he had to be sure of his safety. He didn't think Whelan would be stupid enough to identify him. He had sent him a clear message in prison that his wife's future depended on his silence. Just to make sure, he had come to Montreal to pay Mrs. Whelan a midnight visit. Now she too knew her husband had better keep his mouth shut. Or else. Anyway, Whelan seemed to cherish the prospect of being yet another Irish martyr. The fool.

He was dressed as an Irish workingman with pants that didn't fit and a woven jacket that looked as if he'd slept in it. His hair was jet black and he sported a simple moustache. Soon it would be safe to return to Ottawa. Everyone was convinced that Whelan was guilty.

He looked for John Macdonald, with his clingy young wife, in the procession. He couldn't find him. Probably he was under a table drunk somewhere, mourning his token Irish friend. The Orangeman clearly wanted a quick trial and hanging to get the matter over with. Good. Still, he had better keep a low profile, especially with Thomas O'Dea's irritating son sniffing about.

Thomas O'Dea. *There* was a man with potential. He had the conviction to be another of his soldiers, but he wouldn't be as easy to manipulate as Whelan. O'Dea was motivated by hatred, not by boredom. That could help, or it could be a problem. He had plans for this bartender, but he would have to be careful. That son of his was an issue he would have to consider. He could just kill him and be rid of him, but he was still useful alive. He had seen a man in a grey coat on Sparks Street, and he'd reported the footprints in the snow. Both would be convincing nails in Whelan's coffin. Still, before he left this British soil, he would have to do away with him. He was too close to McGee. He was simply too close to everything.

He would never have dreamed of disobeying his father the way Conor O'Dea had. When he was young, children did what they were told. They learned from their elders. In "rambling houses," people of all generations would gather to tell and hear the old stories—ramble on—and keep the language and traditions alive. He grew up in a kind of rambling house. His home was a hideaway for rebels and spies and patriots, where they kept the fires of revenge burning. From the day he took his first breath, he was taught to hate, and he learned his lessons well.

He taught himself to survive.

His father died in an English jail, wasting away with consumption. An Irish martyr. He was proud of his father's convictions, but despised his failure. Any fool can make himself a victim. That would never happen to him—*he* would be the hunter; *he* would do the killing.

His mother knew he was the most clever of her nine children. She instilled in him a persistent lesson: "The English must pay for what they did to your father, your ancestors, your country." While his older brothers and sisters rotted in a Dublin tenement, their vitality deflating each day their father's prison term dragged on, his energy bubbled. And burst.

When he was Conor O'Dea's age, before he had built calluses around his heart, he also had heroes. His greatest hero was the eloquent, fiery Young Irelander—Thomas D'Arcy McGee. McGee wrote with passion and principle, with words that inspired greatness. He worshipped McGee and built his own dreams around McGee's visions. He followed McGee's early career as if following a pilgrimage; he read McGee's fiery proclamations from Ireland and fierce newspaper articles from America; he hung on his every word. Then McGee rejected everything he had stood for. He moved to British North America, betraying his friends, his cause, himself and everyone who had ever supported him. He became a turncoat—a traitor.

He rubbed his eyes. He clenched his hand into a fist. This was useless nostalgia. He had work to do. McGee was in a coffin on a hearse; soon, he would be on the other side of the grass. He smirked. He had practised that smirk as a child: a slow, sinister grin. He disappeared into the crowd. He had a job to finish.

SIR John and Lady Macdonald did not go to the funeral. Gilbert McMicken felt it was too dangerous, and there was much to do at home. Macdonald sent George-Étienne Cartier in his place.

"But they never got along," Agnes said.

"D'Arcy has no enemies now," he responded. "And George gave a beautiful tribute in the House." Cartier's knighthood had finally been announced. He would officially become Sir George in a few weeks. He seemed more at peace with himself. And with Sir John A. Macdonald.

Agnes had every reason to fear that her husband would hide behind the bottle in his grief, but ever unpredictable, Macdonald instead buckled down to work. He arranged for a pension for Mary McGee, read all of McMicken's reports in detail and planned the next parliamentary session. The country could not descend into gloom or burst into panic. He must show leadership and strength.

And he was worried about Agnes. Since D'Arcy's death, she

hadn't been eating properly and felt ill much of the time. All week, she had looked pale and seemed listless. He gently asked, "Are you all right?"

She choked back tears. "I so wanted this to be a happy time, not a time of murder and funerals."

"What's the matter?" he pleaded awkwardly.

She looked deeply into his sad eyes and quietly sobbed, "I'm going to have a baby." Her tears grew stronger. "But is it safe, John? Is it safe to bring a child into this?"

IN the United States, McGee's murder had turned some people against the Fenians. Many sympathized with the fallen Irish hero. General O'Neill had publicly condemned McGee's murder as "dastardly and cowardly." But Patrick O'Hagan could barely contain his excitement. Alone at night, he toasted the man in Canada and his holy work. And he spent his days preparing, recruiting men and stashing arms by the border.

It was all going according to plan.

PART FIVE

September 1868–February 1869

The fate of our land
God hath placed in your hand;
He hath made you to know
The heart of your foe,
And the schemes he hath plann'd;
Think well who you are,
Know your soul and your star

Lady Macdonald knelt in the straight-backed, uncomfortable pew at St. Alban's Church and prayed heartily. She prayed for her fragile husband; she prayed for the soul of his last wife, the invalid Isabella; she prayed for the soul of his lost son, little Johnny; she prayed for poor Mary McGee and her now-fatherless children. And she prayed for her unborn baby.

She was proud of the new church in Sandy Hill. It reminded her of a country chapel in England. She would have preferred a steeple and a grander altar, but the organ was fine and the woodwork quite magnificent. She was proud of her role raising funds and gathering supporters. D'Arcy McGee, the staunch Roman Catholic, had helped out when she told him that the first minister, Thomas Bedford-Jones, was an Irishman.

Lady Macdonald had started going to St. Alban's Church daily. Sir John didn't mind a weekly sermon and the occasional prayer for forgiveness, but every day, he told her, "was excessively excessive."

John Macdonald had been born into the Church of Scotland—a Presbyterian—but he and his family had joined the Church of England when they came to Canada. He never really took to the kneeling and reciting in the Anglican ritual, but turning C of E was an easy step up the social ladder. And he always had his eye on the top rung.

He had one of his "headaches" this morning and begged off the Sunday service, so her brother Hewitt escorted her.

Agnes paid scant attention to the priest. She found the Reverend Bedford-Jones's sermons wordy and ponderous. "One would think he was lecturing at Trinity," she often complained. This morning's sermon was about St. Alban himself, the first English saint, the namesake of the little gothic church. "Alban was a soldier in the Roman army," Bedford-Jones informed the congregation, "in the second or third century. The scholars are uncertain of the exact date." She nudged her brother, who was in danger of falling asleep. "The Roman authorities were persecuting and hunting down the few Christians on the island, but Alban, even though he was a pagan, gave shelter to a Christian priest." She was feeling the chill in the church. Would she ever become accustomed to this northern country? "The priest converted Alban. When Roman officers came in search of the Christian, Alban met them himself, dressed in the priest's cloak. He was arrested and tried. He refused to renounce his new faith and was executed. He went to his death with the peace and blessing of a Christian."

"So unsatisfactory," she whispered to her brother. "If only he would explain the history less." A man dressed in someone else's clothes, wrongly arrested, refusing to renounce the other man and being executed. What nonsense!

She lined up patiently to approach the altar and take communion, knowing that the parishioners were watching her. She was, after all, a great man's wife. As she took the wafer, the body of Christ, she prayed again for the innocent baby she carried. She prayed for peace and order. And she prayed for the end of Fenians and Irish extremists. As she took the wine, the blood of Christ, she solemnly prayed that this man Whelan, this vicious, cold-blooded murderer, would soon hang from his neck until he was dead.

That would be a blessed thing.

30

onor stood in front of Notre Dame Cathedral, leaning on a gas lamp, watching the people enter the church for Sunday Mass: women in bright bonnets; men in their best suits; some people chattering, others progressing solemnly. It was a dismal early-autumn morning; the dark skies threatened rain and the air had a damp chill in it. Across the river, the Gatineau hills held some autumn colour, but its vibrancy was dulled by the clouds. Flowers that could tough it out to early September brightened the church's front; soon, a blanket of white would cover the gardens.

Conor stayed outside. The priest, the same man he saw the night of his argument with his father, looked out the door and beckoned him inside. He shook his head politely and mouthed, "No, thanks." He thought for a second, and added, "*Non, merci.*"

He walked along the quiet streets of Lowertown. The market stalls were empty, the hawkers and hustlers relaxing before another busy harvest week. As he passed his father's flat on Sussex Street, he hesitated but dared not peek inside. Lapierre's and the many other bars were closed on Sunday, the drinkers sleeping off the night before. Thomas probably was, too.

Ottawa was such a small town, he thought he might have run into his father by now, but Conor spent most of his time in Uppertown and

Thomas rarely left Lowertown. He wasn't sure what lured him to the front of his father's flat. He knew Thomas had been arrested on the night of the assassination and had been freed when all the evidence pointed to James Whelan. He wanted to commiserate with him, but he was afraid of his anger. He wanted to ask Thomas for his forgiveness, but would he allow it? It was all so confusing. He had always craved the spotlight, but now he wanted to hide. He had worked so hard to create an impression of self-assuredness, but now he was uncertain and insecure. He was scared of tomorrow. Tomorrow morning, the trial would begin. Tomorrow, he would see James Whelan face to face.

He kept walking past his father's door.

IT was pandemonium outside the courthouse. The street was over-flowing with people, many of whom had gathered for hours just to catch a glimpse of the bloodthirsty Fenian. A thousand tickets had been issued, but there was room for only four hundred people in the courtroom. Police and citizens were trading insults as Conor and the Trotter family were ushered past the fractious lineup.

They took their seats awaiting judge, jury and accused. A full-length portrait of Queen Victoria, in a gilt frame, hovered over the bench. Her Majesty would be staring down on Patrick James Whelan as his life went on trial.

JAMES Whelan was still blinking, trying to adjust to the bright light, as he was led into the courthouse. The crowd greeted him with hisses, boos and jeers. He hung his head low in self-defence. As long as he could remember, he had been told British justice could not be trusted. Now his life depended on a British North American judge and a system that had failed his people for centuries.

Sitting in his prison cell, he had slowly come to understand his terrible fate. Marshall had used and deserted him. No legendary Fianna soldier would appear and miraculously save him. Only one man stood between him and the gallows, and he was hardly an Irish warrior. His lawyer, John Hillyard Cameron, was impressive, distinguished, eloquent—and also the grand master of the Orange Lodge.

"This should make a few heads turn, over at the lodge," Cameron had joked, trying to cheer Whelan up.

The Orangeman was James Whelan's only hope. He was not going to help himself. In prison, he had decided what he would do: he would not lie; he would declare his innocence, but he would not betray the guilty man. Like the Irish heroes of the past, he would remain faithful and loyal, even to the death. He really had no choice. If he told the truth, Marshall—or whatever his name really was—would certainly have his wife killed, and maybe his family in Ireland. And who would believe him anyway? They all wanted him dead. Everyone wanted him to hang except his "Loyal True Blue and Orange" lawyer.

Whelan took his place in the prisoner's dock in the middle of the courtroom between two grim-faced policemen. His eyes were barely visible under his thick red eyebrows. He had changed in jail. His red beard was fuller, his complexion more pallid, his broad shoulders slumped. He had lost a lot of weight, but he still wore his tailored suit well. He placed his black silk hat neatly on the bench beside him and glanced around the courtroom. He saw his wife, Bridget, dressed in black, already looking like a widow. She had come from Montreal. He supposed she felt it was her duty to be there. She looked at him blankly. He had abandoned her by going to Ottawa, and he had brought shame on her family by associating with Fenians. Did she think he was guilty of this murder? It didn't matter; she probably didn't care anymore.

He searched for other friends or family, saw none and hung his head. He stood impassively when Chief Justice William Buell Richards entered, and he raised his head only when the court clerk read the charge. The first time most people in the room heard him speak was when he declared, in a clear but shaky voice, "Not guilty."

The crowd jumped with excitement. Journalists rushed out of the room to report his impudence. Conor felt his own heart miss a beat, even though he had expected a plea of innocence. Chief Justice Richards pounded his gavel, demanding silence. When the commotion calmed down, he instructed the prosecutor, James O'Reilly, to state the case for the Crown.

James O'Reilly was from County Mayo, just north of Galway, where the O'Dea family was from. Like John Macdonald, he practised law in Kingston. Like D'Arcy McGee, he wore a beard but shaved his moustache. And like both, he was known for his quick wit. He displayed no sense of humour this day, however, as he eased himself out of his chair and walked toward the jurors.

"The evidence we will present will prove beyond the shadow of doubt that James Whelan is guilty of the murder of D'Arcy McGee." Looking each juror in the eyes, he listed the facts of the case: Whelan had told friends in Montreal that he would like to see McGee dead; he had come to Ottawa after the Montreal election to plan the execution; he had been seen in the parliamentary visitors' gallery, shaking his fist at McGee the night of the murder; he had carried a recently fired revolver, and the bullet matched the one that killed McGee; his boots matched one of the footprints, and a man wearing a long grey coat was seen near the scene of the crime.

Conor noticed a fly buzzing about. It landed on James Whelan's forehead. He didn't bother to swat at it. He just stared at the prosecutor. Conor wondered how Whelan felt, listening to such harsh words spoken against him, especially in an Irish accent.

"Patrick James Whelan had the misguided motive of an Irish revolutionary," O'Reilly concluded, "and he shot D'Arcy McGee in cold blood that terrible April night."

The courtroom theatrics fascinated Conor, but as the case proceeded, the plodding nature of the delivery of evidence bored him. He was sure McGee would have approved of the odd casting, though: a Catholic prosecuting a Fenian and a Protestant defending him in front of a stone-faced Irish-Catholic judge. This was the New World in a nutshell. His mind was still wandering when he heard his name.

"The Crown calls Conor O'Dea."

CONOR walked anxiously to the stand. He was certain of what he saw, but uncertain what it meant. As D'Arcy McGee would have said, he knew the bare facts, but he hadn't yet grasped the angle on the story, the perspective that provided its true meaning and significance.

James O'Reilly calmly asked him to recount the events leading up to McGee's murder. Conor retraced his steps as best he could, describing their last words together, how they parted, and where he was when he and Will Trotter heard the gunshot.

"When you turned the corner onto Sparks Street, did you see anybody?" James O'Reilly asked.

"After I heard the shot, I was running at full speed and I might have missed something, but all I saw was Mr. McGee's body lying in front of the boarding house."

"Did you know it was him immediately?"

Conor cleared his throat. "I recognized his white hat on the ground beside him."

"You recognized him from down the street by his clothing?"

"Yes."

"And you were right?"

"Yes, sir."

James O'Reilly walked across the courtroom dramatically, as if deep in thought. He looked at the jurors when he asked Conor, "Did you see anyone else on the street?"

"No, sir," Conor answered. "When I rounded the corner and first saw Mr. McGee, the street was empty."

O'Reilly quickly changed direction. "Then what did you do?"

"I rushed to Mr. McGee's side, and my friend Will Trotter ran to the newspaper office."

"Did you see anybody then?"

Conor knew the importance of his testimony to the prosecution. He couldn't help glancing over at Whelan. The prisoner was watching him with a hint of curiosity.

"I saw a man hiding by the liquor store down the street," Conor continued. "I yelled at him, and he ran away."

"Did you see his face?"

"No, I did not."

"Did you see where he ran to?"

"I thought he ran into Offord's House, across the street from the Toronto House. I followed him there. Or someone there."

"Again, did you see his face?"

"No. The building was vacant and it was dark inside." Conor felt a pang of shame. He knew that many in the courtroom must have felt he had lost the opportunity to catch the killer. He continued, sheepishly, "Someone was in the back. But he got away."

"Did you see any trace of him?"

Conor knew where this was leading, and he got to the inevitable point. "I saw footprints in the snow."

James O'Reilly triumphantly introduced as evidence a boot that matched the footprint. He declared that he would later prove it belonged to James Whelan. Whelan silently shook his head, but all eyes were on O'Reilly as he posed his next question to Conor. "You say you never saw his face, but this man you were pursuing, do you recall what was he wearing?"

"He was wearing a long grey coat and a black cap."

"Are you sure?"

"Yes, sir, I am."

James O'Reilly triumphantly held up a grey coat and showed it to the jurors. "This is the coat found in James Whelan's room. Did the coat look like this?"

Conor had sworn to tell the truth, and the truth was "Yes, sir. The coat looked like that."

Hillyard Cameron rose to cross-examine Conor. He spoke firmly. "Would you please tell the court how many men you saw yesterday wearing a similar coat?"

James O'Reilly jumped up to object that the question was immaterial, and Mr. Justice Richards agreed. Conor thought the question was a good one, but he never got a chance to answer.

THE next witness was Mary Ann Trotter. She recounted the moment of D'Arcy McGee's death. She had heard him fumbling with his keys and was opening the door for him when he was shot. She saw a flash. And McGee's falling body. But she saw no one on the street.

Then she told a story Conor hadn't heard before. Just hours before the murder, James Whelan came to the Toronto House, looking for a drink. Mrs. Trotter served him tea. Whelan insisted she give him a pen and paper, but she refused and he left.

Conor considered the impact of her testimony. O'Reilly was trying to show that Whelan was checking out the location before the murder. But, he thought, so what? A boot print, a grey coat and strange behaviour on the night of the murder did not add up to convincing evidence. The prosecution needed an eyewitness. Rumours were flying through the courtroom. Maybe tomorrow.

THE next day, James Whelan appeared in the prisoner's dock with a green ribbon in his lapel. Again, the courtroom was packed. Everyone was eager to hear from a short, stocky man from Quebec, Jean-Baptiste Lacroix.

Lacroix had appealed to give his testimony in French, but Mr. Justice Richards refused. The predominantly English-speaking crowd in the courtroom was relieved. It didn't strike Conor as fair.

James O'Reilly got to his point quickly. "Tell the court what you saw on Sparks Street the morning of April 7, Monsieur Lacroix."

"I saw two men," Lacroix answered in a thick accent. "One was just about to enter a house on the south side of the street. I saw another man come up behind him, raise his arm and fire a gun." The courtroom crowd rumbled with excitement. The judge scowled, and there was immediate silence. No one wanted to miss a word. "After he fired the shot, the man walked toward me, but I walked away as fast as I could. I did not cross over to see the man. I was too frightened."

Conor was perplexed. He had been there, if not the instant the shot was fired, then just seconds after. Why hadn't he seen Lacroix?

O'Reilly carried on. "Did you ever see the man who fired the shot?"

"Yes."

"Where?"

"In the jailhouse."

"Do you see him in this room?"

Lacroix pointed toward James Whelan in the prisoner's dock. "Yes, that is the man there."

Conor thought Hillyard Cameron appeared shaken. Lacroix claimed to be an eyewitness. There were unanswered questions and clear discrepancies in his testimony. Cameron had to expose them and discredit this witness, or his case would be lost. He walked toward Lacroix like a predatory animal sizing up a smaller beast.

"Mr. Lacroix, did you see anyone else on Sparks Street that night?"

"No. I did not."

"So there is no one who can substantiate your testimony that you were there?"

"I suppose not."

Cameron looked doubtful. "You say you saw Mr. McGee shot?"

"Yes."

"Why didn't you go over to him?"

"As I said, I was much too frightened."

Cameron nodded. A logical answer, he thought. And an opportunity. If he could establish Lacroix as a coward, it would be an easy step to portray him as a liar. He looked at the jury but spoke to Lacroix. "If I have this straight, you abandoned the victim." He paused, sighed and let the thought settle. "Then where did you go?"

"I went home."

"Did you speak to anybody about what you had seen?"

"No. I said I was fright—"

"Ah yes, you were too frightened. Did you go to the police?"

"No."

"Why not?"

Lacroix just stared at him.

Cameron didn't let go. "Were you still too frightened, Mr. Lacroix?"

"Yes," he answered quietly.

"When did you lose your fright? One, two, three days later?"

As O'Reilly jumped to his feet, Cameron waved his arm in the air dismissively. "The important question is, Mr. Lacroix, when did you hear there was a reward for information about the crime?"

Lacroix was starting to sweat. "Wednesday."

"That was three days later."

"Yes."

The smaller animal was now firmly in the predator's grasp.

"Mr. Lacroix, where did you hear that there was a reward?"

"At Lapierre's Tavern."

Conor looked up, startled.

"Please tell the court what you heard about the reward in the . . . uhmm, bar?"

"Some said it was large," Lacroix answered. "Others said it was small. I didn't know."

Cameron paused, then spoke firmly. "It was $16,000, Mr. Lacroix. A lot of money." He was walking away from Lacroix as he asked, "Did you tell people you saw Mr. McGee's murder before or after you heard about the reward?"

"Before," Lacroix practically shouted.

"But you told the authorities after," Cameron shouted back, sarcastically adding, "didn't you?"

As Lacroix nodded, Hillyard Cameron rolled his eyes. But the predator was not finished. "Mr. Lacroix, is it not true that when you first went to see the defendant in jail, you said you did not recognize him?"

"No, I said it was difficult for me to recognize him because he wasn't dressed the same way."

"But if you were able to recognize him by his face, what difference would his clothes make?"

Lacroix looked confused. Cameron deliberately looked exasperated.

"So tell the court when you finally did recognize him."

"I did when I saw him dressed in the same clothes."

"So you recognized him by his grey coat, is that right?"

As Lacroix uttered a feeble "No, it was him," Cameron sadly shook his head. "I'm glad my overcoat is black," he muttered under his breath, but loudly enough for the jury to hear. "No more questions, my Lord."

The predator let the smaller beast go.

31

No matter how Hillyard Cameron tried to prevent it, the noose was tightening around James Whelan's neck. As each new person testified, the defence lawyer did his best to challenge their stories or their credibility. It was an uphill battle.

He knew that for his client to live, he had to deal with the murder weapon. James O'Reilly had made quite a spectacle of brandishing the gun. "It had recently been fired," he declared. "One chamber is empty. It housed the bullet that killed D'Arcy McGee."

Dramatic, impressive and easily refuted, thought Cameron. Yes, Whelan owned a Smith and Wesson, and yes, that was the make of gun that had been used to kill McGee. But it was also the most popular revolver in Canada.

Much of Cameron's case, and James Whelan's fate, would depend on the testimony of Euphemie Lafrance. She was a tiny young woman with fearful eyes, a vicious cough and a thick French accent.

"I used to work for Monsieur Starr," she told the court. "I make the beds."

"Including James Whelan's?"

"Yes."

Cameron could see how nervous she was. She might have expected he would treat her as harshly as he had Lacroix. Instead, he spoke gently and fatherly. "Did you have an accident in Whelan's room?"

"Well, yes, with the pistol."

Cameron picked up Whelan's revolver. "With this pistol?"

"If that is Monsieur Whelan's, then yes." She coughed quickly, then resumed her story. "It was between his mattress and the pillow. I found it making his bed. It was natural."

She stopped talking, as if looking for approval. Hillyard Cameron said simply, "Go on."

"I picked it up and it went off, wounding my arm."

"When did this happen?"

"Maybe six weeks after the new year."

"Before Mr. McGee was killed?"

"*Oui.*"

The word seemed to echo through the courtroom, *Oui.* She was saying that Whelan's gun did not kill McGee. Conor was stunned.

Perhaps Hillyard Cameron should not have smiled so broadly, because juries don't approve of lawyers gloating, but the trial was starting to turn in his favour. He had one more key question: "Do you have a scar?"

Euphemie Lafrance rolled up her sleeve and showed what was clearly a scar. It certainly looked as if a bullet had grazed her arm. There was commotion in the courtroom as people strained to see. John Hillyard Cameron sat down, smiling. But his triumph would be short-lived.

JAMES O'Reilly stood confidently and declared, "I would like to call Joseph Faulkner to the stand." Conor recognized Joe Faulkner immediately from the election campaign in Montreal. Faulkner was one of McGee's critics, but he was no hothead. He sincerely believed

D'Arcy McGee had been inciting the Fenians with his virulent attacks. "A noble man," McGee had described him. "A fool to disagree with me, but true to his convictions nonetheless."

"Do you know the defendant?" O'Reilly asked.

"Yes," Faulkner answered, to Conor's surprise.

"Did you know D'Arcy McGee?"

"Of course."

Conor felt that Joe Faulkner looked very credible on the stand. He wondered where O'Reilly was going to go with his questioning.

"During the election last summer, how would you characterize Mr. Whelan's behaviour?"

"He was against McGee."

"Mr. Faulkner, would it be fair to say that you recall James Whelan as a particularly vocal member of the opposition?"

Faulkner hesitated. Sometimes men said things they didn't mean. Jim Whelan was a braggart, not at all like the quiet, subdued man perched in the prisoner's dock. He drank too much, said too much and said it too loudly.

The judge interrupted his deliberation. "It is a perfectly clear question. Please answer."

"Yes, he was vocal," Faulkner replied, knowing well that further questions would demand a fuller and more damning response.

"Did you overhear any conversations involving Mr. Whelan concerning Mr. McGee?"

"Well, when Mr. McGee was speaking at Jolicoeur's Saloon, I distinctly heard him yell, 'McGee's a traitor and deserves to be shot.'"

"'He deserves to be shot,'" O'Reilly repeated. "What else did you hear?"

"I remember him and another man talking about Mr. McGee. The other man was encouraging Whelan and calling McGee every name in the book. He asked him, 'If you got the chance, would you shoot him?' Whelan said, 'I'd take McGee's life as quick as drink a cup of tea.'"There was a gasp from the courtroom crowd. "Whelan did a lot of bragging. I remember the other man patting his back affectionately. He knew I was listening to their conversation. I don't think Whelan knew."

"What exactly did the defendant say?"

Joseph Faulkner answered carefully and deliberately. Each word seemed to hang in the air. "He said, 'If McGee is elected, the old pig won't reign too long. I'll blow his bloody brains out before the session is over.'"

James O'Reilly smiled proudly. Whelan's eyes were widening with fear. He had developed a slight twitch at the side of his mouth. Conor also noticed that the jurors were no longer looking at the defendant with curiosity; they were glaring at him with contempt.

"Thank you, Mr. Faulkner. No more questions."

HILLYARD Cameron approached Joseph Faulkner carefully. This was not a man to toy with or belittle. No doubt he had heard Whelan say those things, but that did not mean he carried them out. "Mr. Faulkner," he began cordially, "the other man—'the stranger,' as you called him—do you remember what he was wearing?"

"Not really, but he was carrying a grey coat, I believe."

Cameron smiled. Another man with a grey coat. It was a step forward. A small one. But a step nonetheless. "Can you describe the other man?"

"I'm sorry, but not really. He was of medium height and wore a black hat well over his head. He had sideburns, I think. I saw him, but I'm not sure I would recognize him again. I know that's not a very satisfactory answer—in fact, it's rather strange—but it's the truth."

Hillyard Cameron had been taught as a young trial lawyer never to ask a question if he did not know the answer, but he allowed himself to be swayed by the enticing thought of another man as a possible suspect. Was Faulkner thinking what he was thinking? He took a chance and asked an unprepared question. "When you first heard of the murder of D'Arcy McGee, what did you think?"

"I thought, 'Good God! It's nobody but Whelan that shot him!'"

Cameron turned away from the jurors so they would not see his look of horror and embarrassment.

He knows his case is lost, Conor thought.

THE parlour in Mrs. Trotter's boarding house was decorated with large, ornately carved dark furniture. Much of it had come with the place and belonged to the landlord, George Desbarats, but Mary Ann Trotter's own knick-knacks and keepsakes were everywhere, adding her personality to the room. Meg sat alone on the sofa, curled up in a blanket. She had been reading the newspaper reports on the trial, but the paper lay in disarray on her lap. She was breathing deeply, gently falling asleep.

She did not hear him enter the house.

He moved stealthily, settling in a chair across the room. For a few minutes, he simply watched her. In sleep, she was so tranquil, so calm. He could use some serenity now. He kept staring at Meg. Her right eye twitched. She sensed someone in the room. Clutching the blanket, she opened her eyes in terror.

"Conor, what are you doing?" she gasped. "You scared me half to death."

"Sshh," he whispered. "I was thinking."

"About what?"

"Lots of things."

She didn't say anything right away.

He asked, "Do you want me to leave?"

"No, you come over here. Just hold me. Just hold me tight."

32

Thomas O'Dea had been kept in jail for only two nights. His time as a prisoner of the state was uncomfortable, cramped, humiliating, but mercifully short. On the night of his release, he went to work at Lapierre's. The talk at the bar was all about the arrests. A regular customer told him the latest Fenian chant: *It was with the greatest of glee I heard of the death of D'Arcy McGee.* He thought Thomas would enjoy the verse, but he didn't. He found he couldn't savour the taste of death. Not even McGee's. This was a man's life. A father and a husband. What kind of animal could shoot someone from behind in the middle of the night? No, it was not with glee that he heard of McGee's death; it was with emerging shame—shame for Irish vengeance, shame for his own hatred, shame for his wasted life.

He had blamed McGee for deserting the cause of his homeland and for destroying his family. Now he had grounds to blame McGee for his own false arrest. But somehow, he couldn't keep blaming a dead man, and he could find no joy in murder. It made him think: Had D'Arcy McGee caused the mess in his life, or had he done it to himself with a poisonous stew of jealousy, anger and resentment?

Another customer told him that Conor had been the first person to reach McGee's side when he was murdered, that he held his corpse and even ran through the streets, screaming hysterically.

Thomas thought of those hours on Grosse Isle, holding his wife's lifeless body. What about Conor? How was he? He wanted to talk to him, but how could he? He hoped, simply, that his son was all right.

THERE were still some of Conor's papers and books at Thomas O'Dea's flat. In the past, looking at the scribbles, trying in vain to decipher their meaning, made him angry. Now it made him sad. Polly Ryan had urged Thomas to find out what was written there. A teacher who frequented Lapierre's would read Thomas the latest newspaper reports about Whelan's trial in exchange for a free beer or two. One day, Thomas brought in some of Conor's papers and asked him to read them to him.

"Do you really want me to read this one?" the teacher asked. "It's a poem by D'Arcy McGee."

"Read it," Thomas said. "Please."

In the darkness of the tavern, the teacher strained his eyes to read the verses. He started haltingly:

Cling to my breast, my Irish bird,
Poor storm-toss'd stranger, sore afraid!

Thomas interrupted. "When did he write this?"

"It says 1852 on the top of the page, when he was in exile from Ireland."

Thomas nodded. *Poor storm-toss'd stranger*—that's how he'd felt when he arrived in Canada. Did McGee feel the same way when he came to the New World?

"He loved Ireland, didn't he?" Thomas said.

"Yes, he did. And he loved his wife. As I suppose you did, Thomas."

250

And now there was this raven-haired girl with Conor. Were they in love? He asked the teacher to carry on reading.

For you and I are exiles both—
Rest you, wanderer, rest you here!
Soon fair winds shall waft you forth
Back to our beloved North—
Would God I could go with you, dear!

Thomas O'Dea might not have been able to read or write, but his memory was crystal clear. He repeated the verse word for word. Yes, they had been "exiles both," but McGee had made something of his life. He had not. The memories of his past attacked him—the famine . . . the coffin ship to Canada . . . holding his dying wife . . . losing his son.

Would God I could go with you, dear!

Would God, Thomas thought, that I could change what I have done, quell my anger, repair my life. Would God that I could be with Conor again.

WHEN Andrew Cullen was called to the stand, there was confusion in the courtroom. It was not a familiar name among those closely following the trial. Cullen had been sitting with an intense, square-shouldered man Conor couldn't quite place. He spoke with the sing-song accent of County Clare. "I am a detective from Montreal. I got the news of Mr. McGee's death and immediately came to Ottawa." He looked at the man he had been sitting with, and added, "Under orders."

"Are you familiar with the Ottawa jail where the defendant is confined?" James O'Reilly asked.

"Yes, I am. I visited there a number of times."

"Can you describe the arrangement of the cells?"

"Yes, James Whelan was in cell ten and John Doyle in cell seven."

"What was your purpose?"

"To hear what I could hear." There was a burst of laughter in the crowd. It stopped under the glare of Justice Richards.

"And what did you hear?"

"I heard Doyle say, 'James, I'm sorry you ever done it.' Then I heard Whelan say, 'I don't care a damn. I'm prepared for the worst.'" There was now complete silence in the courtroom. "I heard James Whelan say, 'Yes, I shot that fellow. I shot that fellow like a dog.'"

James Whelan watched Cullen in disbelief. Reporters were writing furiously. Conor was shocked. D'Arcy McGee had taught him to think beyond the moment, and this moment was fraught with significance. Conor considered what had really happened. The prosecution was relying on eavesdropping. There was something desperate about that. They would need Doyle to substantiate it. But the fact remained that James O'Reilly did have a confession.

THE new Ottawa jail was on Nicholas Street. Conor stood outside, feeling small and unnerved. He rubbed his hands through his hair, the way D'Arcy McGee used to, and slowly headed along the curved stone walkway toward the cold stone building. A tall, lanky guard opened the door for him. Another guard called out, "How long are you planning to stay?" An old and tired joke. But the guards all laughed. Conor counted four of them. Others must be in the cell blocks.

The jovial mood changed when the tall guard opened the first huge wooden door toward the cells. He and another guard led

Conor up the stairs, past rows of cells filled with petty criminals. Conor tried to ignore the swearing and catcalls from the cells. On the fourth floor, one guard unbolted a thick wooden door. The other stood beside it. Conor entered the hallway where the most dangerous criminals were kept. At the end of the hall, behind another locked door, was death row.

"Whelan, you have a visitor," the jail guard growled.

James Whelan was slumped on a bed that took up most of his tiny, dark cell. He looked up, only slightly curious, as Conor approached the bars. The sole source of light was high above Conor's head. Conor could hear birdsong outside. He wondered if it comforted Whelan or haunted him.

The guard waited down the hall, within both sight and earshot. He was armed and appeared eager to use his weapon if need be. Conor stumbled for his opening words. "How are you?" was the best he could do.

Whelan just shrugged. Life, or the prospect of death, had hardened him. "What are *you* doing here?" he replied bitterly.

Conor answered honestly. "I don't know. I just want to talk to you."

"You worked for McGee. You said you saw me on the street that night. You testified against me." It was as if Whelan was reciting his reasons, in order, for hating Conor.

"I said I saw a man in a grey coat. I never said it was you."

Again, Whelan shrugged. "Are you here to try to sneak another confession out of me? You've heard what they say about me: 'He talks too much.'"

"Actually, I have a feeling that if you told everything you knew, it wouldn't be a confession of guilt."

"Perhaps," Whelan said feebly. "Perhaps you were in court when I pleaded not guilty?"

Conor nodded. He noticed Whelan's eyes were now permanently wide open in fright. Whelan stared above Conor's head, out the high window. Conor let him have some time, then asked, "What about your confession in jail?"

"What confession? I remember saying he was shot like a dog, not that I shot him. Ask Doyle, if he'll talk to you."

"I hear he's been fired at the Russell House."

Whelan just shrugged. "I didn't say it. But it doesn't matter."

Throughout the trial, Conor had been studying Whelan's face, trying to remember him from the Montreal election, from around Parliament Hill. He was familiar, that was all. "When I was in Montreal during the election," Conor said, "there was someone there stirring up trouble, but no one seemed to recognize him."

"I don't know what you're talking about," Whelan responded, but Conor noticed that he was shivering.

"I think you know exactly what I'm saying." He reached out for Whelan and held the bars separating them. Whelan shrank away. "Tell me about the other man Joseph Faulkner was talking about." Conor was practically yelling.

Whelan stared back at Conor with wild, frightened eyes, weighing the odds, considering what to do. "They got to find me guilty yet," was all he said.

But Conor was not about to give up.

"Are you a Fenian?" he asked.

"I don't know anymore," Whelan muttered, but added proudly, "I am an Irishman."

Conor almost left then. In fact, he turned to go but stopped. He owed it to something—to the memory of D'Arcy McGee, maybe; strangely enough, also to his father—to get to the truth. McGee's death would not be avenged by the wrong verdict. Canada would not be a safer place with an assassin at large, and his father . . . well, this terrified man, engulfed by his own hatred, reminded him of his father.

"Mr. Whelan, I'm Irish, too. Tell me what happened. Please. I believe in you."

James Whelan allowed his eyes to close. This young man didn't just believe him; he believed *in* him. When he opened his eyes, they were filled with tears.

"I was there," he said simply. "I held the horse for the man who killed McGee."

"You were just an accomplice."

"Yes, but I cheered him on."

"Is he the man Faulkner talked about?"

Whelan nodded, swallowing hard.

"Where is he?" Conor persisted.

"I don't know."

"You're saying he used you."

"I guess so."

"Then you have a lot in common with D'Arcy McGee. Unless something happens, this man will be responsible for both your deaths."

Whelan dropped his head into his hands, but Conor was relentless. "Who is this man?"

Whelan lurched back, regaining his composure. "I don't know. I knew him only as Marshall. You're right. He was there in Montreal. We had a great time heckling McGee at rallies. He encouraged me and others to take it further—throwing eggs, tomatoes and eventually rocks." He paused before saying, "He led the attack at the Mechanics' Hall." He looked at Conor and smiled. "I remember you there. You looked so hurt whenever we attacked your man."

Conor ignored the jab. "Did he send you to Ottawa?"

"He never told me to move to Ottawa. That was my own doing.

I thought there would be better work here, but when I met up with him by chance, we became friends. I was lonely, and he made me feel important. He asked me to go to the Toronto House and look around, make notes for him. He told me to go to the House of Commons and said I should shake my fist at McGee to remind him of the summer, how Barney Devlin's boys were still around. He even suggested I bring along my gun." Whelan took a deep breath and rubbed his tired eyes. "He lent me his boots. And yes, he wore a grey coat—like the one he gave me." James Whelan had not spoken that many words together in months.

"Tell your story to the court," Conor pleaded. "You must tell people about him."

"Don't you understand, if I do talk, what will happen to my wife in Montreal? Or even my parents in Ireland? This is war, you know. And . . . and . . ."

"And what?"

"And this man named Marshall will be responsible to God for McGee's death."

"And your own."

"Probably," he answered distantly. "Still, I would rather be hanged than be known as a snitch."

Now Conor had the answer. Whelan would rather die a martyr than be called an informer. There was little anyone could do for a man who refused to help himself. Whelan was doomed. But that was only part of the equation: D'Arcy McGee's murderer was still at large.

"I understand now," Conor told him. "I think you are wrong, but you are a very brave man." Conor turned to the guard. He knew he had been listening. "Did you hear that? He's innocent."

"I am here to protect you, not listen to his lies. Your meeting is over."

256

As the guard approached, Whelan asked, "You are Thomas O'Dea's boy, aren't you?"

"Yes."

"Tell your father to be careful."

The guard briskly led Conor away. Conor never had a chance to ask James Whelan what he meant.

34

Conor set up an appointment with Sir John A. Macdonald for eight-thirty the next evening at Macdonald's home. As the former assistant to D'Arcy McGee, he had no trouble arranging an audience with the prime minister. Hewitt Bernard complained about the inconvenience, but added his name to the evening schedule.

Recently, the prime minister had moved his study upstairs. Macdonald's doctor had said the drainage smell drifting into the main-floor office was bad for his health. Conor stayed downstairs, waiting to be announced. He understood the doctor's concerns, but this was a rose garden compared to the outhouse behind his father's flat. Months ago, his old pocket watch had stopped working, but he estimated that he had been waiting for nearly an hour. He could hear Sir John's voice rise in anger from upstairs, but he couldn't distinguish any words.

"Young man."

Lady Macdonald's voice startled Conor. He jumped to his feet, flustered. "I'm sorry, ma'am. I didn't see you there."

"Oh, don't be sorry. You're in good company. D'Arcy used to doze off while I was talking to him, too. Contemplating poetry, I liked to think."

Conor had met Lady Macdonald only a few times before. He was flattered that she remembered him. "How are you, ma'am?" he asked. Lady Macdonald was expecting a baby any day. She looked tired, and Conor was embarrassed to observe how big she was.

"I'm fine, thank you. The baby has the energy of Sir John, I'm afraid. Forever kicking and making its presence known."

Conor was uncomfortable. Working-class pregnant women were often seen in the market or around town, but aristocrats stayed out of society's glare when they were "in the family way." Except for her daily visits to St. Alban's Church, Lady Macdonald had rarely been in public since she started showing. But, he supposed, she was in her house and she could act as she liked.

"The babe wants to help him fight the Grits," Conor joked, wondering if he was being too bold.

Lady Macdonald smiled. "Sir John speaks very highly of you." She left the thought dangling as she walked over to the mantle to rearrange a few flowers. Conor couldn't think of anything to say in return. She broke the silence. "You have been going to court every day, Sir John tells me."

"I was subpoenaed." Conor was afraid she was suggesting that he was lazy. He quickly added, "I'm still working for a few members of Parliament."

"I don't think it's wise," she declared, "to watch that wicked man every day."

"But—"

"It's not right to see such evil." Her face was pained with concern. "They tell me he cannot feel."

Conor thought of the solitary man in jail with eyes alight in fear. "I'm sorry, ma'am," he said. "I think he can feel. I think he feels very deeply."

CONOR recognized the man who marched out of Sir John's study and down the stairs; he was the person sitting with Andrew Cullen in court. He nodded at Lady Macdonald as he passed her and completely ignored Conor. With exaggerated politeness, she called over his shoulder, "And good evening to you, Mr. McMicken." Without turning, he reached up with his hand. It could have been a wave, but it was more like a salute.

"Strange man," Lady Macdonald sighed. "But these are strange times."

"Come in, son, come in," Sir John called impatiently from his study. Conor bowed slightly to Lady Macdonald. She followed him upstairs and turned into her room while he entered the prime minister's home study. The first thing Conor noticed was the huge desk covered with a maze of papers, most of which Old Tomorrow seemed to have cast aside for another day. Macdonald was pouring a glass of sherry from a half-empty decanter. His deep frown indicated that he had been through a very disagreeable meeting.

He looked up from his glass. "How's your work going?" he inquired.

"Well, sir," Conor declared. "I've been quite busy doing odd jobs for members of Parliament and . . ." Conor could see that the prime minister wasn't listening, but was just making conversation, so he let his words trail off. McGee had once told him, "If you lose your audience in the preliminaries, scurry to get back on the track." So Conor came to the point.

"Sir John, I would like to talk to you about Patrick James Whelan."

"A much-discussed man," Macdonald said sarcastically. There was no sparkle in his eyes this night, just a deepening look of concern. Minutes ago, McMicken had told him that an informer in Detroit confirmed other reports that Whelan was not the man who killed McGee. He was an accomplice, but not the murderer. Sir

John, of course, refused to believe it. "Who cares what some fool says in Detroit? The courts in Canada will decide, and the evidence, as D'Arcy would say, is as thick as blackberries. Who cares . . ." he murmured the last two words out loud.

"Pardon me, sir?"

Macdonald realized he had been daydreaming or, if there were such a word, nightmaring.

"I'm sorry. I didn't quite hear what you said," Conor repeated.

"It was nothing. Now, what do you want to say about that fellow Whelan?"

"I don't think he's guilty."

Sir John A. Macdonald almost spit. Conor O'Dea, of all people, McGee's loyal assistant, not wanting the Fenian rebel to hang! He looked at Conor accusingly. "So what makes you think this?"

"He told me," Conor replied.

"He told the court he was innocent, too," the prime minister snapped back. "He pleaded not guilty. Now it's before the courts. Do you not trust our courts?"

"He told me what really happened," Conor said, trying to retain his strength. It took a lot of nerve for him to face the prime minister's assault.

And Sir John had just begun. "Of course he'd tell you he was innocent. The man's life is at stake. He's a cold-blooded murderer. Adding lying to his list of sins is no giant leap."

"But, sir, I believe him. I think he was somehow involved. I think he was part of the crime. But I don't think he killed Mr. McGee."

"What about his confession in jail?"

"He says he was misquoted."

"We all say that!" Macdonald shouted. "So who, pray tell," he asked mockingly, "was the murderer?"

"I don't know. But I am sure that someone else fired the gun."

261

The prime minister's world was in disarray. He wanted this terrible mess cleaned up, once and for all. Surely Whelan was guilty of something, even this young man admitted that, and there was no other suspect except some mysterious, shadowy person. Whelan had the motive and he was there; the evidence was clear. Justice must be done. Because . . . because, he thought with dread, if he wasn't guilty—if someone else was really the assassin—then the murderer was still out there.

"Why are you doing this, young Mr. O'Dea? Don't you think D'Arcy McGee would want his killer brought to justice?"

"Yes, sir, I do." Conor was prepared for this question. He had asked it many times himself. "But I know he would want the truth exposed. He would feel betrayed if the wrong man hanged."

Macdonald sighed deeply. Never before had he felt so alone in the premier's chair. He had a debt to McGee, and it would be met. But he also had a duty to the country not to let this matter grow into hysteria. Anyway, this was the responsibility of the police and the courts, certainly not that of this well-meaning but immature apprentice. A dense silence hung over the room.

Conor, summoning his self-confidence, broke the stalemate. "Do you really think James Whelan is guilty, sir?"

Sir John A. Macdonald had persuaded sworn enemies to work as allies during the Confederation debates, had convinced feuding colonies to unite, had enticed headstrong people to follow him as leader—now he tried his best to convince himself that the matter was under control. "Yes, young man, I do," he affirmed. "The final decision is up to the courts, but I am confident—no, I am certain— that the Fenian is guilty."

But when Conor returned Macdonald's stare, he saw no sign of confidence. He saw the same look he remembered seeing in jail in the eyes of a doomed man. He could tell that the prime minister was frightened. And not in the least bit certain.

The next day, Sir John and Lady Macdonald sat beside Mr. Justice Richards in court. Lady Macdonald sat solemnly, in loose clothes that disguised her pregnancy, but the prime minister made quite a show of it, smiling at friends and acquaintances. Macdonald was both prime minister and attorney general. He was the most powerful man in Canada, and the most persuasive when he wanted to be. He was letting the judge know this was more than just a judicial hearing; it was a political event. He was letting the jury know he wanted James Whelan pronounced guilty.

35

The trial proceeded with enough rumour and hearsay to hang James Whelan many times over, but no real proof of guilt. Conor noted that the prosecution never called John Doyle to confirm the confession. He supposed that a detective with an Irish accent was convincing enough.

It was the dying days of autumn. Meg wanted one last trip to the country before winter took hold of the capital. The court did not sit on Saturday, so Conor rowed Meg up the Rideau Canal to the first set of locks at Hog's Back. The waterfall, with its wondrous sound and the mystic light, had long been one of her favourite spots. It was mid-afternoon by the time they docked; they were alone, sitting on the rocks. They had to speak loudly to hear each other above the crashing sound of the falls.

Conor told her about his meetings with Whelan and the prime minister.

"You have to help Whelan," she urged, shouting over the rushing water.

Conor didn't answer. He stared at the falls, hypnotized by its rhythm. He followed a wave thundering down, thinking about the complexities of life, the horrors of death . . .

Then he heard Meg scream.

Before he could react, a hand reached out and grabbed him from behind, pinning him. He felt ropes burning his wrists and pressure circling his ankles. He hadn't seen his attackers. He tried to speak, but another hand gagged him. Meg was in the grasp of three other people. All wore masks. No one spoke.

Meg tried to pull herself free. Whoever had hold of her tightened his grip. She tried to scream again, but her cry came out as a hollow wail, drowned out by the loud waterfall. She felt another hand groping her, and her scream turned shrill. But it was hopeless. She could hardly breathe. She thought she might be sick.

Even though all their faces were covered, she could tell that this was not the same gang that had threatened her before. These men were older. It was as if the problem had been handed over to a higher authority. The leader, who hadn't touched either of them, spoke almost gently. "Ease off, lads. Not too rough."

But there was nothing gentle about him. He sauntered over to Conor, who lay bound and helpless. "Okay, Paddy, watch what we do to people who go where they don't belong." He took out a long pair of scissors and grabbed Conor by his hair. He snipped at his right sideburn. Then the hair on the left side of his head. Just enough to make Conor look foolish. Conor squirmed, but he couldn't budge the ropes and he was afraid that the scissors might stab him. "If there was a little more of your red whiskers, we might take a scalp," the attacker declared. "But this will do. For now."

And then he looked at Meg.

She closed her eyes in terror as he strolled over to her. He whispered in her ear, "Be fair, Meg. You were warned, but you wouldn't listen." For a few seconds, he played with her hair. He admired it, stroked it, caressed it. Meg's knees buckled, but the three masked attackers propped her up like a prize. Holding up a strand of hair, the leader glanced over at Conor. "Not too brave, are you, Paddy?" They all laughed as Conor wrenched his body, trying to release the ropes. He was powerless, while the person—whoever he was—held the scissors close to Meg's face.

"You have to be taught a lesson," he said. And he cut a chunk of her hair.

She gathered strength and spit at him, hitting his mask.

"Now, Meg," he scolded, "why would you do something like that? It must be the kind of company you've been keeping." One of the people holding her stuffed a handkerchief in her mouth. "That's better," he said and continued cutting Meg's beautiful black hair. He took his time, dramatically holding her curls up and letting strands float in the air. When he was finished, he studied Meg's shorn head. "Can't say it's an improvement, but I think you've got the message: don't go where you don't belong—either of you."

The three people holding Meg released her, and she fell to the ground sobbing. They ran away, leaving Conor and Meg alone, crumpled on the bank of the river.

MEG had to untie Conor's wrists and legs. Her hands were shaking. When he was free, she wouldn't let him comfort her. She crossed her arms, holding on to herself. Holding on for dear life. The waterfall now looked angry and fierce, water pounding into the rocks, attacking them.

They rowed to the Toronto House in silence. Back at the boarding house, Meg ran upstairs, leaving Conor alone in the parlour. Eventually, Mrs. Trotter came downstairs and said to Conor, "I think it is better that you go somewhere else tonight."

AT nine o'clock in the morning, Patrick James Whelan was ushered into the courtroom to hear the jury's verdict. He was dressed in black,

266

his face so pale it was almost white. He sat stiffly in his chair, between the two policemen. He seemed devoid of curiosity or concern. Conor could see why Lady Macdonald thought he had no feeling. He could only guess what dread a man feels when waiting for a sentence of life— or death. After the attack at Hog's Back, he knew the humiliation of helplessness. He watched Whelan with deeper sympathy.

Half an hour after Whelan had taken his seat, the jury filed in. None of the jurors looked at Whelan. Nor he at them. He continued to stare straight ahead.

"Gentlemen," the judge solemnly asked the jury, "have you agreed on your verdict?"

"Yes," the foreman responded, "we have."

"How do you find the defendant: guilty or not guilty?"

James Whelan's life came down to a few simple words. During the trial he had sat silently, listening to men argue his fate. A stream of words. Letters forming thoughts. Thoughts forming sentences. Sentences drawing conclusions. Words with meaning, words that were just sounds. Words that determined his life or death. Now, all the words came down to one, spoken by the jury's foreman.

"Guilty."

The clerk asked, "So say you all?"

In turn, each juror nodded—guilty.

James Whelan swallowed hard. Hillyard Cameron leaned over and spoke to him, but he didn't appear to listen. No other words were important now but that one.

Guilty.

THE judge looked down on the prisoner. "What do you have to say, Patrick James Whelan, that the sentence of the court should not be pronounced against you?" Whelan reached into his pocket and took out some notes. He looked at the judge, then the jury, and stared back into empty space. He had not spoken in court except to assert his innocence. "I have been tried and found guilty of this crime," he began softly. "I am held to be a murderer." He looked over the audience, and his eyes locked onto Conor's. "Here I am, standing on the brink of my grave. I declare to you that I am innocent and never committed this deed. That I know well in my heart and soul."

There was a rumbling in the audience, but Whelan ignored it. "I must say this: if I had been in the same place as one of the gentlemen of the jury, hearing the same evidence, I'd very likely bring in the same verdict. I liberate all the jurors from blame." For a second, it looked as if he might falter, but he didn't. "I am held to be a black assassin. And my blood runs cold. But I am innocent. I never took that man's blood. I know I am not the murderer of the Honourable D'Arcy McGee."

The denial exhausted Whelan. He sank back, his energy spent. He could have spoken longer, but he knew his time was up.

The clerk removed a package from a black bag and handed it to the judge. Chief Justice Richards was clearly moved, maybe even disturbed, by Whelan's speech, but he put on a pair of black gloves, placed a black cap over his head and spoke. "The sentence of this court is that you, Patrick James Whelan, having been found guilty of the murder of Thomas D'Arcy McGee, shall be hanged by the neck until you are dead." He took off his gloves and hat and looked at the condemned man with a blend of pity and disgust. "There is no possible hope on this side of the grave. Let me urge you to make your peace with God."

James Whelan had listened calmly to his sentence of death. As he was being led out of the prisoner's dock, he turned to the judge and said, "All those words, my Lord, still do not make me guilty."

CONOR moved into a small room above a shop on Rideau Street. He went to a barber and, without explanation, had his sideburns evened out and his hair cut short. He still looked rather foolish, but it was the best he could do.

After the verdict, he went back to Sparks Street. There was a sign on the door: THE TORONTO HOUSE IS CLOSED. He still had a key, and he opened the door. Inside, George Desbarats, the Queen's printer who owned the building, was chatting with a solicitor whom Conor didn't recognize. Conor never said his name, but Mr. Desbarats greeted him warmly. "I know you have been through a lot. This is one more shock. The Trotters have moved away and instructed me to ask you kindly not to look for them."

The solicitor added unnecessarily, "Mrs. Trotter doesn't want anyone to know where her family has gone. I'm to deal with her affairs."

"But her furniture is still here," Conor protested. Everything was still in place, as if they had all just gone to the market.

"I own the building and much of the contents," Desbarats said. "Mrs. Trotter will write me and tell me where to send her effects."

The solicitor went back to his paperwork, and George Desbarats took Conor by the arm. "You can stay here as long as you need," he said. "Until I rent the place again, that is."

Conor walked around the parlour, where he had often sat with Meg, where D'Arcy McGee's body had been brought in from the cold and where he had taken Meg in his arms. But the last time they were here, Meg couldn't stand the sight of him. She just rushed upstairs. Out of his life. Who could blame her? He was a coward who did nothing but squirm while she was violated.

"One other thing," the solicitor said. "There was a letter left for you." He handed Conor a scented envelope. Conor did not read it in front of the two men. He waited until he was alone in his room. It read simply,

Conor, I'm sorry. I will contact you as soon as I am ready.
Meg

Conor read the short note three times, then slowly started to cry—weakly at first, but the tears steadily grew until they were unrelenting. He sobbed shamelessly, like a lost child. There was no one there to comfort him.

COLONEL O'Hagan was growing frustrated. He needed publicity. He needed action. He needed something to spur the men on. McGee's assassination was cheered in Irish bars throughout America, but many of his soldiers were drifting back home. They were getting bored. The word from Washington was not good. President Johnson had been impeached; he had come within one vote of being thrown out of the White House, had lost the nomination of his own party and was in disgrace.

The good news was that the new president, General Ulysses S. Grant, was also interested in annexing Canada. He had called the country's existence and actions "vexatious . . . unfriendly . . . unneighbourly." Perfect. But President Grant had no interest in Irish nationalism or Fenian adventures. It remained up to O'Hagan to keep the cause alive. No, it was up to that man in Canada.

O'Hagan was keen to move soon, but he had not heard from him for some time. He paid attention to the trial in Ottawa, but it was largely ignored in American newspapers. Because of a useless appeal, Whelan's hanging was delayed from December to February. How frustrating. O'Hagan had received explicit instructions from Dublin not to do a thing until their man had completed his work in Canada. His hands were tied.

So he sat in New York, waiting impatiently.

36

Mary Ann Trotter hated Toronto. She had named the boarding house in Ottawa the Toronto House to bring in business from the West, not out of admiration for the city's minor glory. Its dull streets, bland buildings and earnest citizens left her dismayed. The town had pretensions of greatness but a musty mood of mediocrity. Muddy York, Hogtown, Toronto the Good. She found Ottawa more interesting: a grimy, young logging town trying to clean itself up. Montreal was her favourite: active and lively, the centre of commerce, with a French joie de vivre. But Toronto was home, and after the attack on Meg, it was a refuge. Mary Ann took her daughter to her sister's stylish house on Sherbourne Street. It was a Protestant area. Her family would stay in Toronto until this Fenian business ended. Then, maybe, they would move back to the capital. She would have to find a job in Toronto, and had already applied to work in the Empire Hotel.

Meg left Ottawa in a daze. She felt she owed Conor more that the cryptic letter she had left behind, but she didn't know what to say. She wanted to disappear. She kept her shorn head covered at all times, even indoors. But she also wanted to attack. She abhorred violence, but deep down, she was ashamed to admit, she wanted revenge.

Will stayed in Ottawa with friends. It pained Mary Ann to leave him there, but he had obligations at school and as a pageboy. He never really liked being surrounded by women at his aunt's house, anyway.

Meg had confided to her aunt that she wanted to protect herself. She wanted to buy a gun and learn how to shoot it. Her mother would never approve, but her aunt told her about the Dominion of Canada Rifle Association. They held target practice on Tuesdays. "Perhaps they'll take you in," her aunt suggested.

But they wouldn't. Meg barely got a hearing at the armouries. The men rejected her simply because she was a woman. "What does a pretty girl like you need to practise shooting for?" the lieutenant taunted her. "Get a strong man at your side."

Meg held her ground. "Who's in charge?" she asked.

"I am," the auxiliary lieutenant declared.

"No, who is *really* in charge?"

"I suppose Colonel Gzowski is."

She looked confused.

"Colonel Casimir Gzowski. Quite a character. And you've never heard of him?"

Gzowski. The name meant nothing to her. She couldn't pronounce it and dared not try to spell it.

"He started the regiment," the lieutenant continued. "He is personally funding it. If he says you can shoot, I'll let you in."

She memorized the strange name. Casimir Gzowski. That night, she asked her aunt if she had ever heard of this man and got an earful back. "He's only one of the most powerful businessmen in Toronto," she responded.

"Why the regiment?"

"Apparently, he was so incensed with the Fenian raids that he organized a militia to defend Canada, even sponsoring shooting teams to go to England for competitions."

"Fenians again," Mary Ann interjected. Meg didn't realize that her mother had been listening.

"Well, he knows a thing or two about revolutionary movements, having been part of one in Poland," her aunt told her.

"Good Lord! Is everyone a former rebel in this country?" Meg exclaimed.

"He's no rebel now. I hear he's a great favourite of Queen Victoria's."

"Why do you want to know about him?" Mary Ann Trotter asked suspiciously.

"Oh, I heard his peculiar name and just wondered," Meg said.

"Well, I know him. He stayed at the boarding house and filled the place with stories one week when you were in London. I can arrange a meeting if you wish. Maybe he can help you get a job. I presume that what's you want."

Meg neglected to tell her otherwise.

MEG expected Colonel Gzowski's King Street office to be over a bank, or in suites shared with other firms, but his engineering business consumed an entire building. Meg was led into his private office, where he was hovering over blueprints and scowling. "Come here, young lady, and look at this. If I get my way, there will be parkland and walkways all along the Toronto waterfront, but the cheapskate politicians won't spend the money and the railwaymen want all the land."

No introduction. No hello. Just straight to his business plans.

"I'm all for railways and money, but there should be land for the people." She had a bit of a problem following his English. Apparently, he learned the language—his fifth—when he arrived in New York a decade ago. She looked at the blueprints for the Toronto waterfront and feigned interest.

She felt pleasantries were in order. "I'm Meg Trotter from Ottawa," she said. "I am Mary Ann Trotter's daughter. My aunt spoke to you."

He had been leaning over the paper. When he stood, he towered over her. He was an imposing man with an upright military bearing. He looked down on her with piercing, enquiring eyes. "You weren't at your mother's charming establishment when I was there."

"No, sir, I was in London."

He nodded. "Good choice."

She looked around the large, profusely decorated room. His writing desk was enormous. Other tables were strewn with more blueprints and contracts and whatever else she couldn't tell. There was a large family crest over the mantle and a fire burning furiously in the fireplace. The crest had a ram in the centre of it, with a cross or a sword in its back. Probably a sword, she thought, skewering the poor sheep. A beautifully ornate chessboard was set up in the corner. It looked as if a game was under way.

"So," she asked, "was Mr. McGee there when you were at my mother's boarding house?"

"Some of the time. We sang songs by the piano. Do you play as well as your mother?"

"Regrettably, no. Do you go to Ottawa often?"

"Regrettably, yes." He smiled at his answer. "My business often takes me there. Usually, I stay at the Russell House. Connections, you know. I must say your mother's company is better, but there is no place in Ottawa like the Russell's bar."

She found his accent rather charming, but was having a little trouble following him.

"When I met your mother, I was trying to get our complacent prime minister to take the military seriously. We don't have a standing army. We don't even have a military school. We can't depend on

Britain anymore. We have to get serious. Mr. McGee and I talked for hours about the Fenians, and I came back to Toronto and started a regiment. As an example, as much as anything."

"I heard you are a man of action," she said.

"An interesting phrase. I get things done. I grew up in a country prone to invasion. I didn't like it."

He walked over to the mantle. He might be the tallest person she had ever met.

"But what about you? You want a job, I assume. I'm always looking for bright young people. Right now, I could use someone who can write. I need help because my English is poor."

His English sounded remarkably good to Meg. In fact, he had a pleasant, rather calming voice, once you were accustomed to the accent.

"I can write, but that's not why I'm here. I actually have a request you might find peculiar. I want to take target practice with your auxiliary regiment."

"Peculiar indeed," he said. "What kind of young woman wants to learn how to shoot? And why?"

"I'd rather not say."

He seemed amused by her conviction. "Tell me, are you like those American women I've read about who dressed as men to fight in the Civil War?"

"No, I loathe war. I want protection."

"Is someone threatening you?"

Again she ignored the direct question. "I don't see why a woman can't take target practice."

"I suppose I don't see why not, either. Convention, I presume." He thought for a second. "Yes, you can shoot. I'll instruct the regiment." And he added, "Remember, I'm looking for bright young people to work for me."

She thought of Conor. In fact, she was almost always thinking of Conor.

MEG was a natural. At first, the gun's recoil surprised her and she wildly missed the target, but she learned to compensate. Aim patiently and precisely. Squeeze the trigger delicately. Fire calmly. The soldiers and volunteers watched her as if she was a novelty, and she supposed that she was. One young man said, loud enough for her to hear, "I was told to touch the trigger like a woman's nipple." The group giggled. She looked directly at him. The laughter stopped and the soldier who cracked the joke turned away.

She wasn't going to be intimidated again.

IT was not an easy delivery. Lady Macdonald went to the General Hospital in the middle of a cold February night and delivered a baby girl. They named her Margaret Mary Theodora. They would call her Mary. D'Arcy McGee's wife's name. A new life. It filled the Macdonalds with joy and hope.

Mary Macdonald was born three days before James Whelan was to hang.

JAMES Whelan sat in his cell, listening to the hammering. He recited his catechism, trying to escape the interminable pounding of nails. But he couldn't drown it out, and he felt each nail as it pierced the wood. He heard the workers chatter and make jokes as they went about their business. He knew they were not skilled labourers. They didn't have to be. They were building a temporary stage with rough, unpainted wood. They were building his scaffold.

37

A t dawn, the blizzard started. By nine o'clock, snow had gathered around the scaffold. It swirled into the faces of the first people to assemble for the spectacle. By ten o'clock, men and women were jostling for the front row, ignoring the snow. Many chose to stay back and nestle comfortably in fur-lined sleighs. People chatted among themselves; children threw snowballs at each other; some paced, either nervously or for warmth. Two children were trying to build a snowman. They laughed and pretended to choke it—and each other. There was an almost-festive mood on the winter morning.

Conor O'Dea decided to go to the hanging so that Jim Whelan might see a friendly face before facing eternity. Many of the people in the crowd were familiar. He wondered if the gang who had attacked Meg and him at Hog's Back were here. Probably. They were likely looking at him and smirking.

Polly Ryan waved hesitantly at him. He pretended not to see her. Was this woman everywhere?

At eleven o'clock, the ghoulish procession began: a jailer, two soldiers and James Whelan, followed by a priest. The priest and the condemned man murmured prayers together; both seemed to be in a trance. Throughout the trial, Whelan had been meticulously dressed, but he walked his final steps in creased pants and scuffed boots. His hair and beard were a tangle of curls, uncombed and uncared for. The procession stopped in front of the scaffold. The crowd quietened in anticipation. The people wanted a speech, a confession, a performance of some sort, but they were disappointed. James Whelan moved his head side to side as if nervously testing his neck muscles. In a high-pitched but feeble voice, he said simply, "God save Ireland and God bless my soul."

He nodded to the hangman.

People in the crowd craned their necks to get a good view. The good citizens of Ottawa leaned forward. It was their last chance to see the mortal face of the killer, to look into his eyes. But his face was as white as the falling snow, and his eyes were closed in dread and agony. No one made a sound as the hooded hangman slipped the noose around Whelan's neck and placed a white hood over his face.

The hangman pulled the bolt; the trap door opened. The crowd gasped. With a thud, Patrick James Whelan's body fell nine feet and his vertebrae snapped.

The crowd quickly dispersed to enjoy a snowy Ottawa day in peace.

CONOR O'Dea wiped a flake of snow from his eye. What had he done to help Jim Whelan? He had spoken to Sir John A. Macdonald, but so what? He should have found the real killer—he had seen him—but he had failed. Meg had moved, probably back to Toronto, but he didn't know where. What had he done to help her? Nothing but watch them insult her, violate her and cut her hair, her dazzling black hair. He walked along Sparks Street toward the Desbarats Block, passing the doorway of what had been the Toronto House, where

Meg had lived, where McGee had died. Offord's House was boarded up. Over by the liquor store, all was quiet. There were no boxes out today. No one was hiding. There was no one to hide from. Ottawa had its killer, and he was dead.

The storm was gaining power and intensity. Conor enjoyed the heaviness of the new snow on his shoulders. He leaned against the force of the wind, trudging on. He turned toward Parliament Hill and headed along Wellington Street. Across Sappers Bridge. Back to Lowertown. Back home. Where he belonged.

It felt curiously comforting to approach his father's door. The gaslight was flickering weakly, so Thomas must be home. Conor peeked inside, through the dirty basement window, and saw two shapes shifting. That's odd, he thought. Thomas rarely had visitors. The window was caked with gas residue, so he couldn't see clearly, but he caught the impression, a familiar form that made his heart almost stop. It was the man he had seen in Montreal, the man in the shadows, the man who killed D'Arcy McGee. He was sure of it.

Conor curled himself into a ball and cowered by the window, desperately trying to listen but terrified of what he might hear.

THOMAS O'Dea was listening, too. "I am ordering you to come with me," the assassin commanded.

Thomas looked into his cold eyes, searching for some emotion, some humanity. He found nothing, just a hardened look of resolve. Well, he was just as resolved. "What happened to Whelan?" Thomas asked. "Did you order him, too?"

The assassin put his right hand in his new coat pocket without taking his eyes off Thomas. He missed his old grey coat with its deep pockets, but it had served him well, and he always knew when to discard things. This man, Thomas O'Dea, was confusing, and he hated being confused. Why these questions about Whelan? Didn't he understand that Whelan was expendable, while he, O'Dea, was more useful alive? It was important that Whelan be caught and hanged, but this time no one would be caught. After the next murder, everyone would think Whelan was innocent, hanged by an incompetent justice system. There would be panic in the streets. If an assassin could kill politicians at random, no one would feel safe.

"I expect some answers before I do anything," Thomas insisted. "First, I want to know about James Whelan."

"Whelan is dead," the assassin answered with a sigh, "because of his own stupidity. You are smarter and much more valuable to our cause."

Thomas wondered, Had he used Whelan and cast him aside?

"It's not Whelan who's important now—" the assassin began, but Thomas interrupted.

"That's right. What's important is you. I want to know who you are. What's your name—your real name?"

The assassin was being tested, and he didn't like that. *He* did the testing, not some simple barman.

Thomas was stalling for time. He was desperately thinking, harnessing courage, but first, he wanted to get a confession out of this murderer.

"Who I am is not the issue," the assassin said impatiently. "I know who you are, Thomas O'Dea. Thrown off your land by the English, dumped like a dog on an evacuation ship. You had a wife, I've heard." He watched the hint of a tear build in Thomas's eyes, and pressed on. "Yes, I know who you are, and you're one of us."

Thomas felt his resolve slipping. He asked, "What is your plan?"

The assassin hesitated. He never told anyone his plans in advance. Still, it could be useful to have at his side a man smart enough to ask a few questions. Only an idiot would follow him as blindly as

Whelan had. And this was not a plan for idiots. Anyway, why not tell O'Dea? If he refused to follow him, he'd kill him.

"The plan is a quick strike against the Orangeman."

"Which one? For God's sake, they are everywhere."

A grin unfurled on the assassin's face as he mouthed the name: "John Macdonald."

Thomas's eyes widened in disbelief. "Assassinate the prime minister?"

"Yes."

"When?"

"On the weekend." He was actually enjoying this. He could already see the shock and disbelief throughout the country when people heard the news: Sir John A. Macdonald dead, struck down by an assassin's bullet.

"Think what a victory it will be for Ireland," he said. "Days after Whelan hangs, the Protestant prime minister is assassinated. They'll pay attention to us then."

Thomas turned away from him, his mind spinning wildly. "Did you kill D'Arcy McGee?"

The assassin ignored the question. He was now caught up in the perfection of his plan. "With McGee and Macdonald gone, Canada will fall to pieces." Thomas turned and looked at him again. The assassin's eyes were no longer cold; they were burning with intensity. "McGee was a traitor to Ireland. That can't be allowed. And Macdonald has to be taught a lesson."

Can't be allowed . . . Taught a lesson . . . He talked like a schoolteacher, but he was describing murder. Thomas was now convinced he was insane.

"Listen, Thomas O'Dea, you will be a hero. You have an obligation to your country."

My country, thought Thomas. *Is this what my country represents?*

Madmen going around, using fellow Irishmen like James Whelan, gunning down politicians, plotting revolution. He wanted no part of it.

The assassin could read the hesitancy in Thomas's expression. "You've changed," he muttered. "You're not with us anymore."

"I'm with those who support a free Ireland," Thomas answered proudly. "I might fight for Irish freedom. But I will not be involved in murder." He glared at the assassin. "And I won't be used by you."

That is too bad, the assassin thought. I have wasted my breath, and my time. Thomas O'Dea has spoken his last.

OUTSIDE, anxiously watching through the filthy window, Conor was shivering, not just from cold but from fright. What were they saying? What was his father up to? His heart raced, his whole body ached in frustration as he crouched, trying to read their lips. *Don't just observe, Conor, study and interpret. Probe, damn it. Probe.* McGee's orders came back to him as he watched the pantomime through the window. There was a curious look on Thomas's face, as if a cloud of anger had lifted.

Then he saw the knife. A flash of light from the gas lamp caught the blade. The other man had pulled it from his coat pocket. He held the weapon behind his back, concealed from Thomas.

There was no time to think. Conor turned the doorknob and lunged through the door, screaming madly, "Da! He has a knife!"

The assassin spun around to see where the shout came from. Conor saw the madness in his eyes and shuddered. It was just a second, but it gave Thomas an opening. He sprang forward and jumped the assassin from behind. But he wasn't fast enough. With the instincts of a panther, the assassin anticipated the move and smashed his elbow into Thomas O'Dea's face. Blood spurted from

Thomas's nose, and as he tumbled to the floor, the assassin slashed at him with the knife, slicing his shoulder.

As the assassin viciously kicked him, Thomas screamed, "Conor, my gun!"

Conor knew where his father kept his gun. He grabbed it from beneath the cloth on the shelf and, without thinking or properly aiming, fired it wildly. It was far too high. His hands were shaking. A second shot was even farther off the mark. The assassin laughed at him. "I thought you said you'd get me," he snarled. But he dared not risk Conor taking a third shot, and he ran out of the room into the snowy, deserted street.

Thomas O'Dea lay slumped on the floor. Conor dropped the gun and reached for him. Thomas opened his eyes and smiled. "I'm fine, son," he said. "A bloody mess, but perfectly fine."

Blood was still pouring from his broken nose; his shoulder was carved and his ribs were bruised. "It's just torn flesh," he insisted as Conor inspected his shoulder. "I don't move as fast as the old days. You won't be telling Gerry O'Beirne back in Galway that I lost a fight, will you? He'd never believe it."

Conor was barely listening to his father's brave front. He mumbled, "I didn't help."

"What do you mean? You saved my life."

"I didn't stop him."

"You missed, that's all. He left me for dead and he was too frightened to tangle with you."

Conor knew no one was frightened of him; not in the least.

Thomas grunted in pain. "And don't be pathetic, son. There are more important matters. Go and get me an old shirt. I need a sling."

Conor knew how to wrap a sling from his days in the lumber camps. While he stopped the bleeding and tended to his father's shoulder, Thomas applied pressure to his broken nose to staunch the bleeding.

"Where are you staying?

"On Rideau Street."

"We'll go there. It's not safe here anymore."

They had been avoiding eye contact until Conor looked straight at Thomas and said, "Da, I'm sorry."

"Me, too. But we can talk of all that later. For now, we have a life to save."

"What?"

"This man . . . he plans to kill Macdonald."

"When?"

"This weekend."

Conor was bewildered. "And you're prepared to help Macdonald?"

After a lifetime of misfortune and tragedy, days of bitterness and jealousy, hours of resentment and hatred, Thomas O'Dea looked at his son with determination and resolve. "Yes, I am. We both are. You and I are going to stop him." He reached out with his good arm. "We are going to end this once and for all."

PART SIX

February 1869

The fate of our land
God hath placed in your hand;
He hath made you to know
The heart of your foe,
And the schemes he hath plann'd;
Think well who you are,
Know your soul and your star;
Persevere—dare—

He walked up the hill, shivering. Would it ever stop snowing in this blessed country? He kept repeating to himself: "I am not defeated. Nobody can stop me." The mess with the O'Dea family was unfortunate. A snag, that's all. But he should have seen the gun. Was the opium making him lose focus? He went back to finish them off that night, but they were gone. Anyway, even if they tried to warn the enemy, no one would believe them.

"No one can stop me. No one ever has."

A reign of terror. *He had to give the colonel credit, for it was a smart plan: Attack Britain from its weakest side. Don't rush. Disrupt the election, then kill McGee. Let Macdonald and his henchmen hang a Catholic, then kill the Orangeman. Brilliant.*

"I am not defeated. I will prevail."

He sometimes wished he could get credit for the work he did. If he were in any other field of work, he would be recognized as the best in the business, a master of his craft. But he had to stay unknown and unheralded. No perks in this job. Just lots of money and, occasionally, great satisfaction. Anyway, the right people knew who he was and what he was doing.

Maybe he should have killed Macdonald right after McGee, get it over with, but he wanted the hanging to add to the confusion. To make them afraid. But this had taken longer than he liked. For his next job, he wanted something fast. A quick shot, and a prince falls.

Christ, it was cold! He longed for a draft of laudanum or the sweet, harsh taste of opium. Comfort and bliss. He would indulge as soon as this job was finished.

He reached the top of the hill and inspected the scene. There was one guard at the top of the slide. It looked as if he was the only one. The fools. At least he wasn't marching back and forth like a sentry; that would make him laugh, and this was no time for a chuckle. He casually walked up to the man and slit his throat.

"I am not defeated. Nobody can stop me."

He had a pack of food and plenty of water. He had learned how to make an enclosure of snow to stay warm. It made him seem to disappear. He would appear when he needed to.

38

The sun had set by the time Thomas and Conor O'Dea left Conor's room and headed south toward Daly Street. The snow had stopped, leaving the city soft and white; the sky was a vivid dark blue, the stars sparkling brightly. It was the kind of crisp, clear night that made you feel you could see into the future. Or wish you could.

Everything was different about Thomas now: the way he talked, even the way he looked. He exuded a new sense of confidence and power. It made Conor beam with pride.

"Da, why the change?"

Thomas smiled and answered thoughtfully, "When I looked into the cruel eyes of that man, everything came into focus. I kept thinking, An eye for an eye, another eye for another eye and another . . . and you know what? I realized how bloody blind I have been."

Conor thought it was the kind of thing D'Arcy McGee might have said. He kept the thought to himself.

"No true Irish revolutionary would shoot a man in the back," Thomas said in disgust. "I don't really trust that Macdonald rascal, but he doesn't deserve to die. And if I can stop it, I will."

They walked silently for several blocks. Thomas was always a man of few words. "Conor, it's grand to be with you again." That was really all that he had to say.

One lonely light flickered upstairs on Daly Street. Conor could picture the prime minister poring over papers and pouring himself "another wee one." Conor and Thomas were met at the door by Hewitt Bernard, Sir John A. Macdonald's principal secretary.

"What do you two want?" he barked. Stuffy and stuffed up.

"And hello to you, too," Thomas said. His voice was pinched and nasal because of his broken nose. "I assume the prime minister is in. We need to see him right away." Conor thought his father might be exaggerating his Irish accent, perhaps to see how Bernard would react.

"What can be so urgent that you arrive at this hour of the night?" Bernard asked.

"The prime minister's life."

Hewitt Bernard looked at Conor, as if for validation; Conor nodded. Bernard was Lady Macdonald's brother, and Conor had met him a number of times on Parliament Hill. He knew he would have more credibility than his father, the barman, but he wanted Thomas to stay in charge.

"It's too cold out here to chat," Bernard said finally. "Follow me."

As they walked the few steps to the door, Bernard turned to Conor and said, "By the looks of you, you'll be needing a better barber." He turned to Thomas and added, "And by the looks of *you*, you'll be needing a doctor."

"Yes," Thomas answered, "but I suggest you send for a policeman."

SIR John A. Macdonald was working in his study—adding, subtracting, multiplying, building railways in his mind. If he was ever going to talk the colonists in the West into joining Confederation, Canada would have to build a transcontinental railway. Connections. Communications. A link from east to west. Nation-building. That's what excited him. Not failing banks in Kingston, and certainly not fanatical gunmen in Ottawa.

Hewitt Bernard informed the prime minister that he had visitors. Macdonald sighed. Railways could wait for an hour. It would be the making of someone else's fortune, anyway. When Conor and Thomas were ushered into his study, Macdonald said coldly, "You keep the strangest hours."

Conor felt he should speak first. He knew the prime minister better than his father did, and more important, he knew the language and grammar of power. "It is very good of you to see us, sir. I believe you know my father from Lapier—"

"Yes," he interjected. "Yes, I do. Mr. O'Dea, could I interest you in a glass of sherry or a dram of whisky?"

"No, thank you," Thomas answered politely.

Sir John poured himself a glass from the crystal decanter. Conor noticed the quality of the vessel—cut glass, handcrafted. A gift, he assumed. He was more aware of these things when he was with his father, knowing how hard Thomas worked for so little money.

Macdonald looked at Thomas O'Dea, his nose broken and arm in a sling, and asked with a devilish grin, "Are you going to say, 'You should see the other fellow'?"

"No, indeed I am not."

Macdonald shrugged and sat down behind his large cluttered desk, gazing at Conor with a pained expression. "Sit down, the two of you, and tell me: Why do I think I'm not going to enjoy this conversation?"

"We have some very distressing news for you, Prime Minister," Thomas began.

"See what I mean," Macdonald muttered.

"The man who killed McGee is still at large."

"The man who killed Mr. McGee," Macdonald barked, "was hanged this morning."

Thomas stood his ground. "Mr. Macdonald, this is too important to dismiss. You must listen to us." Conor watched his father proudly. He noticed that Thomas never called the prime minister "sir." "A man is planning to assassinate you this weekend."

Macdonald stopped short. "How do you know this?"

"It's a long story, but I suggest you trust us."

The prime minister looked around for support. It was a nervous gesture he was using too often these days. As always, he found himself alone. He glared at Thomas suspiciously. "Why should I trust you?"

"Because I'm offering to help."

Macdonald assessed the situation. This is what I have for support, he thought. An Irish immigrant family. A smart young man who is more bookish than rugged and a dispirited lumberman who sells cheap whisky in a common Lowertown bar. Even behind a broken nose, Thomas carried himself with greater authority than he ever had at Lapierre's, but he was hardly the stuff of heroes. The prime minister was a shrewd judge of character, but like anyone, he made mistakes. Would it be a mistake to trust Thomas O'Dea? He couldn't tell. So he went on the offensive.

"I'm not sure, Mr. O'Dea, that there is not a lot that you should be held accountable for. I'm not sure I shouldn't summon the police and have you arrested."

Thomas looked at Conor as if to say, Do you see what these people are really like? "I have asked your brother-in-law to send for a policeman," Thomas answered. "He should be here soon."

Macdonald walked over to the window, refreshed his glass and looked out. Yes, McMicken was marching up the front steps. He wasn't really a policeman, but on Irish matters, he was Macdonald's man.

"If you want to have me arrested," Thomas said defiantly, "I will not resist. It won't be the first time."

"I've never understood you Irishmen," Macdonald whined. Conor was aghast, but Thomas allowed a smile. "McGee, you, the whole lot of you, you're as stubborn as—"

"As you can be, Prime Minister," Thomas interrupted. "I am telling you that a man intends to kill you, and you refuse to listen. No one can be more bullheaded than that."

For a few seconds, Sir John A. Macdonald glared at Thomas O'Dea. How dare he speak to me like that? he thought. The effrontery! He weighed his options and judged this man. Thomas O'Dea looked a wreck but sounded convincing. It took gall for him to come here. Macdonald concluded that trusting this barman was his best option. His *only* option. He smiled grudgingly and got down to business.

"This weekend, I'm going to a public reception at Rideau Hall," he said. "The new governor general, Lord Lisgar, is opening up a toboggan slide, of all things. There will be hundreds of people there. I guess it's a possible opportunity for someone to strike . . ." Macdonald stopped in mid-sentence. He said nothing for a moment, and then looked at Conor. "You have always thought Whelan was innocent."

"He was guilty of something," Conor answered. "Conspiracy, I think. Maybe he helped him escape, I don't know. But I do know someone else was in charge." He looked at his father and added, "*We* know it."

There was a knock on the door. Out of the corner of his eye, Conor thought he saw the prime minister jump with fright. It was Lady Macdonald.

"What is happening here?" she demanded. She walked gingerly. It was still just days since she had given birth, and she was in pain.

But her fury gave her strength. Behind her, Gilbert McMicken stayed safely in her shadow.

"Why have you called for Mr. McMicken? Something horrible is going on, I know it."

Conor gallantly offered her his chair. She accepted it without comment. However weak and tired she felt, she was not going to sit back. There was trouble in her house, and she wanted to know what it was. She looked at Thomas's bruised face and shuddered. "It looks like the day after a drunken brawl in here."

Macdonald smiled.

"John, what is going on?" she persisted.

"Yes, Prime Minister," McMicken asked, "what is the problem?"

Macdonald knew there was no sense in trying to shelter his wife from this, but how he wished he could. "Gilbert McMicken," he said, "meet Thomas O'Dea and his son, Conor. Agnes, I think you've met both gentlemen. Certainly, you know young Conor from D'Arcy McGee's office." He seemed to enjoy not getting to the point. "The O'Dea family has come forward with information about a plot to kill me."

"When?" McMicken asked the question directly of Thomas.

"This weekend."

McMicken turned to the prime minister. "What is your schedule this weekend?" Ever practical, he spoke without a hint of sympathy.

"On Saturday, I am making a speech on the grounds of Rideau Hall. They are opening a toboggan slide. The public is welcome, so it's an ideal time to—"

"Cancel it," Lady Macdonald begged. "Cancel it, John."

Nobody in the room dared challenge her until, to his astonishment, Conor heard his father speak. "With respect, ma'am, I think that would be foolish. He would just strike again, and no one would know when." Thomas turned to the prime minister. "You would forever live in fear. I think you should go ahead and make that speech, and if the good policeman here guards you well, we can get the murderer first."

"We don't know what he looks like," McMicken protested.

"I do, and so does my son."

McMicken lifted himself to attention. "You know the supposed killer?"

"I have met him, yes."

"And he told you he was going to murder the prime minister?"

"Yes."

"Well, then, Sir John, I think we should arrest them both right now. If there is a plot, they are certainly involved. Arresting them might flush out their partner."

Macdonald said nothing.

"We have to be careful here," McMicken continued. "You never know which way these Catholics may go."

Thomas glanced at Conor and raised an eyebrow. This was the kind of talk he had heard all his life. Conor expected his father to stomp out of the room. He wouldn't blame him if he did. In fact, he would follow him. But it didn't come to that. The prime minister spoke first. "I think Thomas O'Dea is not only a loyal Canadian but a very brave man. I'd be more apt to arrest your people for ineptitude."

Gilbert McMicken stood erect, thinly disguising his fury. "But he said he knows this man. He may be part of some plot."

Macdonald had conveniently forgotten that just minutes before, he too had questioned Thomas's loyalty. "I not only trust Thomas O'Dea, but trust that you will apologize to him."

"I will not."

"Then leave my house."

"Stop bickering, for God's sake," Lady Macdonald shrieked. "If what Mr. O'Dea says is true, John, you should go away tomorrow, leave Ottawa, leave all of this." She broke down in tears.

His critics accused Sir John A. Macdonald of indecisiveness, preferring to let problems sit and settle themselves, but there was no way Old Tomorrow could hide from the next day. He stood, walked across the room and rested his hand on his wife's shoulder. "Mr. O'Dea, why are you so certain this man will strike this weekend?"

"He wants to create what he calls 'a reign of terror.' That means he needs this done close to Whelan's hanging. I also think that once a plan is in motion, he won't change. He's too sure of himself, too single-minded. I don't think he'll stop now."

The prime minister was impressed. "All right, I will go to Rideau Hall," he said. "I will deliver my speech, smile appropriately, act like the happy, confident politician. I will even ride down the governor general's silly toboggan ride. And you, Mr. McMicken, will have an army of men in plain clothes there to protect me."

McMicken gestured as if he was about to speak. Sir John did not let him. "You will listen to Thomas O'Dea. He knows what this man looks like. You don't." McMicken made no attempt to hide his offence, but Macdonald simply stared him down. "You will get this man before he gets me."

Painfully, and carefully, Lady Macdonald rose from her chair. Before she could speak, her husband said, "I'm sorry, Agnes. You will stay here. You are far too weak, and I wouldn't put you in danger in any event. It seems my duty is to be the decoy."

Lady Macdonald turned to Conor. "Will this be the end of it?"

"Yes, ma'am," he said, with as much courage as he could muster. And he surprised himself by adding, "God willing."

MEG Trotter arrived at the Ottawa train station early Friday evening. She had taken the long train trip from Toronto. She hated to defy her mother, but she simply had to see Conor again, if only to say a proper goodbye. She didn't know what the trip held in store. She wasn't even sure how she would react when she saw Conor. She might fall into his arms, or she might resist. She burned with confusion.

She still respected his ambition and his eager mind. She was so impressed the day he saved her when they were swimming. Admiration had blossomed into love. But that was a million years ago. There was the stinging memory of the hands grabbing her, the scissors in her hair, and Conor unable to help.

She pulled a furry hat over her ears and hailed a carriage. She ordered the carriage driver to take her to a friend's house in LeBreton Flats.

Conor didn't know she was here. She would see him on the weekend.

39

At Rideau Hall, there was all the excitement and expectation of a winter carnival. The governor general's mansion had been built for a lumber baron, so like most of Ottawa, it had only recently made the transition to politics. Rideau Hall was the cultural centre of Ottawa's fledgling upper class. Young women, of the right class, were introduced to society here, and young men practised diplomacy behind the stone walls. On this winter afternoon, the gathering was unusually large and diverse. The grounds were open to all for the new toboggan slide.

The new governor general, Lord Lisgar, had not been told about the plot against Macdonald. It would have been his duty to report the situation to Britain, and the prime minister insisted upon absolute secrecy.

Plain-clothed police were everywhere. Some blended in; others were so obviously patrolman out of uniform that it almost made Conor laugh.

Sir John, bundled in a lush beaver coat and hat, arrived by carriage with a scowling Gilbert McMicken at his side. "If this man is a fur trapper, I guess I'll be in trouble," Macdonald lamely joked.

"There's no evidence of that, sir," McMicken said.

Macdonald just shook his head.

"Sir John, good morning," the governor general announced, holding out his hand to shake the prime minister's. Lisgar was dressed in a formal topcoat and hat, looking very dignified and viceregal. He was new to Ottawa and new to its winters.

"You might find you need a warmer coat," Macdonald suggested.

"Yes, it's frightfully cold, but one must keep up appearances, mustn't one?"

"Must one?" the prime minister mimicked. "Yes, I suppose one must." He scrutinized the assembling crowd. "Let's go behind the lectern until the speeches begin. I think I'd like to be out of the limelight."

"You? Missing a chance to talk to a voter? That's not how you were described to me."

"Yes, me!" the prime minister snapped back. He led Lisgar to what he hoped would be safety. McMicken stayed at their side.

THOMAS and Conor O'Dea were surveying the crowd, looking for the assassin, when a plain-clothed policeman approached them from behind. "I've been told to keep an eye on you," he said to Thomas, like a babysitter talking to a child.

Thomas glared at him. "We are supposed to help you people."

"And you will. Point out this man, and we'll do the rest."

The silly ass, thought Thomas.

"Give me your gun," the policeman ordered.

"He knows us, you know," Thomas protested. "We are targets."

"I'm under orders that you are not to be armed, and you're to be watched at all times."

Conor spoke up, "But Sir John said—"

"Sir John is in hiding," the policeman interrupted, triumphantly. "No Irishmen like you two are going to be armed on a day like today. Not after what happened to Mr. McGee."

Thomas looked at his son and shook his head in disgust, but there was no time for anger. He asked the policeman, "Where were you born, then?"

"Brockville."

"And your father?"

"Manchester, England."

"Ah, a good Englishman." Thomas stepped closer to the policeman and, without taking his eyes off him, said, "Conor, would you take off your hat for a second?"

Conor did, revealing his almost bald head.

"What do you think of my son's haircut?"

The policeman looked confused and didn't answer.

"You see, that's what English bullies do."

With his one good hand, Thomas grabbed the policeman's ear. As the man gasped in surprise, Thomas lifted his knee hard into the man's arched body. Conor couldn't believe his eyes. The policeman buckled over. Thomas released him and pulled the revolver from his belt, then father and son scurried into the crowd. They were now both armed. Conor laughed wildly; he saw that his father was laughing, too.

"You can tell Gerry O'Beirne about that!"

SIR John A. Macdonald could delay no longer. The prime minister hesitantly followed Lord Lisgar to the stage. He gazed over the faces of Ottawa's citizenry, smiled and quietly gulped. All those people, all bundled up on a winter's day. It would be so easy to conceal a weapon in a fur coat, or pull a hat low and bury your face. He had often said that he trusted his brain but relied on his luck. Now it was truer than ever.

The governor general was going on about something. Perhaps he should pay attention. But then again, perhaps not. He actually liked the man, but he was not in the mood to listen to a speech. He saw

Thomas and Conor O'Dea laughing in the crowd. What in the world could they be laughing at?

When Lisgar finished his speech and welcomed Sir John, the prime minister cautiously walked the few steps to the lectern. "This is not a day for political speeches," he began stiffly, "but I don't know any other kind."

Someone from the crowd yelled, "Give 'em hell, John!" and there was a great cheer. Macdonald smiled. All right, he thought, I might as well have some fun. After all, I've got an audience.

"They say I'm a slippery customer," he began. Some in the crowd laughed, and some cheered. He pointed toward the toboggan slide. "Well, do you see that slide?" he yelled.

"Yes!" the crowd roared.

"Do you know what it reminds me of?"

"Nooo," from the crowd. He was surprised at how much he was enjoying this. Maybe being brave was just a case of ignoring what was terrifying you.

"That slide reminds me of the Liberal party's platform," he continued. "Like the Grits, it's aimed straight downhill, and for the life of me I can't find a rudder on the infernal thing."

The crowd cheered.

"I think we should split up," Thomas told Conor. "I'll stay near the stage. You keep an eye on the back."

Conor held on to his father's elbow. "No, please," he urged. "Let's stay together."

"Okay, son," Thomas said, gently. "We'll work together. But we must think. Where could he be?"

Conor urgently searched the crowd. Faces were hard to distinguish, all covered up from the cold. He searched desperately for an

301

idea, a scent, a clue. D'Arcy McGee had told him that the secret to winning a debate was to put yourself into the mind of your opponent. What was it he said? "Try to understand the heart of your foe." So what would he do if he were the assassin? It would be suicidal to kill Sir John down here. There are too many policemen, the crowd too large; he'd never get away. He might be a maniac, but he has a gift for self-preservation.

"Father," Conor asked, "is Macdonald going to go down the slide?"

"Yes. He and the governor general will be the first to go down it."

Conor watched the prime minister on the stage. He was now talking about a railway to the Pacific, and warming to the subject.

Yes, Conor was sure of it. "He's up top," he said.

"What?" Thomas asked.

Conor took his father by the shoulders. "He's waiting to kill the prime minister at the top of the hill."

MEG first went to her mother's old boarding house. She wondered whether Conor would be there. There was a FOR RENT sign in the window. Mr. Desbarats would know what was happening. She knocked on the door at the Queen's printer's next door, but no one was there. Across the street, Mrs. McKenna said there was a large gathering at the governor general's mansion for the opening of a toboggan slide.

A toboggan slide. This is a strange town, she thought.

She headed toward Rideau Hall. Conor would be there, she figured. She wondered whom else she might see.

40

The toboggan slide was an impressive wooden structure built on stilts up the hill. Tobogganing had been part of winter life at Rideau Hall for years, but the hill on the viceregal property was fairly gentle. The new wooden slide added steepness. This would be the fastest and most thrilling run in the city.

No one could see him huddled at the top of the wooden steps, hidden in the scaffolding. It had been easy. The lone policeman guarding the top of the slide was now his lifeless companion. He had spent the night up here in the dark, sharpening his knife, inspecting his revolver and thinking about the morning. The cold didn't bother him. He was warmed by the excitement of the hunt, anticipating the next kill.

He couldn't see what was happening down below, and he didn't risk looking. His time would come. He was crouched so low that he had no idea Thomas and Conor O'Dea were climbing up the path toward him.

ON the platform at the bottom of the hill, Sir John A. Macdonald's speech was over. Lord Lisgar was telling the crowd that he and the prime minister were going to go down the slide together. "To make sure it's safe for everyone else," Macdonald interjected. The dignitaries started up the wooden steps, watched and guarded by policemen. Sir John hung close to McMicken. He felt like going down a toboggan run about as much as he felt like . . . well, like being used as bait.

Thomas and Conor were well ahead of them, off the path, out of people's sight, trudging through the heavy snow. The steady climb was painful for Thomas. His shoulder ached, but he never complained. They searched along the way for the assassin, for some shape hidden behind a tree, skulking on the other side of a rock—something, anything. They saw nothing.

The platform at the top looked like the scaffolding James Whelan had recently climbed. The sight of it made Conor wince. But he was certain. "He's up there," Conor said. "I know it."

At the top of the hill, just below the platform, Thomas O'Dea assessed the situation. If there was someone up there, he and Conor would be easy targets if they climbed the steps. They would have to stay out of sight and scale the wooden grid work to get to the top. They had time. It should take the politicians a while to get up the hill.

Thomas whispered, "I'll climb up this side. You start from over there." Seeing Conor's dread, he added, "I'll go first."

Thomas quietly started to climb up the grid work to the right of the slide. Conor followed from the other side, slowing his climb to stay in step with his father. Thomas's shoulder slowed him down, and every few rungs his back stiffened, requiring him to rest. But he knew they had to hurry; the politicians were climbing the hill. Fortunately, the structure was stable and their footing was secure.

Governor General Lisgar quickened his pace, bracing himself against the cold in his light jacket. Luckily, Macdonald was dawdling and glad-handing along the way.

A sharp pain flashed through Thomas's back. He faltered and grunted softly.

THE assassin sensed something. He thought he had heard whispering coming from the right side of the slide. Now there was a vibration and a strange sound. Someone must be near, maybe inside the woodwork. He quickly decided gunfire would make too much noise. He crouched low, holding his knife up, about to strike as the intruder—whoever he was—came up the last rung.

MEG had never before been on the grounds of the governor general's residence. She was impressed. She looked up at the toboggan run and decided it was not for her. Conor was probably in the thick of the crowd, where the action was. She could wait.

She went over to the carriages and patted one of the mares. She tried chatting with the man tending to the horses, but he was sullen and withdrawn. Patrick Buckley told her to move on. She was near the front gates. There was no other way out, so she would see Conor when he left.

THOMAS mouthed, "Three, two, one . . ." and they burst to the top together. The assassin was waiting for Thomas, but he wasn't prepared for an attack from both sides. Before he could lurch at Thomas, he saw Conor. He hesitated, confused. His legs were stiff from the night, and he moved more slowly than he wanted. Thomas avoided the thrust of his knife, and Conor grabbed him from behind, spinning him around. He sliced at Conor and struck his right arm. Thomas pushed the assassin as best he could with his one good shoulder and fumbled for his gun. They tried to pin him down. But they couldn't. The assassin glared at Conor—a look of pure hatred—and squirmed away like a fish. He jumped onto the toboggan and pushed off down the slide.

A dead policeman was draped over the edge of the second toboggan. Conor gagged as Thomas pushed the corpse aside. "Come on, son," he cried. They grabbed the other toboggan and followed the assassin down the slide.

"WHAT on earth is that?" the governor general asked as he watched the two toboggans on the track. Macdonald had an idea, but he answered, "I guess someone decided to beat us to the punch." He turned to McMicken and asked, quietly, "Your people?" McMicken shook his head.

MEG had not heard the commotion. In fact, most of the people who had gathered around the slide paid little attention to the two toboggans plunging down ahead of the prime minister. They thought it was just someone checking everything out.

At the bottom of the track, the assassin jumped from the toboggan and ran toward the gates. His plan was in ruins. Macdonald was halfway up the hill. He couldn't get to him. The bastard was safe.

He needed a horse. He saw Patrick Buckley tending to a horse-drawn sleigh. "Get out of my way," he yelled, pushing Buckley aside.

And he could use a hostage, some protection. He thought of Buckley, but he looked too big and burly, and he might be armed. Then he saw her: a girl in a bushy hat languishing behind the crowd, near the entrance. She looked vaguely familiar, but he didn't have time to think of where he might have seen her. He grabbed her, jammed his gun under her chin and pulled her onto the sleigh. He took the whip and thrashed at the horse. They took off together: the assassin and Meg Trotter, racing through the snow- and ice-covered street.

THOMAS and Conor leaped out of their toboggan and chased the murderer through the crowd. Thomas couldn't keep up. He threw Conor the policeman's revolver and fell back, exhausted. Conor pushed ahead. He had lost all sense of fear. It was if he had assumed his father's strength and courage. Memories of D'Arcy McGee lying on Sparks Street, of James Whelan on the scaffold, of a policeman's bloodied corpse—all spurred him on. He ran faster than he knew he could.

He saw her just as the carriage took off. It was like a mirage. Meg . . . what was she doing here? And then panic. Meg . . . with him? Not with him! Meg . . . He jumped on another of Buckley's horses and frantically chased them. He couldn't feel the pain in his arm anymore, and his blood seemed to freeze in the cold.

THE assassin looked behind him. Thomas O'Dea's boy. Following him. Damn it! He should have killed him months ago. Still, he had the girl. He pressed the gun against her throat and urged the horses on.

In the past year, Meg had been threatened and attacked, humiliated and violated. Now she was being held hostage. She'd had enough. She knew this crazed man was going to kill her. She had bought a derringer in Toronto and knew how to use it. It was deep in her purse. She struggled, but couldn't get to it.

Their carriage was speeding ahead, leaving Conor behind. She tried to turn and look, and her hat flew off in the wind. She reached for it, and the assassin struck her face with his gun. The blow thrust her backward with blinding pain, but it gave her a split-second chance to reach her revolver with her other hand. She couldn't quite get her finger on the trigger.

Suddenly, the assassin pulled back on the reins. He had formulated a new plan. He would allow O'Dea's son to get near; it would give him a cleaner shot. And later, he would kill this pretty hostage.

They raced along Sussex Street: a horse-drawn carriage and a lone rider. Conor was gaining on them. Meg watched the man glance back at him, his gun bruising her, holding her back.

When Conor got near, the assassin yelled at him, "Remember me? Jasper Green from Cincinnati."

Meg wondered what on earth he meant.

She heard Conor respond, but she couldn't make out the words. Something threatening. The horrible man flinched. Conor was about to come alongside them. Conor aimed his revolver. He was struggling. She could see blood on his arm. The man pulled the gun from her throat and aimed it at Conor. It gave Meg an opening. She pulled the derringer from her purse, but before she could find the trigger, she heard a shot.

It was as if the world stood still. The gunshot hadn't come from Conor. It hadn't come from the assassin. It had come from in front of them. Meg screamed. The assassin spun around. And Conor looked in wonder. A woman stood defiantly in their path, re-cocking her rifle.

It was Polly Ryan.

Meg threw herself off the carriage, landing hard on the snow-packed road. Her derringer fell in the snow, but she didn't search for it. Instead, she jumped to her feet and ran up Sussex Street, away from Rideau Hall, away from whoever this man was, away from the horror.

Polly's first shot was wild. Her second was closer. She might not have killed him, but she had stopped him. She had done her job. The assassin jumped from the sleigh. He shot recklessly toward her and missed. He quickly thought: Should he kill this woman who had come out of nowhere? Or chase his hostage? Should he try to kill Thomas O'Dea's son? Or should he run?

He ran.

Polly's intervention had stunned Conor as much as it had shocked the assassin. Conor wasted valuable time staring at her in disbelief. When he came to his senses, he jumped from his horse and chased after the assassin. But his energy was drained. His arm was now aching and had started to bleed again. The snow was deep and frustrating. He kept tripping and falling over. The assassin disappeared over a snowbank at the river's edge. There wasn't much land, just a cliff overlooking the Ottawa River. He couldn't go far.

Conor saw that police were converging on them. He yelled, "He went over there. Down there." Conor desperately wanted to chase him down, grab him, look in his eyes while he choked the life out of him. But he decided that Meg was more important. He stumbled after her. "It's all right, he's gone," he shouted. But she was running away, terrified and in shock. She fell in a snowbank, all her strength spent, and leaned on a tree, staring out at the sky. She held her shivering arms around herself for comfort, or protection, just as she had at the Hog's Back waterfall. When Conor reached her, he carefully took her in his arms and silently held her, giving her the warmth of another body, a place to let out her awful fear.

Conor and Meg were together when Thomas caught up to them. Conor mouthed the words "We're not hurt" and held Meg tightly, her face now deep in his shoulder. Thomas sat down beside them in the snow. When Meg looked up, Thomas startled her, not just because he was cut and bruised, but because he looked so different. He seemed twice the man she had met the year before.

Thomas thought of apologizing for how he had treated her when they first met, but he said nothing. There would be time for that later. They listened to the sound of the police calling out to each other, frenetically searching the riverside and down the cliff. Finally, she said, "Mr. O'Dea, let's pretend we're meeting for the first time."

Thomas smiled, kindly.

The three of them sat in silence, an exhausted trinity.

No one paid attention to Polly Ryan, who was calmly walking back to Lowertown, her rifle at her side.

42

≡

He lay in the covering of snow and rock, safe and secure. He knew they wouldn't find him. He had prepared this reserve position days ago. He was dry, but soaking in his misery. He was not a man who knew failure. This should not have happened. His plan was in shambles. He had to escape. Get out of Canada. But was there anything else he could do before leaving this wretched British country?

THE Toronto House burned down the next week. The building just burst into flames in the middle of a moonless night. The offices of the Queen's printer burned to the ground with it. There was a masquerade ball at the Desbarats home, and the guests watched the inferno in fancy costumes. Miraculously, no one was killed or injured. George Desbarats had insurance, but that didn't compensate for the loss. A part of Canada's young history had disappeared overnight.

Fires were common among the lumber town's many wooden structures, especially in winter, when wood stoves threw flames about. Still, the police believed it might have been arson. Fenians were suspected, but when police searched through the rubble and ashes, they found no clues. No one had been seen around the boarding house the night of the fire. No one was arrested. Somehow, the suspicions didn't linger. The country wanted to get back to the business of living.

The fire seemed to help put the Fenian–D'Arcy McGee matter to rest.

TWO WEEKS LATER

===

"**HOW** are you, Sir John?" Conor asked.

"Can't complain," the prime minister answered. "Well, I can, but no one would pay attention." He looked over at Thomas and winked. The mood was jovial in Macdonald's study. There was a sense of relief, as if a sick friend had been cured. Everyone was smiling, except for Meg, who was still anxious and tentative. Conor was beside his father. Meg held back, just slightly behind.

Polly Ryan stood tall beside a beaming Gilbert McMicken.

"How long were you working for the government?" Conor asked.

"Since the Ridgeway invasion. So I guess about three years. My husband was killed in the Fenian attack."

"I recruited her myself," McMicken declared.

"I tried to keep an eye on you both," she told Thomas.

So many things started to make sense to Conor. He turned to the prime minister. "So what are we going to do, sir, about the murderer?"

"Mr. McMicken here has people chasing the man. I don't have to tell you that he hasn't caught him."

Conor nodded. McMicken stared straight ahead.

"What about the fire at my mother's boarding house?" Meg asked.

"What a blessing no one was hurt," Macdonald answered. "These wooden buildings are such fire traps."

"Do you think it was the work of Fenians—or that man?" Conor added.

"Good Lord, no. Just a coincidence. I'm just glad, Miss Trotter, that you and your family were not there."

Conor glanced at McMicken, who ignored him.

Meg pressed on. "The trouble at Rideau Hall . . . it never made the newspapers?" Her voice had a slight waver to it. Her stunning blue eyes still held a trace of fear.

"No," Macdonald said proudly. "Not a word. No talk of assassins and gun battles. We told everybody that some petty thief was hanging around the toboggan run. The story is sticking." Conor considered how it must irk a man like Macdonald, who loved to bask in the light of his successes, to keep this one quiet. Pragmatism won over pride.

"A policeman was killed," Thomas reminded him.

"Don't worry, I've explained it," McMicken declared. "A freak accident while we were chasing the thief."

His answer didn't please the O'Deas, but before either could object, Macdonald announced, "I have some news for you, though. Our sources in New York say the Fenians are devastated by their failure here. Apparently, the powers that be in Dublin have lost interest in these Canadian dreams. We think it's over."

It looked as if McMicken might disagree when Thomas asked, "What about Jim Whelan?"

Macdonald frowned deeply. "Whelan admitted that he was part of the conspiracy. A jury would still have found him guilty, and he would still have hanged. I know that isn't very satisfactory, but it is the truth."

Neither Thomas nor Conor looked impressed. A jury might well have acquitted Whelan if they knew the whole story. To serve his purposes, Macdonald was prepared to sweep the facts under the rug and be done with it. The prime minister knew he was losing the convivial spirit in the room and quickly changed the subject. "What about you people?" he asked.

"I don't know what I'm going to do," Meg said softly. "I know a man in Toronto who might be able to give Conor a job. I believe you know him. Casimir Gzowski."

"Ah, the Polish count."

"He is looking for someone to help him write speeches, prepare business briefs; someone proficient in English."

"I think working for D'Arcy was as good as a university education. Conor, I will give you a reference so glorious he might name a bank vault after you."

Conor took Meg's hand; she held it, gently.

"This has been horrible for you, I know," the prime minister said, stumbling for the right words. "But let me tell you, this country is in great shape with people like you two growing up to replace old fools like Thomas and me."

Thomas laughed. How Conor loved to watch him laugh.

"Thomas," Macdonald said, "I wonder if you would do me a favour?"

Thomas looked at him, puzzled.

"There is a delegation travelling to Ireland next month. Would you go along as an extra adviser, an emissary from the prime minister's office?"

"You know I can't read or write."

"But you can think. We need people with good, old-fashioned common sense. I know you're a good listener. I'll give you some people to keep an eye on for me, and maybe, if you would, say a few nice things about me over a dram. Don't worry, I'll pick your brain. You'll earn your keep." There was a sparkle in Macdonald's eye that Conor hadn't seen in months. "And the pay will be better than Lapierre's, even counting my tips."

Thomas just nodded. "Thanks."

Macdonald shook his hand warmly.

"Thank you, sir," Thomas said again, emphasizing the "sir."

Thomas gently touched Polly's shoulder. "You're a woman of mystery."

"Oh, I think I wear my heart on my sleeve." She smiled at Thomas. And Conor didn't mind.

"Now," Sir John A. Macdonald wondered, "who would like a wee glass of whisky?"

The fate of our land
God hath placed in your hand;
He hath made you to know
The heart of your foe,
And the schemes he hath plann'd;
Think well who you are,
Know your soul and your star;
Persevere—dare—
Be wise and beware—

THOMAS D'ARCY MCGEE

The voyage across the Atlantic was like a dream. Two decades ago, Thomas O'Dea and his wife and baby were crammed like cargo in a crumbling, disease-infected ship, treated like rotting merchandise. Now, he was surrounded by elegance and treated with respect. He was a gentleman, a representative of the Canadian government. It was marvellous.

One especially clear evening, midway across the ocean, Thomas stepped out on the deck to spend a few minutes alone. Watching the moonlight reflect on the waves, he considered the turns his life had taken. The hours of draining physical labour in the lumber camps, the nights of misery in Ottawa, the hardening of his heart, and now, the new opportunities. He was so proud of his relationship with Conor. They were a family again. He had not felt such contentment since he was a young man.

There was another person on the deck: a priest whom Thomas hadn't noticed before. "Lovely evening, Father," Thomas said cordially.

The priest did not return the greeting. He quickly looked away from Thomas, but not before Thomas caught a glimpse of his face.

COLONEL Patrick O'Hagan opened the letter from Dublin. He read it three times before crumpling up the paper and throwing it in the wastebasket. It read, simply, "There was an accident at sea. Our man is missing." His dream had floated briefly, swum with promise, but in the end, gasped for air and sunk.

It was over.

What's True and What's Not

===

When D'Arcy McGee was murdered, the first person to reach his side was Will Trotter, a pageboy and the son of McGee's landlady. There were no eyewitnesses to the crime. Patrick James Whelan never denied that he was part of a conspiracy, but he always claimed he was not the man who killed D'Arcy McGee. He said that on the night of the assassination, he was drinking with "a fellow called Marshall."

With those facts in mind, I wrote this story.

CONOR O'Dea and his father, Thomas, are fictitious. The death of Conor's mother, Margaret, is based on actual accounts of hellish voyages from Ireland to North America.

Mrs. Trotter, who ran the Toronto House, was a widow, and her son, Will Trotter, was a pageboy. She also had a daughter. I know nothing about her, not even her name. So Meg Trotter is fictitious. I have no reason to believe that Mary Ann Trotter was a transcendentalist.

Clearly, this is a story set in the past, not a history text. I tried to stay as close to the facts as possible, but veered off them when I felt it useful to do so. The events of Confederation Day, the troubled election in Montreal, the Fenians gathering in the United States, McGee's life as an Irish rebel and Canadian Father of Confederation, even his prophetic dream—they are all based on recorded accounts.

I played with time quite a bit and compressed much of the trial. For example, Joseph Faulkner did testify at the trial, but in the novel he is actually a combination of three people who testified. Whelan's confession to Doyle in jail was reported by Andrew Cullen. I slightly changed the circumstances. The testimony about the footprints was raised in the police magistrate's inquiry, not the trial itself. Much of the dialogue from the trial is taken from actual testimony. But the trial is much condensed and simplified.

I tried to make D'Arcy McGee, Sir John A. and Lady Macdonald as true to life as possible. From their speeches and diaries, one can get a sense of their personalities. I embellished things, certainly, but in an attempt to breathe life into their characters. Whenever possible, I used actual words and reported anecdotes. I pulled sentences and fragments from speeches and letters, and inserted them into dialogue. I admit to modernizing their speech at times to make conversation more readable.

The Macdonalds did live in a rented house called Quadrilateral on Daly Street in this era, and it did have terrible drainage problems. Later, they would move to Stadacona Hall, and later still to the much grander Earnscliffe, overlooking the Ottawa River.

Many of the anecdotes regarding Sir John A. Macdonald are based on reported stories. Some would have happened after the novel's time period. For example, Lady Macdonald did discover toys that had belonged to her husband's dead son, but she found them much later in their marriage. Macdonald reportedly did quip about not knowing ancient Greek but knowing politics; however, it was at McGill University, not Queen's, and it was a later governor general speaking, not a professor. It simply made sense to place him in his beloved Kingston. There was a secret means of escape from the prime minister's parliamentary office, but it was put in by Alexander Mackenzie, so while it makes sense to imagine Macdonald sitting at his desk, looking longingly for escape routes, he could not have done so until his second tenure as prime minister. Lady Macdonald did have a child in February 1869. It was a very difficult birth, and she could not have participated in the meeting as described. The Macdonalds would soon discover that their daughter, Mary Theodora, had been born with hydroencephalitis, better known as water on the brain. She would never fully be able to take care of herself.

The Toronto House burned down in January 1869. My timing is a bit off. Many felt the fire was set by Fenians. I should also note that the wooden toboggan slide was not built until the 1870s. It was a keen part of Ottawa's winter life. But not yet.

Tex is loosely based on Morley Roberts, a British adventurer who worked on the Canadian Pacific Railway in 1883. He was nicknamed Tex because he wore a Stetson hat. Roberts, by the way, was a transcendentalist.

Patrick Buckley was Macdonald's favourite driver. He was charged with conspiracy and acquitted. Many people in Ottawa wouldn't hire Buckley because of his alleged association with McGee's murder, but Sir John employed him until the prime minister's death, and Buckley remained steadfastly loyal to his employer.

D'Arcy McGee's brother reported that Patrick James Whelan visited McGee at his home during the election campaign. It was used against him at the trial. I have the assassin visiting McGee instead, as it gave me an opportunity to have McGee tell the story of his rebellious past.

Gilbert McMicken did head a clandestine spying operation. Henri Le Caron, in his book: *Twenty-Five Years in the Secret Service: A British Spy Among the Fenians*, praises McMicken. Sir John

A. Macdonald called him "a shrewd, cool and determined man who won't easily lose his head." He was not in Ottawa on July 1, 1867, but it was convenient to have him report to Macdonald on the day of Confederation.

Colonel Patrick O'Hagan is fictitious. There were many rogue officers in the Fenian movement, but he is an invention. Fenian general John O'Neill did invade Canada at Ridgeway and planned two more invasions—one in Quebec and one in Manitoba—but he was appalled by the murder of D'Arcy McGee. The meeting between the American president, Andrew Johnson, and O'Neill is from Le Caron's book. I added O'Hagan to the mix.

The Fenian threat was real, or certainly perceived to be very real. The Fenian letters, chants and proclamations are shortened, but they are presented as they were written. The Fenians certainly saw McGee as a turncoat and an enemy, and he denounced their activities with passion, as depicted in this story. The threats to McGee's and John A. Macdonald's lives are accurate.

It was indeed a troubled time.

NOW, the fundamental question: Was there an assassin? Perhaps. Whelan was identified by his clothing and a matching boot print. He went to the gallows not only claiming his innocence but stating, "I know the man who shot Mr. McGee." Many in the Irish community in Ottawa and Montreal felt that there definitely was a conspiracy, and that Whelan was not the murderer. After Whelan's arrest, an informer reported to Gilbert McMicken that he was "almost sure that Whelan is not the man that assassinated McGee." The rumour in Montreal, which has been passed down through the generations and was reported in T. P. Slattery's *They Got to Find Mee Guilty Yet*, was that "Whelan didn't shoot McGee. Whelan held the horse for the man who shot McGee." David A. Wilson, McGee's biographer, told me that "by the criminal law criterion of reasonable doubt, Whelan should be found not guilty. But by the criterion of the balance of probabilities, Whelan either shot McGee or was part of a hit squad that did."

But who knows? An innocent man may well have hanged for the murder of Thomas D'Arcy McGee.

Acknowledgments

===

My friend, the late broadcaster, journalist and novelist Bill Cameron, urged me not to give up on this novel. But I did. For a decade, the manuscript lay parked in a lonely folder on my computer, out of sight and out of mind. With the 150th anniversary of Confederation approaching, I decided to look at it again and set about rewriting the story. It goes to show two things: never give up, and always listen to Bill Cameron. If only I could. I deeply miss Bill's witty conversation and wise advice.

Along with Bill, a few people read early versions of this book. Liam O'Rinn read a very early draft, and Andrew Gregg and Geoff Matheson read a recent draft. All offered useful comments and advice. Michael Levine sent it to Patrick Watson. Kind words from such a prominent Canadian really meant a lot to me. My wife, Pam, was a sharp-eyed copy editor and grammarian. Pam is actually related to Sir John A. Macdonald. Her mother was a Macpherson from Kingston and Ottawa. The Macphersons and the Macdonalds were cousins. Pam wanted me to cut back on his drinking, but I thought that was really more up to him. I like to think that some of Sir John A.'s common sense and endearing charm runs in her blood, and that of our children, Stuart, Kate and Elizabeth.

The historian David A. Wilson's comments were particularly

valuable. I admit that I worried about asking D'Arcy's McGee's biographer to read the manuscript. After all, the book wanders— or stomps—through his academic territory, creating characters, changing circumstances and describing events he has studied and analyzed. I was sure he would take me to task for playing with time and messing with history. Instead, David was full of encouragement. He said he imagined McGee just as I had. That was Celtic music to my ears! He corrected small points—who knew they would have played a fife and not a tin flute at an Orange Parade?—and pointed me in better directions on larger issues. Most important, he understood that this is a story, not a history textbook, so it was all right to let my imagination run wild. I happily remember us sitting in pubs, pencils in hand, discussing Canada and Canadians 150 years ago. What fun!

A huge thanks is owed to my lawyer and agent, Michael Levine. What can I say about Michael that hasn't been said by so many other people he has helped? He is a whirlwind—tireless, tenacious, enthusiastic and also very pleasant company. Thank you, my friend. Iris Tupholme at HarperCollins championed the book, and for that I am forever grateful. Jane Warren was a diligent editor. She caught inconsistencies and trimmed what needed to be trimmed. Lloyd Davis was an excellent copy editor. He was eagle-eyed, spotting errors and pointing out some embarrassing mistakes. Many thanks to you both.

I mentioned my proofreader, Pam Henderson, but she deserves a much more heartfelt mention than that. I am blessed to have her as my wife. To Pam goes my deepest thanks, and to her the book is dedicated.